PATRICIA WE

WHO PAYS T... ER?

Patricia Wentworth was born Dora Amy Elles in India in 1877 (not 1878 as has sometimes been stated). She was first educated privately in India, and later at Blackheath School for Girls. Her first husband was George Dillon, with whom she had her only child, a daughter. She also had two stepsons from her first marriage, one of whom died in the Somme during World War I.

Her first novel was published in 1910, but it wasn't until the 1920's that she embarked on her long career as a writer of mysteries. Her most famous creation was Miss Maud Silver, who appeared in 32 novels, though there were a further 33 full-length mysteries not featuring Miss Silver—the entire run of these is now reissued by Dean Street Press.

Patricia Wentworth died in 1961. She is recognized today as one of the pre-eminent exponents of the classic British golden age mystery novel.

By Patricia Wentworth

PATRICIA WENTWORTH

WHO PAYS THE PIPER?

With an introduction by
Curtis Evans

DEAN STREET PRESS

Introduction

BRITISH AUTHOR Patricia Wentworth published her first novel, a gripping tale of desperate love during the French Revolution entitled *A Marriage under the Terror*, a little over a century ago, in 1910. The book won first prize in the Melrose Novel Competition and was a popular success in both the United States and the United Kingdom. Over the next five years Wentworth published five additional novels, the majority of them historical fiction, the best-known of which today is *The Devil's Wind* (1912), another sweeping period romance, this one set during the Sepoy Mutiny (1857-58) in India, a region with which the author, as we shall see, had extensive familiarity. Like *A Marriage under the Terror*, *The Devil's Wind* received much praise from reviewers for its sheer storytelling élan. One notice, for example, pronounced the novel "an achievement of some magnitude" on account of "the extraordinary vividness...the reality of the atmosphere...the scenes that shift and move with the swiftness of a moving picture...." (*The Bookman*, August 1912) With her knack for spinning a yarn, it perhaps should come as no surprise that Patricia Wentworth during the early years of the Golden Age of mystery fiction (roughly from 1920 into the 1940s) launched upon her own mystery-writing career, a course charted most successfully for nearly four decades by the prolific author, right up to the year of her death in 1961.

Considering that Patricia Wentworth belongs to the select company of Golden Age mystery writers with books which have remained in print in every decade for nearly a century now (the centenary of Agatha Christie's first mystery, *The Mysterious Affair at Styles*, is in 2020; the centenary of Wentworth's first mystery, *The Astonishing Adventure of Jane Smith*, follows merely three years later, in 2023), relatively little is known about the author herself. It appears, for example, that even the widely given year of Wentworth's birth, 1878, is incorrect. Yet it is sufficiently clear that Wentworth lived a varied and intriguing life that provided her ample inspiration for a writing career devoted to imaginative fiction.

It is usually stated that Patricia Wentworth was born Dora Amy Elles on 10 November 1878 in Mussoorie, India, during the heyday of the British Raj; however, her Indian birth and baptismal record states that she in fact was born on 15 October 1877 and was baptized on 26 November of that same year in Gwalior. Whatever doubts surround her actual birth year, however, unquestionably the future author came from a prominent Anglo-Indian military family. Her father, Edmond Roche Elles, a son of Malcolm Jamieson Elles, a Porto, Portugal wine merchant originally from Ardrossan, Scotland, entered the British Royal Artillery in 1867, a decade before Wentworth's birth, and first saw service in India during the Lushai Expedition of 1871-72. The next year Elles in India wed Clara Gertrude Rothney, daughter of Brigadier-General Octavius Edward Rothney, commander of the Gwalior District, and Maria (Dempster) Rothney, daughter of a surgeon in the Bengal Medical Service. Four children were born of the union of Edmond and Clara Elles, Wentworth being the only daughter.

Before his retirement from the army in 1908, Edmond Elles rose to the rank of lieutenant-general and was awarded the KCB (Knight Commander of the Order of Bath), as was the case with his elder brother, Wentworth's uncle, Lieutenant-General Sir William Kidston Elles, of the Bengal Command. Edmond Elles also served as Military Member to the Council of the Governor-General of India from 1901 to 1905. Two of Wentworth's brothers, Malcolm Rothney Elles and Edmond Claude Elles, served in the Indian Army as well, though both of them died young (Malcolm in 1906 drowned in the Ganges Canal while attempting to rescue his orderly, who had fallen into the water), while her youngest brother, Hugh Jamieson Elles, achieved great distinction in the British Army. During the First World War he catapulted, at the relatively youthful age of 37, to the rank of brigadier-general and the command of the British Tank Corps, at the Battle of Cambrai personally leading the advance of more than 350 tanks against the German line. Years later Hugh Elles also played a major role in British civil defense during the Second World War. In the event of a German invasion of Great Britain, something which seemed all too possible in 1940, he was tasked with leading the defense of southwestern England. Like Sir Edmond and Sir William, Hugh Elles attained the rank of lieutenant-general and was awarded the KCB.

Although she was born in India, Patricia Wentworth spent much of her childhood in England. In 1881 she with her mother and two younger brothers was at Tunbridge Wells, Kent, on what appears to have been a rather extended visit in her ancestral country; while a decade later the same family group resided at Blackheath, London at Lennox House, domicile of Wentworth's widowed maternal grandmother, Maria Rothney. (Her eldest brother, Malcolm, was in Bristol attending Clifton College.) During her years at Lennox House, Wentworth attended Blackheath High School for Girls, then only recently founded as "one of the first schools in the country to give girls a proper education" (*The London Encyclopaedia*, 3rd ed., p. 74). Lennox House was an ample Victorian villa with a great glassed-in conservatory running all along the back and a substantial garden--most happily, one presumes, for Wentworth, who resided there not only with her grandmother, mother and two brothers, but also five aunts (Maria Rothney's unmarried daughters, aged 26 to 42), one adult first cousin once removed and nine first cousins, adolescents like Wentworth herself, from no less than three different families (one Barrow, three Masons and five Dempsters); their parents, like Wentworth's father, presumably were living many miles away in various far-flung British dominions. Three servants--a cook, parlourmaid and housemaid--were tasked with serving this full score of individuals.

Sometime after graduating from Blackheath High School in the mid-1890s, Wentworth returned to India, where in a local British newspaper she is said to have published her first fiction. In 1901 the 23-year-old Wentworth married widower George Fredrick Horace Dillon, a 41-year-old lieutenant-colonel in the Indian Army with three sons from his prior marriage. Two years later Wentworth gave birth to her only child, a daughter named Clare Roche Dillon. (In some sources it is erroneously stated that Clare was the offspring of Wentworth's second marriage.) However in 1906, after just five years of marriage, George Dillon died suddenly on a sea voyage, leaving Wentworth with sole responsibly for her three teenaged stepsons and baby daughter. A very short span of years, 1904 to 1907, saw the deaths of Wentworth's husband, mother, grandmother and brothers Malcolm and Edmond, removing much of her support network. In 1908, however, her father, who was now sixty years old, retired from the army and returned to England, settling at Guildford, Surrey with an older unmarried sister named Dora (for whom his daughter presumably had been named). Wentworth joined this household as well, along with her daughter and her youngest stepson. Here in Surrey Wentworth, presumably with the goal of making herself financially independent for the first time in her life (she was now in her early thirties), wrote the novel that changed the course of her life, *A Marriage under the Terror*, for the first time we know of utilizing her famous *nom de plume*.

The burst of creative energy that resulted in Wentworth's publication of six novels in six years suddenly halted after the appearance of *Queen Anne Is Dead* in 1915. It seems not unlikely that the Great War impinged in various ways on her writing. One tragic episode was the death on the western front of one of her stepsons, George Charles Tracey Dillon. Mining in Colorado when war was declared, young Dillon worked his passage from Galveston, Texas to Bristol, England as a shipboard muleteer (mule-tender) and joined the Gloucestershire Regiment. In 1916 he died at the Somme at the age of 29 (about the age of Wentworth's two brothers when they had passed away in India).

A couple of years after the conflict's cessation in 1918, a happy event occurred in Wentworth's life when at Frimley, Surrey she wed George Oliver Turnbull, up to this time a lifelong bachelor who like the author's first husband was a lieutenant-colonel in the Indian Army. Like his bride now forty-two years old, George Turnbull as a younger man had distinguished himself for his athletic prowess, playing forward for eight years for the Scottish rugby team and while a student at the Royal Military Academy winning the medal awarded the best athlete of his term. It seems not unlikely that Turnbull played a role in his wife's turn toward writing mystery fiction, for he is said to have strongly supported Wentworth's career, even assisting her in preparing manuscripts for publication. In 1936 the couple in Camberley, Surrey built Heatherglade House, a large two-story structure on substantial grounds, where they resided until Wentworth's death a quarter of a century later. (George Turnbull survived his wife by nearly a decade, passing away in 1970 at the age of 92.) This highly successful middle-aged companionate marriage contrasts sharply with the more youthful yet rocky union of Agatha and Archie Christie, which was three years away from sundering when Wentworth published *The Astonishing Adventure of Jane Smith* (1923), the first of her sixty-five mystery novels.

Although Patricia Wentworth became best-known for her cozy tales of the criminal investigations of consulting detective Miss Maud Silver, one of the mystery genre's most prominent spinster sleuths, in truth the Miss Silver tales account for just under half of Wentworth's 65 mystery novels. Miss Silver did not make her debut until 1928 and she did not come to predominate in Wentworth's fictional criminous output until the 1940s. Between 1923 and 1945 Wentworth published 33 mystery novels without Miss Silver, a handsome and substantial legacy in and of itself to vintage crime fiction fans. Many of these books are standalone tales of mystery, but nine of them have series characters. Debuting in the novel *Fool Errant* in 1929, a year after Miss Silver first appeared in print, was the enigmatic, nautically-named *eminence grise* Benbow Collingwood Horatio Smith, owner of a most expressively opinionated parrot named Ananias (and quite a colorful character in his own right). Benbow Smith went on to appear in three additional Wentworth mysteries: *Danger Calling* (1931), *Walk with Care* (1933) and *Down Under* (1937). Working in tandem with Smith in the investigation of sinister affairs threatening the security of Great Britain in *Danger*

Calling and *Walk with Care* is Frank Garrett, Head of Intelligence for the Foreign Office, who also appears solo in *Dead or Alive* (1936) and *Rolling Stone* (1940) and collaborates with additional series characters, Scotland Yard's Inspector Ernest Lamb and Sergeant Frank Abbott, in *Pursuit of a Parcel* (1942). Inspector Lamb and Sergeant Abbott headlined a further pair of mysteries, *The Blind Side* (1939) and *Who Pays the Piper?* (1940), before they became absorbed, beginning with *Miss Silver Deals with Death* (1943), into the burgeoning Miss Silver canon. Lamb would make his farewell appearance in 1955 in *The Listening Eye*, while Abbott would take his final bow in mystery fiction with Wentworth's last published novel, *The Girl in the Cellar* (1961), which went into print the year of the author's death at the age of 83.

The remaining two dozen Wentworth mysteries, from the fantastical *The Astonishing Adventure of Jane Smith* in 1923 to the intense legal drama *Silence in Court* in 1945, are, like the author's series novels, highly imaginative and entertaining tales of mystery and adventure, told by a writer gifted with a consummate flair for storytelling. As one confirmed Patricia Wentworth mystery fiction addict, American Golden Age mystery writer Todd Downing, admiringly declared in the 1930s, "There's something about Miss Wentworth's yarns that is contagious." This attractive new series of Patricia Wentworth reissues by Dean Street Press provides modern fans of vintage mystery a splendid opportunity to catch the Wentworth fever.

Curtis Evans

Chapter One

"I ALWAYS GET what I want," said Lucas Dale. He stood with his back to the fire, a tall, well setup man in his easy forties, and smiled at his guests.

In the chair beside the fire Mrs. Mickleham, the Vicar's wife, was balancing rather unhandily the glass of sherry which she had not liked to refuse but did not really want to drink. She had the air of a hen confronted by a worm of some unknown species. She was not exactly a teetotaller, but she did not drink wine. Her expression became that of a hen with grave moral scruples.

Next to her, but farther from the fire, a square, dumpy woman with boot-button eyes and short grizzled hair. She wore the roughest of rough tweeds, shoes with square heels and soles half an inch thick, and ribbed hand-knitted stockings, all in a fierce shade of ginger. She was the wife of the thickset man with a thatch of white hair who was on the far side of the fire talking to the cheerful, rosy-faced Vicar. They were Sir John and Lady Vere, and they owned between them as much of the neighbourhood as did not belong by recent purchase to Lucas Dale.

Their daughter, Lydia Hammond, was sitting a little way off talking to Susan Lenox. They made a pretty contrast—Lydia small, dark, vivaciously pretty, with birdlike movements and rich carnation flush; and Susan with her fair, pearly skin where the colour came and went so readily, her dark blue eyes, and the hair like corn which is so ripe that it has begun to turn brown. There was gold in it still when she moved and the light caught the wave.

Lucas Dale was watching the gold. This was where Susan should be—here in the home where she had grown up, and not in the little house down the hill where she waited for a lover without a penny and nursed a fretful ailing aunt. This was Susan's place, in her drawing-room at King's Bourne, entertaining her guests, hostess to his host. But he would put better clothes on her than those shabby old blue tweeds, and give her a better ring, by heck, than the trumpery sapphire she had from Bill Carrick.

Lucas Dale did not have to formulate these thoughts. They were always present in his mind. When he looked at Susan as he was looking now, they merely became more insistent, and his desire for her more clamorous.

He looked away.

Cathleen O'Hara was coming from the door which led by a short length of passage to the library, a little, plain-faced thing with a shy charm for those who loved her. She was Lucas Dale's social secretary, and first cousin to Susan Lenox. Like Susan she had grown up in this house. She worked in it now, but she lived with her mother and Susan in the Little House down the hill. She came up the room now with a key-ring dangling from the little finger of her right hand, and between her two hands a shallow drawer or tray of some dark wood. The tray was lined with black velvet, and, disposed upon that flattering background, there were pearls, and pearls, and pearls.

Cathy walked very carefully indeed. People always made her feel rather nervous, and it would be quite dreadful if she were to knock against anyone or drop the tray. It was a great responsibility to have the handling of such valuable things. It frightened her to think how much they must be worth. She hadn't really liked having to take Mr. Dale's keys and get the pearls out of his safe, but she hadn't liked to say so. As she came into the room she heard him say in that very strong voice of his, "I always get what I want." Well, he had wanted money, and he had wanted King's Bourne, and he had wanted these pearls. If he wanted anything he would get it.... Something looked out of her thoughts and frightened her so much that she did very nearly drop the tray. But not quite. She brought it carefully to Lucas Dale, and gave a small breath of relief as he lifted it from her hands.

"And the keys, Mr. Dale—" She held them out.

Lucas Dale smiled. He was a big, dark man, very well shaved, very well groomed. He wore a loose brown shooting-coat, not too new. He had well kept hands, but the nails were square and ugly, and the three middle fingers all of the same length. When he smiled he showed strong white teeth. He said in the kind voice which didn't frighten her,

"Keep them, Cathy. I shall want you to put the tray away when we've finished."

He set it down on a small walnut table. Lady Vere and Mrs. Mickleham both leaned forward, the one intent, the other fluttering. It was Mrs. Mickleham who said,

"Oh, Mr. Dale, what lovely pearls!"

Lucas Dale was looking at Susan. She hadn't moved, or turned her head, or stopped her talk. A rough, pleasurable anger possessed him. It was that way, was it? "All right then, we'll see." He lifted his voice and called across the room.

"Mrs. Hammond—don't you like pearls? Come along and look at mine."

He felt a dark amusement at the alacrity with which Lydia responded. She jumped up, pulling Susan with her.

"Don't give them all away till I come!" she cried, and came running.

Susan Lenox followed slowly.

Dale was holding up a lovely milky string of perfectly matched pearls, and the Vicar was saying,

"Really, you know, they must be very valuable. I suppose you are well covered by insurance? I shouldn't care to have such valuable things in the house myself."

Lucas Dale laughed.

"I keep a loaded revolver, and take care that everyone knows it. Anyway what's the good of having a thing if you're going to keep it shut up in a bank? It might just as well be stolen and have done with it. As a matter of fact it would be stolen. I should be letting my own fear of a possible burglary rob me of my everyday enjoyment. Not that I look at these pretty things every day by any means. In fact I don't know when I had them out last, or when I shall have them out again. Perhaps not for months. But I like to feel I've got them under my hand."

"Pearls ought to be worn," said Lydia Hammond. She put out her hands with a quick, darting movement, took them, and looped them about her neck. They hung down over her honey-coloured jumper in two rows. Her colour glowed and her dark eyes sparkled. "Oh, I must see how I look!" she cried, and ran down the room to the tall Venice glass between the two end windows.

Sir John watched her go indulgently, but Lady Vere stiffened a little. "Lydia is so impulsive, and I'm sure neither her father nor I—" The thought just stirred, and was gone again.

Lydia gazed ecstatically at her own reflection. This room and the pearls suited each other. She could see the whole of it in the glass. The old ivory panelling, with electric candles in gilt sconces lighting it. The Adam mantelpiece. The dark polished floor with its beautiful Persian rugs. The long windows, curtained in a deep lovely shade of blue. The little group about the fire. "Mummy's getting stouter—she ought to slim.... Cathy is exactly like a mouse. I can't think how she ever plucked up enough spirit to take a secretarial course, but *what* a good thing she did.... Susan and Lucas Dale—Well, Bill Carrick or no Bill Carrick, they make a very good-looking couple. And this is Susan's room. If he had furnished it for her—perhaps he did.... And she ought to be wearing the pearls—perhaps she will. She'd be quite breath-taking. Oh, bother Bill Carrick!"

Lydia's reflection stopped pleasing her. She came running back and pulled off the pearls as she came.

"Too much temptation, Mr. Dale. You'd better take them. But it does seem a shame that they shouldn't be worn."

"Oh, I hope my wife will wear them some day," said Lucas Dale.

Lydia had a way of saying the first thing that came into her head. She did it now.

"Oh, *what* a pity I'm married!"

Lady Vere said, "Lydia!" and Mrs. Mickleham said, "Lydia—*dear!*" Sir John Vere chuckled, and Lucas Dale threw back his head and laughed.

Lydia laughed too.

"It isn't fair to come dangling pearls like that at a poor sailor's wife. Freddy's an angel, and he'd give me the world if he'd got it, but he hasn't and he never will have, so it's Woolworths for me and for ever and ever, amen."

Mrs. Mickleham broke in eagerly.

"And they're really wonderful, are they not?" (Dear Lydia, how heedless—how very heedless! I don't wonder Lady Vere looks vexed. And what Mr. Dale can be *thinking*!) She felt extremely fluttered, but she pressed on. "Do you know, with all these wonderful imitations, I am not sure, Mr. Dale, that I would not rather be spared the anxiety of owning valuable pearls."

Sir John burst out laughing.

"I don't believe it, Mrs. Mickleham. The woman isn't born who can resist pearls—and did you ever hear of Jenny Baxter who refused the man before he axed her?"

Mrs. Mickleham looked down the long nose which so strongly resembled a hen's beak. Sir John might come of a very old family, but there were times when she considered that he forgot himself. That remark was in decidedly bad taste—like Lydia's. But Lydia was only heedless. Everyone knew that she was devoted to Freddy Hammond, but it was a pity to say things like that, especially when he had to be away so much at sea.

Sir John stopped laughing and addressed his host.

"Seriously, Dale, I wonder you're not afraid of having those things in the house. They're a temptation, that's what they are—and that's the Vicar's department. Hi, Vicar, you'll have to preach him a sermon about it next Sunday." He only half dropped his voice before adding—"make a nice change."

All this time Cathleen O'Hara had stood silently by the table which held the tray. Lydia pounced on her now.

"Come along, Cathy, let's be tempted together. What's your fancy? Me for the black pearls. Oh, Mr. Dale—how divine!"

"I shall count them before you go, Mrs. Hammond, so take care."

He still held the long string in his hand. He turned away with it now to Susan Lenox, who was standing behind Cathy.

"Will you put them on for a minute? I'd like to see what they look like. Mrs. Hammond is too dark for them really—pearls are for fair women. I'd like very much to see them on you, if you would be so good." Words and voice were formal.

Susan had no excuse for refusing. She had a feeling that the whole scene had been contrived for just this very end—to make her try on the pearls. And Lydia had made it impossible for her to refuse. A glow of anger stained her cheeks and brightened there as the thought went through her mind, "He'll think I'm blushing—they'll all think so." But her voice was cool and detached as she said,

"Oh, certainly, if you want me to. But I'm one of the people whom Sir John won't believe in—I don't really care for pearls." She held them up against her for a moment without fastening the clasp.

She became aware that they were all watching her—Mrs. Mickleham nervously, Lady Vere with her shallow stare, Sir John prodigiously amused, the Vicar kindly and unaware, Lydia's eyes dancing with mischief, Cathy with something scared about her, and Lucas Dale with the smouldering look which made her come near to hating him. They could all see how pale she turned.

She dropped her hands from her neck and gave him back the pearls.

"And I must say goodnight, Mr. Dale. Aunt Milly will be wanting me."

Lydia jumped up from where she had been kneeling by the tray.

"I'll walk down the hill with you, darling, and the parents can pick me up when they go. Daddy hasn't nearly finished drinking sherry yet, and it's so much cheaper for him not to drink his own these stony-broke days. Goodbye, Mr. Dale. I simply daren't stay near those pearls any longer, but I call you to witness they're all there, even the loose ones which would be so frightfully easy to pinch. Here, you'd better count them. If you go and lose them, I'm not going to have you say it's me. Freddy wouldn't like it—his family are all fearfully respectable. Come on—count them!"

Mrs. Mickleham said, "Lydia—*dear!*" Lucas Dale said, "It's all right, Mrs. Hammond, they're all there. You can leave the room without a stain on your character. And now, Cathy, I think you might put them away again. They don't come out more than once in a blue moon anyhow."

Chapter Two

THE PROPER WAY to reach the Little House was down half a mile of drive and along the road into Netherbourne village, but it was less than a quarter of a mile as the crow flies, and no more even without wings, if you went straight down past the three terraces and the tennis courts, through the vegetable garden, to the orchard which ran right down to Mrs. O'Hara's fence.

Mrs. O'Hara had been Millicent Bourne—one of the beautiful Bourne twins. She and her sister Laura were the talk of their first season. And then the war came. Millicent married a penniless Irishman who was killed in 1917, leaving her with a delicate baby and no income. Laura married John Lenox. He was killed in 1916, and Laura died the following year. Millicent O'Hara came back to her brother at King's Bourne. Everyone said that she would marry again, but she did not. She kept house very inefficiently for James, who was twenty years older than his young sister, and by degrees she lost her looks and her health and became a rather tiresome invalid. James Bourne was a confirmed bachelor. He was very glad to have poor Milly there, and to have her little girl and poor Laura's little girl. He became, in fact, extremely fond of the children, but being a most amiable, indolent and inconsequent-minded man, it never occurred to him to make any provision for them. When he died there was really nothing left. The estate had paid death-duties twice during the war, and everything that could be mortgaged was mortgaged. For the last couple of years things had been kept going with borrowed money. Lucas Dale stepped in and bought the place lock, stock and barrel. He was English, though he had made his great fortune in America, and he meant to settle in England and marry an English wife. He meant to marry Susan Lenox.

Mrs. O'Hara moved into the Little House with Susan and Cathy. She supposed they would get along somehow. There was about two hundred and fifty pounds a year. They couldn't afford a servant. One of the girls could look after her and the house, and the other could be earning something. Susan would have been the one to go out and earn, but it was no use wasting a training on her if she was going to marry Bill Carrick, so it was Cathy who went to stay with old Cousin Emma in London and took a three months secretarial course, the enterprise being financed by the sale of Mrs. O'Hara's Brussels flounce. She wept over the sacrifice at the time, and would probably never stop talking about it, because of course Cathy ought to have the lace for her wedding dress, but on the other hand they really couldn't live on two hundred and fifty a year, and how fortunate that Cathy should step straight into such an unexceptionable post. Mrs. O'Hara quite brightened when she talked it over with Mrs. Mickleham—"He treats her perfectly, like the nicest uncle. And she comes back to all her meals."

"But I thought—surely the Vicar was told—that Mr. Dale had a secretary already. He has been superintending all the alterations. A Mr. Phipson—yes, that's it—Mr. Montague Phipson. Quite a pleasant little man."

"Oh, yes, but he's the business secretary. Mr. Dale has a great many business interests. He doesn't want Cathy for that sort of thing. She is to do the flowers and—well, all the sort of things she and Susan used to do for my brother—only of course there will be far more entertaining now. He came to see me about it and was quite charming."

This was three months ago. Tonight Susan and Lydia took the garden way to the Little House. They came out on to the first of the terraces and saw the whole slope of the hill under a waning moon and a dappled sky, and the lights in the village far below.

Susan stood for a moment and looked. She felt Lydia's hand on her arm.

"I don't know how you can bear it. It isn't his—it's yours. It will always be yours."

"But I don't want it, Lydia—I never did. I've seen too much of trying to keep up a big place on a small income—" her soft laugh broke in—"or no income at all."

"I didn't mean that," said Lydia—"I didn't mean that at all. What about having the income to match the place? Wouldn't you like that?"

Susan laughed again.

"Bill wouldn't. He wants to build everything we live in. He says what's the good of being an architect if you don't. So we shall start in a three-roomed cottage and work up."

Lydia's eyes sparkled in the moonlight. She said crisply,

"And *when* do you start?"

They had been standing still, but Susan moved now. It was not until they reached the next terrace that she answered Lydia's question.

"It is so dreadfully hard for an architect to get a start. They mustn't advertise, and it's uphill work getting known. The Maynards were awfully pleased with the house he did for them. He proposed to me on the strength of that. But he's only had small jobs since then. People say they're going to build, and then building costs go up, or something like that, and they don't do it. If we had any capital, it would be different, because then he could build to sell or let without waiting for orders, and get known that way."

"It sounds like waiting a long time," said Lydia. She paused and added, with the effect of flinging a dart, *"Are you going to wait?"*

Susan stopped at the top of the steps to the last terrace. The moonlight stole all her colour, but it wasn't the moonlight which made her look so stern.

"What do you mean? Of course I'm going to wait."

"Are you?" said Lydia. "Are you? *Are you, Susan?* I wouldn't if I were you. Do you remember how Lolly Smith got engaged to a boy who had just gone into the army, and he went out to India, and they went on being engaged for years and years and years till she'd completely gone down the drain, and then he married a girl of eighteen whom he'd known for a month?"

"Lydia!"

"Well, suppose you both go on waiting. What a look-out! You'll begin to lose your looks, and either he'll get plodding and dull and won't care, or else he'll get worked up and nervy and feel that he's spoiling your life. You can take your pick of which you'd rather have on your hands, but you can bet your life, whichever it is, it'll be hell for you."

"Lydia!"

"Oh, you don't think so now. Look at me. I was crazy to marry Freddy—we were crazy about each other. And what's the good of it? I'm sitting at home with the parents, and he's in China. I can't go out, and he can't come home. What's the good of it?"

Susan laughed.

"You'd do it again tomorrow."

Lydia stamped her foot.

"Because I'm a fool! And now you're angry with me—Susan—"

Susan put out a hand and touched her.

"I'm not really. But you mustn't say things about Bill."

They went down the steps together and across the last terrace. As they began to skirt the tennis courts, Lydia said in something just above a whisper,

"It was seeing you at King's Bourne again, and—and—the pearls. I *wanted* you to have them."

Susan was so secure that she could let a laugh come into her voice.

"It's no good, Lyddy."

"You *might*—" Lydia was breathless with her own daring.

"No."

"What's the good of saying no? He's in love with you—he'd give you anything in the world. He only had those pearls out because he wanted to see them on you." She broke into sudden laughter. "And I ran off with them! You bet he hated me quite a lot for that. But you can't say he hasn't got good manners. I piled it on on purpose just to see how he'd react, and he bore up nobly. Oh, Susan, *think* of lifting about half an eyelash and having King's Bourne, and a millionaire, and those divine pearls all put down at your feet just waiting for you to pick them up."

"I should find them too heavy. And I'd much rather not think about it, if you don't mind. And, Lyddy, if you don't want to make me angry, you'll stop. Up to now I've laughed, but I'm not going to go on laughing."

"Well, I wouldn't like to make you really angry, darling. You know, the only time I did you nearly scared me dead. I believe if you were really roused you might do something rather frightful."

They passed the tennis courts and took the orchard path.

"You do talk a lot of nonsense, Lyddy," said Susan.

Chapter Three

LYDIA CAME IN and prattled to Mrs. O'Hara about Freddy, about the climate of China and how dreadful the war was, about Lucas Dale and the drawing-room curtains at King's Bourne, and about the pearls.

"Rows and rows and rows of them—pink ones, and black ones, and white ones—enough to undermine any woman. Wouldn't it be too marvellous if he put them into a lucky bag and let us all have a dip?"

"I had quite a nice little string when I was a girl," said Mrs. O'Hara in her plaintive voice.

She lay propped up with cushions on the comfortable deep sofa which she had brought from her own room at King's Bourne. When Lucas Dale bought the whole place as it stood he had begged Mrs. O'Hara to take with her to the Little House whatever she needed in the way of furniture. She had protested gracefully and then interpreted her needs with the utmost liberality. The room was full, and overfull. The sofa was too large for it. There were too many chairs, too many knick-knacks, and far too much china. It was obvious that the furnishings of a much larger room or rooms had been crammed into the small space. The walls were crowded too.. A dark portrait over the mantelpiece was jostled by sketches which grandmamma had brought from Venice. A reproduction in red of Titian's Assumption hung side by side with The Soul's Awakening in sepia. On another wall an enlargement of her own wedding group was surrounded by some really lovely Chinese paintings of butterflies, birds and flowers.

Mrs. O'Hara herself resembled a faded watercolour. Her hair had not turned grey. It had become dull like her skin, her lips, her eyes. She was not at all unhappy, because she loved Cathy and Susan, and derived a great deal of pleasure from the precarious condition of her health. Her drops, her tonics, her pills, her little bottle of tablets, the sympathetic visits of Dr. Matthews who had been an early admirer—all these stood between her and the actual drabness of her life. She played with them as a girl plays with her dolls. She had seen herself as the admired young girl, the lovely bride, the pathetic widow. Now she was the brave invalid, pale, fragile, interesting. And of course if you are an invalid you do escape life's duller duties—taking the dog for a walk when you would rather sit by the fire, visiting the—sometimes—ungrateful poor, and going to church in the rain.

"Quite a nice little string," said Mrs. O'Hara. "And Susan's mother had one too. They were a coming-out present from our father. Laura sold hers for the Red Cross—after her husband was killed, you know—but I kept mine until the other day, and it only fetched twenty pounds, though I am sure it cost a great deal more than that. Does Freddy *like* being in China, my dear? And I hope you have good news of Roger. Are they together? Because that would be so nice. I do think it is so delightful that you should have married someone who was such a friend of your brother's. But of course that is how you came to meet Freddy—isn't it? I remember your bringing them both up to King's Bourne, and I thought then what friends they were. Of course, you know, my dear, I always have thought your brother Roger one of the handsomest young men I ever met. And you were all such friends, you, and Roger, and Susan, and Cathy—oh, yes—thank you, my dear—I am always dropping my handkerchief, I can't think why."

The conversation went on. Susan went away.

Roger Vere certainly was very good-looking. He had a way with him too, a sailor's way, and when he came home on leave he added considerably to the gaiety of the countryside by making love to every girl he met. He had made rather special love to Susan a year ago when she and Cathy were bridesmaids at Lydia's wedding and he was Freddy Hammond's best man. Bill had been jealous. Susan caught her breath as she remembered just how jealous Bill had been. It had really been a thankful day when Roger took his irresponsible charm to the China Station. Hong Kong might have him and welcome as far as Susan Lenox was concerned.

She began to prepare the evening meal, and presently a loud hooting announced the fact that Sir John Vere had finished his sherry and was in a hurry to get home. Susan pushed her soup to the side of the range and went out to the gate with Lydia. It opened straight upon the village street, with the front door almost in reach. Lydia kissed her with a little extra warmth. The door banged. The car moved off.

Susan stood a moment to see the tail-light disappear. The sound of the engine died away. She could hear the water flowing on the other side of the street—the little deep stream which gave the village its name. Each house had its own culvert. Under all these tiny bridges the water flowed ceaselessly, sometimes flooding out into the roadway after heavy rain, never failing through the longest drought. Susan's room looked this way. She loved the voice of the stream, she loved to wake and hear it in the night. She lingered and listened to it now.

She had turned to go in, when she heard another sound, a man's footsteps coming nearer. She stood with the gate in her hand. Bill— but it couldn't be Bill—he would have let her know. And then the dark shape loomed. Warmth and happiness flooded up in her. She let go of the gate and was in his arms.

"Bill!"

"Susan!"

They stood holding one another close. She put up her face and they kissed. It did not matter how long or how short a time it was since they had met, there was always this rush of happiness, this deep contentment when they were together again.

Susan spoke first.

"Oh, Bill—why didn't you ring up? We've got a dreadfully female meal."

"I knew you lived on buns when I wasn't here."

"It isn't buns—it's eggs."

"I'm strong on eggs. And as a matter of fact I did ring up, but they couldn't get any reply."

"That's Aunt Milly. It's too naughty—she just won't get up off her sofa. And it's no good saying anything, because she's got it firmly embedded in her mind that the telephone means bad news. I did hound her into answering it when we moved down here, and the very first time she did, it was Uncle James' lawyer to say those mining shares of hers were a total loss. I found her having palpitations, and after that she simply wouldn't go near the thing again. Oh, Bill, how did you come?"

"Car. Ted Walters has taken her on. He'll pick me up in the morning."

"Come along in and help me cook the eggs. Cathy'll be back any time now."

"Wait a minute. Susan, I've had a nibble. I had to come and tell you about it."

"Oh, Bill!"

"It's the most wonderful chance if it comes off. But you won't count on it—will you? I mean, it's no good counting on it—not with people who come and talk about building houses anyway. They're all over you one minute, and everything you say goes, and the next thing you know they're as flat as yesterday's beer and you wouldn't think they knew what an architect was for. All the same, listen, Susan. You know the Maynards really are pleased with their house.

Well, Mrs. Maynard's got a second cousin, who's got a third cousin umpty-ump times removed, who is married to Gilbert Garnish—"

Susan said in a faint, flabbergasted voice,

"Darling, *who* is Gilbert Garnish?"

"You don't read the papers. Gilbert is a pillar of our Empire trade—things in tins, things in bottles. 'Mr. Smith will never leave home again now that Mrs. Smith has learned that Garnish's Grand Goods are what keep husbands at home. Do you want to keep your husband at home? Give him Garnish's Turkey in a Tablet on his toast! Give him Garnish's Grand Jams! Give him Garnish's Glorious Jellies! Give him—' "

"Oh, Bill, stop!"

"Well, have you got Garnish?"

"Yes, yes—what about him?"

Bill picked her up and hugged her.

"Well, I hope I've got him too."

"Oh, Bill—how marvellous!"

"We mustn't count on it, but he did seem awfully keen. He took about three hours telling me what he wanted—and when you're a Garnish time is money. The trouble is he wants something as much like Balmoral as possible. Not quite so big, of course, and the last thing in plumbing, but the date-stamp on his mind is definitely of the Balmoral period." He began to sing at the top of his voice, "My heart's in the Highlands, my heart is not here."

"Bill! The whole village will think you're drunk!"

"I am. I've been bottling it up all the way down, and it's gone to my head with a rush." A powerful hug took all the breath out of her body. "Susan—oh, Susan, if it comes off, we can get married at once! He's going to let me know on Monday, and I oughtn't to have told you, but I just couldn't keep it in. And it doesn't take more than three days to get a licence, so if it comes off—Susan, if it comes off— we'll get married on Thursday!"

Susan had the strangest feeling of unreality. Bill's arms had been round her like this in so many a dream, his coat rough against her cheek—rough and a little wet. It hadn't been raining. She must have cried to make his shoulder wet like this.

She said in a straining voice, "Don't count on it so much, my darling—*don't*," and knew that the words went past him.

"Susan—you will—if it comes off. You will, darling, you will!"

A shiver went over her. It was a dream like all those other dreams. She would wake up. It wasn't real. But even in a dream kisses are sweet and love is dear. She put up her lips to Bill and clung to him.

Everything seemed much more real again when they were heating up the soup and scrambling the eggs together. Bill let the soup boil over whilst he went poaching amongst Susan's tins looking for candied peel. In the light he could be seen as a hefty, upstanding young man with dark hair and rather nondescript grey eyes, rather square features, rather a jutting chin, rather the look of a man who likes having his own way but will take it with a due regard for other people just so long and just so far as the bounds set by a hot temper and a cool sense of justice. The temper was hot enough. Susan had seen it directed against other people, never yet against herself. She had seen him fight a carter twice his weight when he was fifteen because the man was lashing a horse that was unfit for work. She had seen him throw a tramp who had frightened Cathy into the middle of the village pond a couple of years later. The temper was there all right, but at twenty-seven he had it under control.

He was sitting on the dresser eating his stolen peel, when Cathy slipped in like a little mouse, with her brown dress, her mousy brown hair, and her soft brown eyes.

"Mummy says are you nearly ready, because—"

"She's going to swoon," said Bill.

He got down from the dresser with a large piece of green peel in his hand and gave her a sticky kiss.

Susan laughed.

"I shall have to lock everything up when we're married, or he'll ruin us. We're just coming, Cathy. He let the soup boil over."

They went in processionally, each girl with a soup-plate, and Bill in front with two.

Rather to Susan's dismay, Bill poured out the whole story of Mr. Garnish to the assembled family.

"But, Bill, we mustn't count on it—"

"Who's counting?"

"You are."

"I'm not. I'm living in the present. If Gilbert comes off, well, it's all right—it's all stupendously right. And if Gilbert doesn't come off, a good time will have been had by all over his castle in the air." He threw back his head and laughed. "I know a chap who says we're going to be able to photograph thoughts—dreams—things like that. I bet Gilbert's castle in the air would come out something like the result of putting Balmoral and the Regent Palace Hotel and one of those big hydropathics into a cocked hat and shaking them up. And Susan and I are going to be married on Thursday, Aunt Milly. No relations, by request, but you and Cathy can come if you're good. Have some more. Susan scrambles a very good egg—that's why I'm marrying her. Lots of vitamins in scrambled eggs, if you want to get up your strength for the wedding."

Mrs. O'Hara passed up her plate. She had an excellent appetite.

"My dear boy, how you do run on," she said in an indulgent voice.

When the meal was over and cleared away there came out of a cardboard cylinder the plans, brought up to date, of the house which they would build if Gilbert came off. Bill had produced the first sketch within twenty-four hours of their engagement two years ago. It had to be as cheap as possible. But it wasn't going to be just like everybody else's house. It was going to be different—it was going to be theirs. Only three rooms to start with—kitchen and good-sized living-room downstairs and bedroom above. The latest sketch, encouraged by Gilbert, had rather let itself go. The squeezed-in bathroom had become comparatively palatial, and the most exciting things had happened to the garden. They sat with their heads together and babbled about cherry trees and lavender hedges.

It was all very comfortable and comforting, but in the middle Susan looked up and saw Cathy looking at them. She had been reading, but her hands had dropped and her book had fallen. She sat on a square brocaded stool with her back to the fire watching Susan and Bill. Her eyes were frightened. Susan looked back quickly at the plans of her little house. But it didn't look real any more. It was just pencil marks on a sheet of drawing-paper.

Chapter Four

BILL WENT OFF in the morning. Somewhere round about twelve o'clock, when Susan was just going to make a cake, the telephone bell rang. Well, at least it hadn't waited until she had got her hands in the flour. She picked up the receiver and heard Cathy say, "Is that you?"

Susan laughed a little.

"Who else could it possibly be?"

"I know—but you see—" Cathy sounded a little breathless. "Are you very busy? Because Mr. Dale is planning the new lily pool, and he wondered if you could possibly spare the time to come with us and have a look at the place."

"I'm making a cake," said Susan, not quite truthfully.

There was an indistinct murmur from the telephone, and then Lucas Dale's voice.

"Miss Lenox, Cathy has told you we are planning the pool. She says you are much better at that sort of thing than she is. You don't know how grateful I'd be if you would come and have a finger in the pie."

"But I've got to make a cake, Mr. Dale—to say nothing of lunch."

"I see—" He sounded as if he were considering a point of importance. "Well then—I ought to have thought of that—we must just make it after lunch. How would that do?"

Susan said, "I could come after lunch."

There was colour in her cheeks as she hung up the receiver. She could not refuse without rudeness, and he had given her no reason to be rude. On the contrary he had been all that was kind and considerate to Aunt Milly, and, she supposed, to her. He paid Cathy three pounds a week for doing very much what she had done for Uncle James without being paid at all. It would be cutting off the family nose to spite her face if she were to offend Lucas Dale, and she really had not the slightest reason for offending him. He had never said or done anything to which she could take exception. All he had done was to look at her rather longer and rather more often than she liked, and the long, frequent looks had said what she did not choose that anyone except Bill should say—"You're lovely. I love to look at you."

Well, if he got no farther than that.... Other men's eyes had said the same things, but he knew, everyone knew, that she was engaged to Bill. And it would be fun to plan the lily pool. It was fun to plan anything when you could go absolutely all out without having to think what it would cost.

She went up through the garden after lunch. There were snowdrops sheltering among ivy leaves in the orchard bank. The green spikes of the crocuses were pushing through. The air was damp and mild, the sky patched blue and grey.

She came out on the upper terrace, and found Lucas Dale waiting for her. He said, "Cathy had some letters to finish," and she felt that she had been trapped. He had used Cathy to trap her, and she found that hard to forgive. Her temper stiffened. If he asked for a snub he would get one, and he would have no one but himself to thank for it.

But for the moment no one could have stood in less need of snubbing. They went across the rose garden to the far end where a hedge shut off the view.

"You see, this is what I thought. An archway here, so that you can see down the valley, and beyond the arch—well, that is really what I wanted your advice about. Would you have the pool there, and should the hedge be carried round it?"

Susan considered.

"If you have the pool, I think it would have to be enclosed. It would need a formal setting—you couldn't just put it down in the open. I think we ought to go round to the other side of the hedge and see if there's enough flat ground there."

They turned, but when they came to where the sundial waited to record a sunny hour Lucas Dale took a step ahead and stopped there right in her path.

"It will do another time," he said. "I want it to be just as you would like, but just now—I want to talk to you."

Susan stood and looked at him.

"What do you want to talk to me about?"

A little dark colour came into his face. There was a sense of emotion kept in check. He said,

"Don't you know, Susan?" And then, "I think you do."

Susan kept her eyes on his face. She said,

"I don't want to know."

"Is that because you want to save my feelings? But suppose I don't want to have them saved. It won't hurt you to listen to me, will it? I won't make a scene or distress you. I only want a hearing—I only want to put my case."

"You haven't got a case," said Susan quickly.

"You mean you have prejudiced it. Well, even so, it can't possibly hurt you to listen to what I have got to say."

"But it's no use—"

He smiled.

"How do you know that? I have got things that I want to say to you. I shall never rest until I have said them—I shall never stop trying to make you listen. You know, I am not asking so much—I only want you to listen. You will do that, won't you?"

Susan looked away. There was something in his eyes—something. She said,

"Very well, I'll listen—but it isn't any good."

There was a little pause. She thought he came a step nearer, and she thought that he was smiling.

"We are both taking a good deal for granted—aren't we, Susan? You're quite right of course. How soon did you find out that I was in love with you?"

Her colour rose. She made no reply. He said,

"I wanted you to know. It happened the first time I saw you. You had on a blue dress—you had caught it on a rose bush—you asked me if I had a pin, and I gave you one to pin it up with. I fell in love with you then. Whilst you were pinning your dress I said to myself, 'That's my wife. She doesn't know it yet, but that's my wife.' "

Susan made an abrupt movement.

"I can't listen to this sort of thing, Mr. Dale."

"Why? It doesn't hurt you, does it? And you promised to listen. I was trying to explain. I don't want you to think I fell in love with you in just the ordinary way—I didn't. You got me the way a woman does get a man once in a while. I'm not saying much about how I feel, but if there's any way a man can love a woman more than I love you, I'd like to know about it so that I can love you that way too."

The tears stung in Susan's eyes.

"Oh, Mr. Dale, *don't!*"

"Because of Bill Carrick?"

"You know we're going to be married—you've always known."

He shook his head.

"I don't know it now. You're going to marry me."

Susan flamed with anger.

"How dare you say a thing like that to me? I'm engaged to Bill, and I'm going to marry him—sooner than you think perhaps."

"What does that mean?"

"It might mean next week."

Anger had ripped up her discretion. She wanted only to convince him and to convince herself. Because she was frightened—she was frightened. There was nothing to be frightened about. There were gardeners within call. What could he do? She couldn't guess. He was smiling. His smile frightened her. He said easily,

"Look here, Susan—have you ever thought what you are doing to Bill Carrick? If you were fond of him you wouldn't want to do it.

He may be as clever as paint and as good at his job as you think he is, but how is a young fellow going to get on if he's got a wife tied round his neck just when he wants all his thoughts and energies for his work? It's a hard scramble getting up the ladder, and the married men don't make it. They're carrying two, and the last little bit of push that means success peters out over trying to make both ends meet round the family bills."

Susan said, "Stop!" Her eyes were wide and frightened. This wasn't Lucas Dale's voice. It was a voice that talked with her when she was tired, when she was discouraged, when she couldn't sleep.

He said, "It's true."

Susan tried for words. She couldn't get the right ones. She tried again.

"People have to make up their own minds about that sort of thing. No one else can say."

"That's true enough," said Lucas Dale. "And you're putting it kindly. You might have told me to mind my own business, and if you had, I should have told you that it was my business because I love you, and because I know what I'm talking about. You see, when I was Carrick's age I did just that very thing—I fell in love and I married with nothing in the cupboard and my way to make. That's why I could say what I did just now—I've been there. It was just plain hell. You don't know what it does to a man, trying to be in two places at once, live two lives, work double tides, never get anywhere, and come home at night to a girl who hasn't known what to do with herself all day. There wasn't much left of our fine romance after six months. We had to count every penny. Sometimes there weren't any pennies to count. She was very pretty, and she'd been used to more money than I could give her—she was on the stage. We'd been married just a year when she walked out on me."

"Is she dead?" said Susan. Her soft heart was touched. She was sorry for him.

He gave a short laugh.

"No, she's not dead. You know the first thing I did when I struck a bit of luck? I got my divorce, and I was every bit as glad to get it as I had been to get the licence to marry her. That makes you stop and think a bit, doesn't it? She'd been bad luck to me all right, and when I got rid of her I got rid of my bad luck too. That's when I went out to my first job in the States, and from then on everything went right. I couldn't put a foot wrong if I tried. Well, I didn't mean to go into all that. I only wanted to show you that I knew what I was talking about. And if you marry me, I'd know how to make you a good husband. I'd make you happy, Susan."

She looked at him without anger and shook her head. There was pity in her eyes, and something that wasn't quite a smile.

"You don't think so now," said Lucas Dale. "But I'll make you happy, and I'll make you love me." His voice was suddenly rough with feeling.

"I can't listen," said Susan. "*Please*, Mr. Dale—"

He stood out of her way.

"That's all," he said.

Chapter Five

COMING UP the garden, Susan met Montague Phipson. He had an inky forefinger, and his usually sleek fair hair was slightly ruffled. His pince-nez dangled by the cord, and without it his pale blue eyes had a vague, short-sighted look. He was hurrying, but when he saw Susan he stopped.

"Oh, Miss Lenox, have you seen Mr. Dale anywhere?"

"He is in the rose garden—I've just left him there."

He looked worried.

"Then perhaps I—or is he just coming, do you think?"

Susan hoped not.

She said, "I'm late—I must fly," and hurried on. She was angry, resentful, and frightened, but in some odd way Dale had touched her. There had been tears in her eyes. She wanted to get away, to be alone, to think about Gilbert Garnish and fees—lots and lots of comfortable fat fees for Bill, so that they could have their house and make the two ends of their income not only meet but overlap.

It was an insult for this other man to call her his wife. What was it Miranda said to Ferdinand in The Tempest? "I am your wife if you will marry me. If not, I'll die your maid." She was Bill's wife and she would marry him. There wasn't anyone else—there would never be anyone else.

Half way across the terrace she came face to face with a spruce little man she had never seen before. He had rather upstanding black hair and a Charlie Chaplin moustache. His eyes snapped brightly here, there and everywhere. He reminded her of a squirrel looking for nuts. He took off his hat and addressed her politely.

"Have I the pleasure of speaking to Mrs. Dale?" Voice and accent were American.

To her annoyance Susan's colour rose. It was the flush of anger, but he wasn't to know that. He thought she was a mighty pretty girl, and he thought Dale was in luck.

"Oh, no—I'm Miss Lenox. If you are looking for Mr. Dale you will find him in the rose garden just down there."

She pointed, but he stood there and showed a disposition to talk.

"I'm a very old friend of Mr. Dale's. And will he be pleased to see me!"

Judging this to be a rhetorical question, Susan made no attempt to answer it. The little man threw back his head and laughed.

"And that depends on how much store Mr. Dale sets by his old friends, doesn't it? That was what you were going to say if I'd given you time. Did you ever hear him speak of Capper G. Bell? That's my father. Or Vincent C. Bell? That's me—and very pleased to meet you, Miss Lenox."

"Thank you," said Susan. "I have only known Mr. Dale a very short time. If you go down that path at the end of the terrace you will find him."

She got away this time with a slight inclination of the head and the faintest of smiles. The audience was closed. Vincent Bell considered that he had been given the air. He felt a trifle aggrieved. He was anxious to see Lucas Dale, but business which had kept for a couple of years would have kept for another ten minutes or so. He had an eye for a pretty girl. He looked after her with some regret before taking the path to the rose garden.

He encountered Mr. Montague Phipson coming back.

"Oh, Mr. Bell, I'm sorry you didn't wait in the drawing-room. Mr. Dale is just coming in."

Vincent Bell appeared to be amused.

"He's coming in, and I'm going out. What happens next? I'd say we'd meet—wouldn't you? We're very old friends, your Mr. Dale and me, and if you've been with him long you'll know just how much ice that cuts."

He laughed and went on down the path, leaving Mr. Phipson rather at a loss. Perhaps he ought to have stopped him. Perhaps Mr. Dale would be angry. It was at all times most necessary to know just what would or would not anger Mr. Dale. There seemed to be no rule about it, but just now, when he had announced the arrival of an old friend, there had certainly been no enthusiasm—rather, a certain tension.

Mr. Phipson didn't really know what to do. Lucas Dale had said quickly, "Where is he—in the drawing-room? All right, keep him there. I'm coming." And he had had no chance of keeping him there, because Mr. Bell had already followed him. It was quite on the cards that Mr. Dale would be furious. It was equally on the cards that he would be indifferent or amused. It was very worrying indeed not to know where you were. It might be as well to find out.

Mr. Phipson turned and went back along the path towards the rose garden, but before coming to it he struck across the grass and, arriving at the outer side of the fine yew hedge which kept the wind from the roses, proceeded to skirt it, head a little on one side and ears cocked, rather after the manner of the nervous terrier who smells a rat but is almost certain to turn tail and bolt if the rat comes out of his hole.

He had not gone more than a dozen yards, when Lucas Dale's voice made him start. It was raised above its normal tone, and there was no doubt that it was raised in anger.

"And what do you think you'll get by coming over here and pitching that sort of tale? You've come to the wrong shop, and the sooner you make up your mind to that the better! Not a penny—not a cent—not the smell of half a dime! Do you get that? You'd better!"

Mr. Phipson found himself very much interested. The hedge made a perfect screen, but it afforded no obstacle to sound. He could hear every word. He heard Vincent Bell laugh, and he heard him say in a tone of what he supposed to be mock admiration,

"If that isn't interesting!"

"I hope it interests you," said Lucas Dale.

"Very much—very much indeed. I like to see a man change his mind and change his tune, and I'm looking forward to seeing you change yours."

"You won't."

"Will you bet on it? I shouldn't if I were you, Dale, because you'd lose. You see, I've got you in a cinch. And how? You can't go into court, and I can." He laughed with apparent enjoyment. "Why, I'd be tickled to death! Too bad, isn't it? But that's the way I'm playing. Very nice place you've got here too. It would be a pity to have anything happen so that you'd have to move on—wouldn't it? You think it over, and when you've made up your mind you'll play my way you can let me know."

There was a pause. Then Mr. Phipson heard his employer say in a slow, harsh voice,

"Where are you staying?"

Vincent Bell sounded more amused than ever. He said,

"I'm stopping here."

Chapter Six

CATHLEEN O'HARA looked up from the letter she was writing. She had caught the sound of a footstep on the flagged path outside. Her writing-table faced the windows of a deep recess which gave her what amounted to a room of her own to work in, though it was open to the study. Lucas Dale's table, large, masculine, and in perfect order, stood on the far side of the large room. When he sat there he had only to lift his eyes to see across the terrace, and across the valley to the line of distant hills.

Cathy's windows were at the side of the house. The flagged walk ran below them. She looked over it to a small sunk garden which would be bright with spring bulbs later on. She wondered if it was Lucas Dale who was coming along the path, or his American friend who had dropped from the blue yesterday afternoon. She liked him very much. Or did she? She wasn't really sure. She liked the way he spoke. It was different—amusing. She liked his being so new, so different, but she wasn't sure whether she really liked him. When you have lived in a place all your life, you know everyone so very well. You know just what they will think and what they will say, and what they will do, and that may be dull, but it gives you a very safe feeling. When you don't really know people you don't feel quite so safe. Cathy liked to feel safe.

But it was neither Lucas Dale nor Vincent Bell who was coming along the path. It was a woman. She came up to the casement window and leaned on the sill, looking in. Cathy had never seen her before. As she met the bold, challenging stare she began to wish that she hadn't opened that window. The sun on the glass had tempted her.

The woman leaned right in with her head and shoulders in the room and said,

"Lucas at home?"

Cathy was startled and showed it. She was a little bit of a thing, and the woman leaning in at the window was a haggard, strapping creature with big black eyes and bare sinewy hands. A lot of black hair in untidy loops and braids, and a bright handkerchief at her throat like a gipsy woman. If she hadn't used Dale's Christian name in the way she had, that is just what Cathy would have taken her for—one of those women who come swinging round to the back door, basket on hip, trying to sell rubbish to the maids and tell their fortunes. Maids don't like to send them away.

Cathy wouldn't have liked to send this woman away. She had on an old black cloth coat with a collar of draggled fur, and a black hat with a scarlet feather. There was a red dress under the coat, and the silk handkerchief was as bright as a parrot's wing. Long gold earrings bobbed and swung amongst the untidy braids. She laughed jeeringly at Cathy's dismay, and said in a deep voice that was sometimes harsh and sometimes musical,

"Come—I won't eat you. Where's Lucas? I want to see him."

Cathy collected herself. The woman had probably come to beg. Or had she? Her clothes were shabby, all except the coloured handkerchief, which was shiny and new. But she had said "Lucas"—

Cathy drew her chair back a little.

"I don't know if Mr. Dale is in. And—and—he doesn't see anyone without an appointment. Is he expecting you?"

"I don't know," said the woman. "He might be. He ought to have got my letter yesterday, but I don't suppose he'd tell you about it. He can be pretty close when it suits his book." She laughed a little. "He'll see me all right—you don't need to worry about that. Oh, yes, yes—he'll see me." She straightened up and took a look about her, left, right, over her shoulder, and back into the room again. "He's got a nice place here—I'll say that for it."

She had some kind of an accent which Cathy couldn't place. It would be very strong, and then it would fade right out. It was very strong as she spoke now.

"What's anyone want with a place like this? It wouldn't be my choice, I can tell you. What's he want it for?"

"You could ask him," said Cathy.

She got a sharp look. Her lips trembled unwillingly into a smile. The woman said quick and hard,

"Are you the girl?"

The smile vanished. Cathy's head lifted.

"I am one of Mr. Dale's secretaries. I will find out if he is in."

But before she could rise from her chair the woman said,

"What are you taking offence about? If you're the girl, you can say so, can't you? And if you're not, well, I suppose you can give a civil answer to a civil question."

"I think you had better put your questions to Mr. Dale," said Cathy. She crossed the room and rang the bell.

She was watched as she went and came again. There was a frown for her return.

"What's that picture over there above the chimney-piece?"

Cathy looked round, because although she knew it so well, she could always look at it again with a secret pleasure and emotion. The picture hung upon the jutting chimney-breast. It had hung there for as long as Cathy could remember. Two young girls in white dresses looked out from it at the room—at the unknown. One of them was dark and pale, with her hair in a mist about her face. The other was fair and golden, with deep dreaming eyes. Both had beauty. She said,

"It is Lazlo's portrait of my mother and her twin sister."

"Not much alike for twins."

"No—they were not at all alike."

"The dark one's your mother, I suppose. You don't favour her much." She gave a short laugh.

Cathy blushed and was glad to see the door open. The butler came in. She said with relief,

"Oh, Raby, is Mr. Dale in the house, do you know? This lady—" She turned to the woman. "What name shall he say?"

A card was produced, rather to Cathy's surprise. She would not have expected that such a gipsy-looking woman would have a card, but if she had one, it would be like this, very large and square, with a wild flourish of ornamental lettering. She glanced at the name as she handed it to Raby—Miss Cora de Lisle. And under that in pencil, Theatre Royal, Ledlington.

Before Raby had crossed to the door Miss de Lisle was back at the portrait.

"If that's your mother, why has Lucas got the picture?"

"It's valuable," said Cathy simply. "Mr. Dale bought all the pictures with the house."

"He can buy anything he's got a fancy for these days, or he thinks he can," said Cora de Lisle. "What about the other girl—the fair one?"

"She died a long time ago—in the war."

"Married?"

"Oh, yes. Her husband was killed."

"Any family?"

Cathy felt that she ought to be able to stop this inquisition. The woman gave her a helpless feeling. She said,

"My cousin Susan Lenox is her daughter."

And then she wished she hadn't answered. The haggard, sallow face waked up suddenly. It had a moment of fierce beauty as Cora de Lisle repeated the name Cathy had just spoken.

"Susan Lenox—that's the girl—that's the one I've been hearing about! What's she like?"

Cathy hoped earnestly that Raby would not be long. There was no harm in Miss de Lisle's questions, she supposed, but they made her feel dreadfully nervous. She said in a stumbling voice,

"Oh, Susan is fair."

"Like that girl in the picture?" Cora de Lisle laughed angrily. "Lucas would fancy that all right! And he'd fancy having her picture stuck up there where he could look at it. Come on—give us an answer, can't you! Is that what she's like?"

Cathy said "Yes" in a small, displeased voice. She felt offended, but too nervous and inadequate to check the woman's impertinence. Susan would have been able to do it—Susan—

Cora de Lisle said harshly, "If Lucas wants anything he gets it. If he wants that girl he'll get her, and she'll be as sorry for it as I was."

Cathy plucked up a little trembling courage.

"Please—"

"Well?"

"You mustn't say things like that."

"And who's going to stop me? I've got the free use of my tongue, and I'll say what I like with it to Lucas, and to you, and to Miss Susan Lenox!" She repeated the name with a sort of mocking music. "Miss Susan Lenox—and as pretty as a picture. He likes them pretty. I wasn't so bad myself. And now it's Miss Susan Lenox!" She laughed derisively. "I wonder how she'll like my cast-off shoes. I wouldn't fancy another woman's leavings myself."

Cathy was as white as a sheet. She thought Miss de Lisle had been drinking though it was so early in the day. She had always been terrified of anyone who drank. She got up and did her best to be brave.

"Please stop talking about Susan. I don't know what you've heard, but it's not true. She is engaged to someone else."

Cora de Lisle stared at her.

"Oh lord—so was I!" she said. "What difference does that make?"

"I don't know who you are," said Cathy, "but—oh, please go away!"

"I was Mrs. Lucas Dale for five years—and damned miserable ones too," said Cora de Lisle.

Cathy said, "Oh!"

And then she heard the sound she had been waiting for, the door opening and Raby coming in. He came right up to them and said in a low, respectful voice,

"Mr. Dale has gone out in the Daimler. He left word that he would not be back till late."

Chapter Seven

SUSAN WOKE in the night and heard a cry. It must have been the cry that waked her, and just for a moment her heart beat strongly. Then she knew what it was—Cathy calling out in her sleep as she had often done in their nursery days when anything had happened to disturb or frighten her. She jumped out of bed, caught up her dressing-gown without stopping to put it on, and ran barefoot into Cathy's room.

There were just the three bedrooms in the Little House, and because they had no maid they could have one each. When Bill stayed he got the drawing-room sofa, and said it spoilt him for his hard London bed. Cathy's room looked to the garden. The window stood wide to a cloudy sky and a soft, damp air.

Susan shut the door behind her and felt her way to the bed. She had reached the foot, when she heard a smothered sob. She was on her knees in a moment, holding Cathy close and speaking her name.

"Cathy—what is it? Are you ill?"

The little figure trembled. A shaky voice said, "Oh, Susan!" and was choked by another sob.

"My lamb, what is it? Tell Susan—"

"It—it—was a dream—a horrible dream—"

Susan had both arms round her, rocking her like a baby.

"Silly little thing! A dream isn't anything to be frightened about. It's gone. You've waked up, and I'm here. Everything's all right. Would you like the light?"

"Not with you—" There was a long quivering breath. "Lovely to wake up. But oh, I wish I didn't dream."

"You haven't done it for a long time, have you? And it's not true—it's never true, darling."

"It's just as bad while it lasts," said Cathy. She sat up and clutched at Susan. "It was a most horrid dream about being in a cage. I was locked in, and I couldn't get out, and they came and pointed at me through the bars. It was just as bad as if it was true, because as long as you don't wake up it is true in the dream."

She shook so much that the whole bed shook too.

Susan said "Nonsense!" in a brisk voice. She leaned sideways, found a box of matches, and lit the candle. It showed Cathy very much as the nursery candlelight had showed her when she was eight years old and afraid of the dark, like a little white ghost with her hair damp on her forehead and her hands clenched together under her chin.

"There—that's better," said Susan. "You don't wake right up in the dark. Shall I make you a cup of tea?"

"No—don't go—" There was another of those long breaths. "I'll be all right again soon, but—stay a little. I don't want it to come back."

Susan said, "It won't."

She put on her blue dressing-gown and came and sat on the bed, her hair loose on her neck and golden in the candlelight. She had been lying on her side before she woke, and that cheek was warmly flushed. Her eyes were very kind, and soft with sleep. Cathy looked at her and said,

"I don't want you to be cold. It's going away. Stay just a little."

"I'm not cold," said Susan.

"It's really going. I think that woman frightened me. She wasn't like anyone I've ever talked to before. There was something fierce about her. I expect that's what made me have that dream."

Susan said, "Silly little thing—" in a warm, sleepy voice. The candlelight flickered in her eyes, the flame had a halo round it. She blinked, and heard Cathy say as if from a long way off,

"Did you know he was married, Susan?"

It was like cold water in her face. The drowsy feeling left her. She said,

"Oh, yes—he told me. But they are divorced."

Cathy said, "Oh!" The frightened feeling touched her again. She said in a whisper,

"When did he tell you that?"

"Day before yesterday, when I came up about the lily pond."

"Why did he tell you?" said Cathy, still in that whisper.

There was no sleep in Susan now. She said in a clear, reserved voice,

"I suppose he wanted me to know."

"She wrote to him," said Cathy. "She said so. She wrote and said she was coming. He must have had the letter that morning before he asked you to come up and talk about the pool. If he told you then—Susan, why did he tell you then? I don't like it—it frightens me."

It didn't frighten Susan, it displeased her. She said,

"It doesn't matter, Cathy. If he knew she was coming he might have thought he would rather tell us himself that he had been married."

"He didn't tell *us*, he told you. Why did he do that?"

Susan made no answer.

All at once Cathy leaned forward and caught her wrist.

"He's in love with you—that's why he told you. It frightens me."

"I think you're being silly," said Susan. Her voice changed suddenly. "Cathy! You mustn't say things like that!"

"It's true."

Susan stood up.

"That's all the more reason for not talking about it," she said.

Chapter Eight

THAT WAS Friday night, the night between Friday and the Saturday morning which Susan was never to forget—a soft, cloudy night, with Cathy's dream of being in a cage set in it like a frightening picture.

The morning came up in a mist. Cathy came down to breakfast rather paler than usual and with dark smudges under her eyes, but she said no more about her dream or about being frightened, and went off up to King's Bourne at her usual time.

Susan took up Mrs. O'Hara's tray, washed up the breakfast things, made her own bed and Cathy's, and ran down to the gate to meet the postman. He was a very nice old man called Jeremiah Hill, and he was almost as pleased as Susan when he could bring out her letter with a flourish and say, "Morning, Miss Susan—here 'tis."

There was a letter this morning, but not a fat one. She took it into the kitchen and read it with sparkling eyes. There was the loveliest colour in her cheeks. There wasn't much in the letter, but there was enough good news for twenty letters. And it was short, because Bill had had only five minutes to catch the post.

"Garnish has just rung up, and I'm to come and see him in his London office first thing on Monday morning. He said he'd made up his mind to let me have a go at it. Said he thought a man did his best work when he'd got his way to make, and was bound to go all out if he wants to get anywhere at all. Said that's how it had been with him, and he expected it to be that way with me. Oh, *Susan—*"

She had got as far as that, when the telephone bell rang. The fixture was in the dining-room. She had only to push the communicating door and she could lift the receiver without really leaving the kitchen at all, which was very convenient, because you can't always take your eye off the stove. Just now there was nothing to watch. She picked up the receiver, put it to her ear, and heard Lucas Dale say,

"Susan, is that you?" His voice hurried on the words.

She said, "Yes—what is it?"

"Something's happened. Can you come up here at once?"

"What is it? Cathy—"

"She's not well. Will you come?"

"What is it? Please tell me, Mr. Dale."

"She is—upset. I can't tell you on the telephone. Will you come at once?"

She said "Yes", and hung up the receiver. She felt cold and sick. Cathy…. No, it was stupid to feel like this. Cathy had had a bad night. Perhaps she had turned faint. Men always got frightened. It was nothing.

She ran upstairs and told Mrs. O'Hara that she was going out. The breakfast tray was done with, and she took it away. After which she had to fetch a book from the drawing-room—"and oh dear, my knitting!"—before she could snatch down an old tweed coat and make her way up the hill.

As she came up on to the terrace outside the house she saw Lucas Dale at the glass door which led to the study. He had it in his hand, half open, and beckoned her in. She thought she had mastered her foolish fears, but the urgency with which he beckoned her and the sight of his grave, dark face set them all free again.

He brought her in and shut the door. There was a big leather-covered chair on either side of the hearth. In the farther one Cathy crouched, her face hidden in her hands. Her body had a stiff and twisted look. She did not move or turn when Susan said her name and came to her.

Susan's arms were round her.

"Cathy—what is it?" she said, as she had said it in the night. "What is it, darling—what is the matter?"

She felt Cathy stiffen.

Lucas Dale spoke.

"Something very unpleasant has happened, Susan. Perhaps I had better tell you about it."

She looked round, startled. He was over by the writing-table, looking down at it, moving some papers, not looking at her. That frightened her too. She got up and went over to him.

"What has happened, Mr. Dale?"

He did look at her then.

"I hate telling you, but there's no way out of it—you've got to know. It's those pearls, the ones I had out to show you all on Wednesday. You remember?"

"Yes."

"Cathy fetched them, and Cathy put them away again. I went to look at them last night, and some of them are missing."

The change from what she had been afraid of was so sudden, so direct, that it left her mind empty. She stared at Lucas Dale and said,

"I don't understand."

"I wish you didn't have to, Susan, but there's no other way. I haven't done anything about sending for the police—I wanted to see you first. I'm afraid it's a perfectly clear case. Unfortunately there was a lot of talk about how seldom I looked at the pearls. And that's true. I hadn't had them out for six months before last Wednesday, and I mightn't have had them out for six months again, only last night I had a fancy to look at them because—because—oh, well, I'm a fool, Susan—I was thinking about you, and I got out the pearls because I wanted to make a picture to myself of what they'd look like on your neck. Then when I came to take them out I saw at once that some of the loose ones were gone. Do you remember, Mrs. Hammond asked me to count them? She was joking, but I did count them—I always do. And they were all right when Cathy took them away. You remember she had my keys. I never dreamed of not trusting her as if she had been myself, but—there are twenty of the loose pearls missing, and twenty-five very well matched ones which I got last year in case I wanted to have the big necklace lengthened. They were very good pearls, just loosely strung, and the ends knotted to keep them safe."

Whilst he talked, understanding came to Susan, and a blinding anger. Everything in her flamed. She said, "Stop! How dare you say a thing like that about Cathy!"

He looked at her, and looked away.

"Do you think I want to say it?"

"Mr. Dale, you can't mean that you think Cathy took your pearls—*Cathy!*"

"What *can* I think? The pearls were all there on Wednesday evening—I can swear to that. Everyone in the room heard Mrs. Hammond tell me to count them. No one touched them after that except Cathy. She put them away and brought me back my keys. When I got them out last night there were forty-five pearls missing."

Susan turned. Cathy had lifted her head. Her face was white and wet, her eyes wide with fright. Susan said,

"Cathy—you hear what he says. What did you do when you put the tray away? Try and think."

Cathy opened her lips to speak. She had to try twice before any sound came. She said at last,

"I put—it away—"

"Think, Cathy—*think*! Did you put it down anywhere, or go out of the room? Did you put the keys down?"

Cathy shook her head. Words came a little more easily.

"No—I put it away."

"At once?"

"Yes."

Susan turned to Dale. He said,

"She didn't give me back the keys till everyone had gone. There was time enough and to spare."

There was a gasp from Cathy. Her face went back into her hands again. Lucas Dale said,

"There it is."

"What are you going to do?" said Susan in an icy voice.

She saw him frown.

"I've been thinking it out since last night. If she took those pearls—and I can't see how anyone else can have taken them—well, they won't have gone very far. She hasn't been out of the place since Wednesday, and she wouldn't risk posting them in the village—if she did, they'll be easily traced. But this afternoon she was going into Ledlington by the two o'clock bus—she might have reckoned on getting them away then. Now look here, Cathy, I've got a name for being a hard man, but I don't want to be hard on you. I don't know what you wanted money for, but I'd have given you anything in reason if you'd come and asked me to help you. You took my pearls instead. Well, I want them back. Make a clean breast of it and give them up, and I won't prosecute."

Cathy lifted her head again. She had a lost look.

"I—can't—"

Susan had a stab of fear.

"Why can't you?" said Lucas Dale.

Cathy began to shake. Between chattering teeth she stammered,

"I—don't—know—I didn't take them—oh, I *didn't*!"

Dale shrugged his shoulders.

"You see—that's all she says. I did my best before you came, but she won't speak. Well, she's had her chance. I asked you to come here because I think it's most likely she's got the pearls on her. Either that or they're in her room at the Little House. If she's got them here, they'll be on her or in her bag. Will you turn out her bag first, and if they're not there, will you take her up into one of the bedrooms and search her? I want to be quite sure before I ring up the police. You see, I'm trusting you."

Susan walked over to the chair with her head very high.

"Where's your bag, Cathy?"

It was Lucas Dale who answered.

"It's over there on her table. Perhaps you wouldn't mind getting it. I don't want to have it in my hands."

Susan fetched the bag—Cathy's old brown bag which went everywhere with her. It was when she was coming back with it that Cathy started up and ran to meet her.

"Give it to me!"

"Cathy—"

"You mustn't open it—" The words were in a stuttering whisper. They chilled Susan's anger. They chilled her to her bones.

"Cathy—"

"You mustn't, you mustn't, you *mustn't*!"

"Go and sit down!"

Cathy had never heard this voice from Susan before. She went back to the big chair and cowered down in it as if for shelter.

Susan went up to the writing-table. She faced Lucas Dale across it and opened Cathy's bag. It had an inner compartment which shut with a clasp. The two sides of it were stuffed quite full of odds and ends. Susan took them out one by one—an almost empty purse, two handkerchiefs, three pencils, a pencil sharpener, two bills and a receipt from shops in Ledlington, a letter in a bright blue envelope, a shopping list, a yard of brown ribbon, a powder compact, lipstick and a little round box of rouge, some acid drops in a paper bag, a small square pincushion stuffed full of pins, a ring of safety pins. There seemed to be no end.

Susan came at last to the inner compartment. With her fingers on the clasp, she heard Cathy take a hard-drawn breath. Her fingers were like ice as they opened the clasp. There were two little pockets, one of silk, the other lined with white leather. In the silk pocket there was a hair-net and hair-pins, in the other a snapshot of Roger Vere. It had been stuck on a piece of card, and at the bottom there was fastened on one side a spray of white heather, and on the other a snippet of curly black hair. Oh, poor Cathy! Susan glanced round with a jab of pity and relief. Cathy's face was hidden again.

Susan held the card up with its back to Lucas Dale.

"It's only a photograph. There's nothing else." She turned out the two little pockets as she spoke, and some dust with them. There was nothing else.

Dale looked impassively.

"Will you do the same with the rest of it?"

It was when she took hold of the lining and pulled that the slit became visible. It ran down the side of the lining. She hadn't noticed anything until she pulled the silk. It tore now with a small, sharp sound. She put her hand into the hole and felt the pearls.

Dale had his eyes on her face. He had not meant to watch her, but he found himself unable to look away. Anger gave her a brilliance which fairly took his breath. Her colour glowed, her eyes shone. And then all at once everything hardened, sharpened. Her hand stayed where she had thrust it, and slowly all the colour drained away, the brightness left her eyes. It was like watching her die. There seemed to be nothing left. He leaned across the table and said in an agitated voice,

"Susan—what is it? Don't look like that!"

She looked at him. Her hand came slowly back, holding a string of pearls knotted at either end, each pearl the size of a pea, smooth and iridescent. She moved her hand with the pearls a little towards him and dropped them down. She did not look at them. She groped for the bag and pushed it towards him.

Lucas Dale took it up and turned it inside out. The loose pearls that were in the lining came pattering down. He swept them together, picked up a straggler here and there, and counted them.

"Twenty—and twenty-five in the string. They're all here."

Susan turned and went to Cathy. She felt as if she was bleeding to death. Her body was slow and stiff. Her mind had come to a standstill. Cathy and Lucas Dale's pearls.... Lucas Dale's pearls in Cathy's bag.... Cathy saying, "You mustn't open it—you *mustn't*!"... But that was because of Roger's photograph.... Was it?... The pearls were in the lining of Cathy's bag.... These thoughts had been in her mind when it stopped. They stayed there without her having any power to change them.

She came to Cathy and pulled her hands away from her face.

"The pearls were in your bag."

Cathy stared up at her. A look of blind terror crossed her face. She put out a groping hand and slipped sideways to the floor.

Chapter Nine

"ARE YOU BETTER, Cathy?"

The brown eyes opened blankly and closed again. Susan felt a rush of pity and terror. Four years ago, when Cathy had been so ill, she had looked like that day after day for all those horrible weeks— just there, just on the edge of death, just living and no more. Her heart broke in her. She said softly,

"Won't you tell me about it—won't you?"

The eyelids lifted again. The eyes looked blankly. The eyelids fell. Susan said in an urgent voice,

"I must talk to him. You'll be all right, won't you? Just lie still."

There was a sighing breath. She did not dare to wait. If he were to ring up the police, it would be out of his hands.

They had carried Cathy into the recess where her writing-table stood and laid her down on the padded window-seat. She had come out of her faint almost at once, but she had not uttered a word. Susan dared not stay. She got to her feet, pulled back the curtain which screened the recess, and saw with relief that Dale had not left the study. He was standing by the hearth, his elbow on the chimney ledge, looking down into the fire. As the curtain slid back he turned, waiting for her. She came slowly to stand beside him and say in a faltering voice,

"What are you going to do?"

"That's for you to say, Susan."

She looked at the burning logs.

"That is very kind—very generous. I—I don't know what to say. She's ill. There must be some dreadful mistake, or else she didn't know what she was doing. Cathy couldn't do anything like that if she was herself—you must know that."

Lucas Dale said, choosing his words,

"That would be taken into consideration in preparing her defence."

Her head came up. She said,

"What are you saying? What are you going to do?"

He was looking at her gravely and sternly.

"Do you really expect me not to prosecute?"

"Mr. Dale!"

"You must forgive me if I don't look at it quite as you do. It's a pretty bad case, you know. She was in a position of trust, and I did trust her implicitly. She has abused that trust in the most flagrant way. The whole thing seems to me to have been quite cleverly calculated. Don't look like that, Susan—I am bound to let you see my point of view. It's not only the loss of the pearls, but it was just an outside chance my looking at them again like that. It might have been six months before I had them out—or longer. And who would have fallen under suspicion then? Monty Phipson, or Raby, or one of the servants. I'm not a suspicious man. After months had passed I couldn't say or swear that my keys had never been left about, or that I hadn't let Monty have them to fetch something from the safe. The last person on earth to be suspected would be Miss Cathleen O'Hara, and that's what she was counting on. How can you expect me just to pass it over and let her go to play the same kind of trick on someone else? If you're kind to a criminal you may be letting a lot of other people down, and the way the law looks at it, you would be compounding a felony."

"You said—"

"I gave her a chance before you found the pearls. If she'd owned up then and given them back, I could have believed she had given way to some sudden temptation and been sorry for it ever since. But you saw how it was—she thought she could get away with it. They were cleverly hidden, and she held right on. Well, there it is—she made her choice. And that was the last minute I was going to feel justified in letting her go."

Susan watched his face, and found no comfort there. He had the look of a man who has made up his mind. There was no anger—she would have had more hope if he had been angry. There was a settled purpose, and that purpose to—send—Cathy—to—prison....
Her lips moved very stiffly.

"You said it was for me to say—"

Dale said, "Yes."

He turned from her abruptly and went to the glass door by which she had come in. He opened it and stood there, letting the wind blow through. There was a streak of sun between grey clouds. There was a yellow crocus out below the window. He shut the door and came back.

"Yes, it's for you to say, Susan. I've got a duty to society, and a duty to the law, and a duty, as I feel it, to the other members of my household. But there's a duty that one puts before all these. It may be right or it may be wrong, but there it is. It's nature, and you can't go against nature. If a thing like this happens in a man's own family, he's got a right to keep it in the family, and no one can blame him. I shouldn't prosecute my wife's cousin."

She had known what was coming before it came, but the shock was no less for that. A car on a straight road and another car coming right at it—the inevitable head-on collision. You know just when it will come and where. There is nothing to do but to wait for the crash. It was like that. At first just the hint of danger, then danger looming, coming nearer, nearer. Then the words, "I should not prosecute my wife's cousin."

Susan walked to a chair and sat down. She closed her eyes and steadied herself as best she could to fight for everything that mattered to her in the world—Cathy, Bill, their little house, Aunt Milly, friends, the place they had lived in not only for her lifetime and Cathy's but for all those generations that had gone before—men and women who had taken their name from King's Bourne, lived out their lives there, and were remembered by cross and slab, by effigy and brass, in the churchyard and in the church under the hill—not many wise, not many noble, but a race of honourable people, faithful in their obligations, gallant in stress, kindly and upright. She had to fight for them, and she went into the battle shocked and dazed, her heart betraying her, because how can you think clearly or know what you should do when you love two people and they pull different ways?

Lucas Dale had never admired her so much as when she lifted eyes that were dark with pain to his and said,

"Will you sit down? I can't stand any longer, and we must talk."

He moved the chair in which Cathy had sat, leaned back in it, and spoke more gently,

"It rests with you."

It was some time before she said anything. When she did her voice was steady.

"You have said that you care for me. I think you do. I am very grateful. I shall be grateful to you every day of my life if you will be generous about this."

"I don't see it that way, Susan. You mayn't think I've got a code, but I have. I won't break it. If this is a family affair it can be settled in the family. If it isn't it's a case for the police. It's for you to say whether it's a family affair or not."

She took that blow, and came back with a pathetic courage.

"Please, will you let me tell you about Cathy? She isn't strong—she hasn't ever really been strong. About four years ago she had a very bad illness. She very nearly died. They said then that she mustn't ever have any strain or shock. If there were a case and she had to go into court, I think it would kill her. There must be some mistake, and it would come out in the end, but I don't think Cathy would ever get over it. Mr. Dale—if you care for me at all—"

He said harshly, "That's not fair." And then, "I want you to listen to me. You say if I care for you I'll break through my code. If I was that sort of man I wouldn't be worth caring for you at all. If I'd no more stuffing in me than that, do you think I'd ever have got where I am? Do you know what I was? A charity boy—no father, no mother, no name. You don't get from that to where I am now by being soft, nor by giving up because a thing's hard to get. The harder it's been, the harder I've had to try, but what I've wanted I've got, all through. Don't you think that you can turn me, Susan. No one ever has, and no one ever will—not when I've set my mind on a thing. What I want I get, and what I get I keep."

There was a pause on that. The room was very still. His last words said themselves over and over in Susan's mind. She broke from them at last. Some colour came to her cheeks. She said in a stronger voice,

"It's not possible—none of it. Cathy couldn't do a thing like that."

"Who did it then? The pearls were in her bag. She begged you not to open it. Why did she do that? She crouched right down in that chair and hid her face when you began to turn it out."

"There was a photograph there—a boy she's fond of. She didn't want anyone to know."

She saw him smile.

"You can't really believe that—or if you can, I can't. What does it matter whose photograph she's got? What's the use, Susan? She did it, and she'll have to stand by it, unless—"

Susan's face burned.

"Blackmail?" she said, and felt her heart stop with terror at the change in his face.

He looked like murder as he jerked her out of her chair and held her facing him.

"Say that again and there will be no unless! Do you want me to ring up the police—now, at once? Because I will if you like—you've only to say so. Well, what is it to be?" He was rough in voice and action. His hands bruised her with their hard strength. But she kept her eyes on his. If she died for it she wouldn't look away.

"Let me go, Mr. Dale."

He let go of her at once, walked to the writing-table, and reached for the telephone. With his hand on it he looked back at her and said,

"Well—make up your mind."

Susan looked across to the recess where Cathy lay. She hadn't moved. Perhaps she wouldn't move for hours. She had had these turns before—when her kitten had been killed by a strange dog—when a tramp had frightened her. She had lain stunned and dazed for hours, and afterwards she had been ill. The doctors called it shock. They had said, "Leave it to time." The word was in Susan's mind as she turned to Lucas Dale. She heard herself saying it out loud,

"I must have time."

He left the table and came back to her. The gust of anger was gone. He said,

"How much time? I could give you an hour."

"That's not enough. Cathy is ill. I can't ask her anything until she's well again. It may be days. And sometimes she doesn't remember—she didn't when her kitten was killed. It's shock."

"I'm afraid I can't give you days—you must see that. I couldn't explain to the police why I had put off reporting the theft of the pearls. I can give you an hour. Would you like me to leave you alone here?"

"Yes, please."

"Is there anything you would like for yourself or for Cathy?"

She said "No."

He went out and shut the door.

Chapter Ten

THAT HOUR was the strangest one in Susan's life. She could not have told how it went. It was like the time in a dream, when moments lengthen into ages or contract to a dizzy flash. She tried to rouse Cathy, to get an answer from her, but achieved nothing but a dull state of distress without coherent speech. Dr. Carrick had always told them to let her alone and she would sleep it off. In the midst of all that was so unreal she had the clearest picture of Bill's father saying that in his warm, reassuring voice.

She began to walk up and down in the long room. Two windows on to the terrace and the glass door between them. Everything grey and misty outside. The ray of sun had gone. She turned and walked back, leaving the windows behind her. The door on the right, Dale's writing-table, the chimney-breast, the logs on the hearth fallen down in a bed of white ash. Above, on the panelling, Lazio's picture of Millicent and Laura Bourne. On the left the recess, Cathy's writing-table. Cathy lying motionless on the window-seat very small and frail. She walked on to the end of the room. There was another door on the right. It led by a narrow passage to a back stair.

Susan turned and came back again. Her eyes went to the picture. Millicent and Laura Bourne.... How lovely and serene they looked—Aunt Milly who was a fretful invalid—Laura who was dead.... She thought. "I'm twenty-two. I'm older than she was when she died." She thought how easy it would be to be dead and not to have to break your heart.

She stood there and thought about Bill—"I've got a right to break my heart for Cathy, but I'm breaking Bill's heart too—" A small, cold voice answered her. It said, "He'll get over it. *Cathy wouldn't.* Men have died and worms have eaten them, but not for love." Cathy could be broken like a leaf. Bill would suffer, but he wouldn't break. She didn't think about herself at all. There was no feeling there—it was all numb. She thought about Bill, and Cathy, and Aunt Milly. She thought Aunt Milly would crumple up if anything happened to Cathy. She sat down in the big leather chair and stopped thinking.

The door near the windows opened. Mr. Vincent C. Bell looked in. When he saw Susan he came right in.

"When I had the pleasure of meeting you the other day I called you out of your name, so I'm very glad to have the opportunity of saying how do you do all over again. I'm very pleased to meet you, Miss Lenox."

Susan looked at him vaguely—the man she had met, coming up from the rose garden—Cathy had said he was staying—She said,

"Are you looking for Mr. Dale?"

He said, "Mr. Phipson."

"If you go out by that other door you will see the back stairs on your left. Mr. Phipson's room is at the end of the long passage at the top of the stairs."

"Well, there's no hurry," said Vincent Bell.

Susan said in a tired voice, "My cousin is ill. I am just waiting to take her home. I think if you don't mind—"

He seemed a long way off as he apologized and went.

Susan waited. It was a relief when Dale came into the room. She stood up to meet him and said what she had planned to say.

"You know I am engaged to Bill Carrick—"

"You have been engaged."

"You know we love each other—very much—"

"I love you too," said Lucas Dale.

"But I love Bill. I shall always love him."

"Always is a long time."

Susan shivered.

"What good will it be to you if I don't love you—if I love Bill?"

He gave her a strange look.

"I think that's my look-out. Are you going to marry me?"

Her control broke.

"Don't make me—don't make me!"

Dale said, "I'm not making you do anything. I've come here to get your answer."

She said, "I can't!" and saw him go to the table and pick up the telephone.

"Is that your last word? Once I call up the police station there'll be no going back."

"No—no—don't ring! I didn't mean that. You mustn't ring."

"Well, I don't want to," said Dale. "But you'll have to know your own mind, because, you see, I've got to trust you. I've got to be sure that you won't let me down. I've got to take my decision right away. If I don't ring up the police now, it's not going to be easy to ring them up later on, in a day or two, if you come to me and say you've changed your mind. How am I going to guard against that?"

Susan's lips said stiffly, "If I say I'll do it—"

"I could guard myself," said Dale. "I could get you to sign a statement to say you'd found my pearls in your cousin's bag. But I'm not going to do that—I'm going to trust your word. You see, that's how I think of you. If you gave your word you wouldn't go back on it. Are you going to marry me, Susan?"

"Yes."

"Next week?"

"No."

"Yes, Susan—yes." His voice changed suddenly, softened. "What's the good of putting it off, my dear?"

That was true. It was no good putting it off.

"Well? Is it yes?"

Susan said, "Yes."

"Is that your word of honour?"

"Yes."

He went to the bell and pressed it.

"The car is waiting. I'll carry Cathy out."

Chapter Eleven

SATURDAY TO SUNDAY—Sunday to Monday. Susan walked in a nightmare. Her mind was clogged and dull. Past, present and future lay under a heavy weight of dread, and there was nothing she could do to break it or get free. Nothing she could do to get free, but endless tasks to take up every moment of her time.

Cathy lay in her bed and neither moved nor spoke. She had to be fed and tended. Aunt Milly cried a good deal, and said darling Cathy had never been really strong and it was very hard to feel resigned. The house had to be kept, meals cooked and served, plates and dishes washed. Susan did everything. She remembered Aunt Milly's fads, she remembered just how Cathy liked her hot milk.

In the middle of the Sunday afternoon she sat down to write to Bill. The post went out at five. If she posted her letter then, he would get it by the second post on Monday morning. That would be all right. He mustn't get it by the first post, because he was to see Gilbert Garnish at nine o'clock and he must be at his very best for that. She sat and looked at the paper for a long time. It had always been so easy to write to Bill, but it wasn't easy now. She wrote:

"I can't marry you, Bill. I'm going to marry Lucas Dale."

She looked at the words, and it seemed to her that they were nonsense. Bill wouldn't believe them. She would have to write something that would make him believe. She wrote again, adding word to word like a child writing from a copy:

"It doesn't matter what you think about me, but you mustn't let it spoil your work."

She wrote her name, and folded the sheet quickly without reading it through. When she had addressed and stamped the envelope she walked down the street and posted it at Mrs. Gill's general shop, which was also the post office. Then she came home and told Mrs. O'Hara that she had broken off her engagement. Aunt Milly had a great deal to say about it, and Susan had to listen.

"Of course, my dear, I wouldn't interfere for the world. And no one could say he was any sort of a match for you, though his father being so much respected and such an old friend did make a difference, as I told poor James at the time. And no one can be fonder of Bill than I am, but if you don't feel quite sure about marrying him, it is really much better to break it off—I have always said so. Because, after all, an engagement isn't a marriage, and divorce is a thing we haven't ever had in our family, and I hope we never shall. So don't marry him on any account unless you feel perfectly sure of yourself, though I'd like to see you happy and in a home of your own."

"I'm going to marry Mr. Dale," said Susan, and went out of the room.

Lucas Dale left her alone. He rang up once to inquire about Cathy, and said,

"I'm writing to you. I won't come and see you for a day or two. That's what you'd like, isn't it?"

There was a faint relief in her voice as she said "Yes".

She got his letter an hour later. He wrote:

"I will make everything as easy for you as I can. I know that I shall have all my courting to do after we are married. Please don't be afraid of me. Please don't think that I shall try and rush you. Once we are married you shall have all the time you want. I will go into Ledlington and make arrangements tomorrow morning. I won't bother you till everything is settled. I thought perhaps Thursday—"

Susan felt a piercing stab. Bill had said Thursday—if Gilbert Garnish gave him the job. But she wasn't marrying Bill on Thursday, she was marrying Lucas Dale. Something in her said *"I can't"*. Something that was stronger than that said "I must".

Chapter Twelve

BILL CARRICK stopped the car which he had borrowed from Ted Walters and got out. There were no lights on this side of the Little House, and no Susan at the gate. It hit him, but he didn't stop to think about it. He walked straight into the unlighted hall, where he stood and listened. There was no sound of any kind. He went through the dining-room to the kitchen and saw Susan standing there as white as paper. He shut the door behind him and stood against it. Neither of them spoke, until at last he said in the same rough tone which he had used over the telephone,

"What's all this nonsense?"

Susan went back till she could lean against the dresser.

"You shouldn't have come," she said in a desolate tone.

"I have come. And you've got to explain. On Wednesday when I was down here everything was all right—I was going to get Garnish's job, and you were going to marry me. Now I've got the job, and you're going to marry Dale. I suppose you don't think that needs any explanation. I'm sorry, but I don't agree. I've come here to get an explanation, and I'm not going away till I've got one. If you haven't got a story ready, you'd better do some quick thinking."

Bill had never spoken to her like that in his life before. They had disagreed and argued, they had quarrelled and made it up again, but he had never looked as if he hated her before, never used that rough, cold voice of sarcasm. It hurt unbelievably, but it steadied her. She said,

"It's no use trying to explain. It was no use your coming down. We mustn't see each other, we mustn't talk. It's no use—"

He left the door and came towards her.

"Look here, Susan, if you think you can come that sort of thing over me, you can't! We're engaged. If you want to break the engagement you can, but you must tell me why." He dropped his hands on her shoulders and let them lie there heavy and strong. "Look at me!"

Susan looked at him. She did not know how wretched a look it was. The hands that held her tightened.

"What's the matter? What's happened? You've got to tell me."

"Bill, it's no use. Oh, Bill—please go!"

"What's the good of saying things like that? There's something behind this, and I'm going to know what it is. Are you going to look me in the face and say that you care for this fellow?"

She went on looking, but she did not speak.

"Come along—say it! You wouldn't marry a man you didn't care for. Don't mind my feelings—they don't matter to you any more. Go on—tell me you love him—a little—much—passionately—not at all! Which of them is it? Or shall I tell you that you don't care a snap of your fingers about him? Susan, you don't—you *can't*!"

She put up her hands and took him by the wrists to push him away.

"Stop! It's no good, Bill."

"Then you've got to tell me why."

She freed herself.

"I can't tell you why—I can't tell you anything. We're not engaged any more. I can't marry you—I'm going to marry him. That's all there is to say." Her colour had risen, her breath came quickly. There was a desperate sound in her voice.

Bill's manner changed suddenly. The roughness went out of it. He said,

"Look here, Susan, this is no good. You were all right on Wednesday. Something has happened since then, and you're going to tell me what it is. If you've fallen out of love with me you've only got to say so. If you've fallen in love with him you've only got to tell me. But if you love me and I love you, do you suppose for a moment that anything you say or do is going to make me stand on one side whilst you marry him? I don't know what's happened, but you're not using your brain. Get on and use it. You're no fool, but you're behaving like the village idiot. Drop it, and tell me what's been happening."

Susan leaned back against the dresser.

"It won't do any good."

"It won't do any harm."

"I don't know—it might. There's Cathy—"

His face changed.

"Oh, Cathy's in it, is she? How?"

"He said—she took—his pearls—"

"*What?*"

Susan looked at him in a lost sort of way.

"He said so."

"What are you talking about?"

"He had them out on Wednesday. The Veres were there, and the Micklehams, and Lydia. Cathy brought the pearls."

"*What?*"

"The pearls—from his safe—in a tray. They are worth a lot of money. There were some loose ones. Everyone said wasn't he afraid to keep them in the house, and he said no, he liked to have them there, even though sometimes he didn't look at them for months. Lydia and I got up to go. He gave Cathy his keys and told her to put the pearls away. Lydia said he had better count them—" Her voice went down into a whisper and stopped.

"Go on."

"On Saturday morning he rang up and said there was something wrong. I went up. Cathy was there—you know how she is when she's frightened. He said she had taken some of the pearls—twenty loose ones and a string of twenty-five that he had got to lengthen one of the other necklaces. He said if she would give them back he wouldn't prosecute. She was all to bits. He said would I look for the pearls. I turned out Cathy's bag—and they were in the lining. Cathy fainted."

"Susan!"

It was an extraordinary relief to speak—to tell Bill. She went on telling him.

"He said it was a very bad case. He said anyone else in the house might have been suspected. He said he must ring up the police. I told him Cathy would die. He said it was his duty, but—"

"Go on," said Bill.

She looked away.

"He said he wouldn't prosecute his wife's cousin—"

There was a pause. Susan felt herself gripped and held.

"Look at me!"

She looked, and saw a stranger. Bill would look like this in thirty years time perhaps—features sharpened, lines bitten in, youth gone. It frightened her, and the hard anger in his eyes set her heart beating.

"Blackmail! And you knuckled down to it!"

She said, "Cathy—the police—I couldn't let him. That time the tramp frightened her your father said it was touch and go. She's upstairs now, just lying there. She hasn't spoken. It *would* have killed her."

"If she did it she's better dead," said Bill Carrick.

Susan cried out.

"She didn't—she couldn't!"

"Then who did? Dale—Dale himself? Had he made love to you—before this happened?"

"Yes—he asked me to marry him—on Thursday."

"And you said?"

Susan's head came up.

"What do you think?"

"And then Cathy takes the pearls and they are found in her bag. That's damned convenient! And you walked right into the trap!"

"What could I do? I couldn't kill Cathy."

"You could have called his bluff. It was bluff all right. You don't imagine he would really have rung up the police, do you?"

"Oh, he would."

"He wouldn't. If he thought he'd a hold on you he wouldn't have been in a hurry to give it up. You've been a damned fool!" He caught her suddenly in a hard clasp. "You can imagine a lot, can't you? All right, imagine that I'll let you go to that swine! Go on—try hard! Oh, Susan, you fool—you fool! You blasted *darling* fool!"

Just for a moment Susan let herself go. The frightful strain and tension eased. She had a flashing sense of relief. Right in the midst of unimaginable darkness, thirst, and terror there was light—spring water—comfort. The moment came and went, the flash died, the comfort was gone. She lifted her head.

"Bill—I've promised—"

"You can't keep that sort of promise."

"He said, 'Is that your word of honour?'—and I said 'Yes'."

Bill let go of her. She thought, "He's letting me go." And then she saw his face set in hard, obstinate lines. His eyes, angry and determined, held hers.

"Suppose you promised to murder someone—would you do it?"

"I shouldn't promise."

"That's shuffling!" His voice was contemptuous. "Suppose you were my wife—what would you have said then? Would you have let him blackmail you into going to him?"

"Bill!"

"What's the good of saying 'Bill!'? And where's the difference? Would anyone say or think that a promise like that ought to be kept?"

She said in a fainting voice, "We're—not—married," and saw him whiten.

"And that's all the tie you recognize—a legal tie, a physical one? Nothing else—nothing sacred and binding between us? Are you going to look at me and say that—and are you going to expect me to believe it if you do?"

"Bill!"

He came quite close, but he did not touch her.

"Wake up! You're going to marry me. If Dale or anyone else tries to butt in he'll get what's coming to him."

Behind him the door into the dining-room moved. The faint click of the latch had passed unheard. Mrs. Mickleham stood with her hand on the knob in a state of worried indecision. The Vicar had sent her—but on the other hand—a private conversation—Bill Carrick—naturally very upset—oh dear, dear, *dear*—really no attempt to keep his voice down—anyone in the house might have heard him—and oh, really, he *ought not* to go up to King's Bourne in such a state—very natural of course, but most unwise, and sure to lead to a really terrible quarrel—oh, *yes*—and Susan trying to stop him and keeping on saying she had promised—

Inside the room Bill Carrick said with frightful distinctness,

"Do you want me to kill him, Susan? I think I'm going to."

Chapter Thirteen

MRS. MICKLEHAM pushed the door wide open and stepped over the threshold. She saw Susan holding Bill Carrick by the arm, and she saw Bill turn his head and look at her standing there in the doorway. He was quite white, and his eyes blazed. As soon as he saw her he twisted himself free and rushed out through the scullery, slamming the door behind him. Susan went back against the dresser and stood there shaking. She stared at Mrs. Mickleham, but she didn't seem to see her.

"My dear—my dear Susan—the Vicar sent me—but oh dear, I feel I am intruding—only we were both so distressed—indeed he did not feel that he could perform the ceremony—unless he felt assured that it was going to be for your happiness, my dear—he had to go to Mrs. Brain, and he thought perhaps you could talk more freely to me—"

Susan went on staring. Mrs. Mickleham's voice was a long way off.... she was talking about someone being married.... It came to her that Mrs. Mickleham was talking about the marriage of Susan Lenox and Lucas Dale—and the Vicar was distressed—*the Vicar*—

Lucas Dale.... Sharp and clear on that the voice in which Bill had said, "Do you want me to kill him? I think I'm going to." *And she had let him go.*

She put out her hands as if she was pushing something away and went running through the scullery and out of the back door as Bill had done.

Mrs. Mickleham was left in a state of considerable agitation. If one could only be sure that one had done the right thing—one tried, but oh dear—and the Vicar had wanted her to come—a woman's intuition—and of course if old Mrs. Brain was really dying, he had to go to her—*oh dear!*

She went slowly back into the hall. The drawing-room door was ajar and she could see that the room was in darkness. Mrs. O'Hara must be in her room. There was a light on the upper landing. She did not know whether to go up or not. She listened, and could not hear anyone moving. A lorry went by in the road. The Little House must be very noisy—only of course there wasn't much traffic—Mrs. O'Hara didn't seem to mind—poor thing, such an invalid—perhaps she was resting—better not disturb her—better just slip away. ... Mrs. Mickleham slipped away.

Susan went running and stumbling up the hill. She was so terrified and confused that she hardly knew what she was doing. She only knew that Bill was beside himself with anger, and that she had let him go to meet Lucas Dale. It was quite dark in the orchard, but even in her confusion her feet found their own way and brought her out from among the trees. There was low cloud overhead, very little light from the sky, damp air on her face.

She was just beyond the trees, when she heard a shot. It did not frighten her at first. When you have lived in the country all your life the sound of a stray shot is neither here nor there. She heard it, but her mind had its own fear, the fear of Bill's hands—his very strong hands. She saw them striking Dale, flinging him down, closing about his throat. The shot meant nothing to her at all.

She came to the paved terrace, as she had come to it on the Saturday morning when Lucas Dale had let her in. There was a light in the study, and as she saw that, she saw the curtain move, and the door. Bill Carrick passed the lighted space and came out upon the terrace. She ran to him.

"Bill!"

He caught her arm.

"What are you doing here? Come away!"

"Bill!"

"He's dead."

Susan heard the words as she had heard the shot. They began to draw together in her mind. They didn't mean anything yet.

Bill had his arm round her, hurrying her down the steps, across the lower terrace, down the slope—down, down, and on amongst the trees. They came to the garden of the Little House, to the back door, to the dark scullery, and there stood. Bill said in a sharp whisper,

"Is she gone—Mrs. Mickleham?"

She said, "I'll see."

She went through the lower rooms. She listened in the hall. There was no sound at all. She came back across the dining-room, shutting both the doors behind her.

Bill Carrick was standing by the kitchen window. He turned, and the light fell on his face. Until that moment Susan had not thought—there had been no time to think. She had heard Bill say "He's dead." The words were there in her mind, but she hadn't begun to think about them. What she had had to do was to run, to get back into the shelter of the Little House, to make sure that Mrs. Mickleham was gone. Now these things were done.

She looked at Bill, saw something in his face which she had never seen there before, and with a dreadful rush thought began. Lucas Dale was dead. She remembered the shot, and her knees began to shake. She took hold of the edge of the kitchen table and leaned on it. Bill said,

"He's dead." And then, "I didn't kill him."

She said, "Who killed him?"

"I don't know. He was lying there dead."

Susan thought about that vaguely. She was shaking so much that she was afraid she was going to fall. She said,

"You came out of the study—"

"Yes—I found the glass door open. Don't you believe me?"

What were they saying to one another? What was between them? What had he done?

He leaned across the table and spoke low.

"I wanted to kill him—I might have killed him—but I didn't. You've got to believe me."

"I'll try."

That was all wrong—dreadfully wrong. You believe, or you don't believe—it's no good trying. Her lips were quite dry. She moistened them and said,

"Tell me."

Bill put his hands over hers and pressed them down.

"If you don't believe me, no one will. You've got to believe me. I heard the shot. I went up to the house. There was a light in the study. I went round to the side where Cathy has her table and looked in. One of the windows was open and the curtain flapping. I could see the other writing-table across the room. I couldn't see Dale—only a hand and arm stretched out along the carpet. I went back to the terrace. The glass door was open. I went in, and there he was, fallen down behind the writing-table. I went and looked at him. I didn't know what to do. He'd been shot through the head. There was a revolver on the writing-table. I didn't touch anything. I was trying to think what I ought to do, when I heard someone on the terrace. I came out to see who it was, and when I found it was you I lost my head. I only thought about getting you away. I didn't want you to get mixed up in it, and I didn't want you to see him. I ought to have sent you home and called up the police. I think I ought to go back now."

She shook her head.

"They'll think you did it."

"They'll think so anyhow. Mrs. Mickleham heard me say I wanted to. Susan, I'd better go back."

"It's too late."

"I expect it is. I don't want to say you were there."

Susan was steadying.

"Bill, you heard the shot. I did, but I didn't think it was anything. I was just clear of the orchard. Where were you?"

"On the lower terrace. I didn't go straight up to the house. That's what is going to look bad for me. If I'd gone straight to the house, I'd have been there when the shot was fired. But I wasn't—I wasn't there. I was on the lower terrace trying to get hold of myself a bit. You see, I did want to kill him—"

"Bill!"

"So I had to get myself in hand. Then I heard the shot, and I stopped where I was for about a minute, because I wasn't sure where the sound came from. It sounded awfully close. That was because the door was open. I was listening for footsteps—anyone moving. When I couldn't hear anything I went on up to the house and looked in."

"You didn't see anyone or hear anyone?"

"No."

"Could he have done it himself?"

"No, he couldn't, Susan."

Susan pulled her hands away and stood up.

"We heard the shot. Why didn't anyone in the house hear it—why didn't they come?"

"I don't know," said Bill Carrick.

Chapter Fourteen

ILL NEWS travels apace. By eight o'clock it would have been hard to find anyone within a mile radius who did not know that Mr. Dale up at King's Bourne had been found murdered in his own study—"and Scotland Yard called in, they do say."

Mr. Pipe, the landlord of the Crown and Magpie, knew all about that. He was a man of slow but interminable speech delivered weightily in a deep booming voice, small and thin of person but mighty with the tongue. There must have been times when he stopped talking to listen, for he was always full of information, but behind his own bar he talked, and listened to none. He knew all about the death of Lucas Dale and why Scotland Yard had been called in.

"Shot right through the back of the head, he was, pore gentleman, and dead as mutton. If all the best doctors in the kingdom had been called in there wasn't nothing they could have done for him. Alive and hearty one minute, as it might be you or me, and shot down the next as if he wasn't no better than a rabbit. And when the police come they gets word as nothing's to be touched on account of Scotland Yard being called in. And the reason for that, as I hear, is along of Colonel Rutland, the new Chief Constable, being down with the influenza. Leastways some say it's that, and some say there's other reasons—like them that's suspected being a bit too well known locally. And there's others'll tell you 'tis because the ones they think done it belongs to London, and it stands to reason that London police 'ud have a better chance of ferreting out whatever it was as went before. We all know as you don't just up and murder a man on account of not liking the look of him. It's bad feeling and bitter 'atred as goes before murder, and no one won't find out how it was done without they find out where the 'atred was."

"They say he was going to marry Miss Susan," said a hefty young man who was drinking beer.

"*And* that's nonsense, William Cole!" retorted a thin woman in a draggled coat. "Everyone knows as Miss Susan and Mr. Bill's been going together for years. Pint of bitter, Mr. Pipe."

William grinned.

"Have it your own way, but Mr. Dale, he come up and fixed with Vicar to marry Miss Susan Thursday, and Vicar wasn't none too pleased. Said just what you say, that Miss Susan was going with Mr. Bill. And Mr. Dale, he said, 'Well, she's marrying me on Thursday'. And that I heard with my own ears on account of the window being open and me putting lime on the rose-beds just outside."

"Well then, I don't believe it."

"All right, you needn't."

"Next thing you'll be saying is Mr. Bill shot him."

"Not me—but the police will most likely."

The talk went this way and that. Old Mr. Gill, whose grand-daughter was kitchen-maid at King's Bourne, said he did hear tell there was bad blood between Mr. Dale and the American gentleman that was staying.

Mr. Pipe took up the tale again.

"There's a good many of us could have something to say if it comes to that. The one it's most likely to be is the one you wouldn't be likely to think of, because it stands to reason if there was 'atred and ill will right down here in Bourne, we'd know about it, wouldn't we? It stands to reason we would, for if there's one thing more than another that can't be hid it's 'atred."

"Well, I'd 'ate a man as took my girl," said William Cole.

The thin woman flashed round on him.

"What's Mr. Bill done to you for you to keep picking on him?" William grinned.

"He hasn't done nothing to me. 'Twasn't me as took his girl."

Mr. Pipe's voice boomed out.

"There's ladies to be considered as well as men. 'Atred isn't one of those things as the men have got a prerogative for. Why, there was a lady in here no later than this very afternoon round about five o'clock or a bit later, and she had a double brandy, and the way she took it off, well, you wouldn't often see anything like it. And if I told you what she said, well, you wouldn't believe me, and if you would, it's not the time for me to be telling it. I don't say as how she's got anything to do with Mr. Dale, and I don't say as how she hasn't, but I do say as 'atred will out."

"It's *murder* will out," said the thin woman.

"There's no murder without 'atred," said Mr. Pipe in a resounding voice.

Chapter Fifteen

THERE IS A ROUTINE which waits upon murder. It is a matter for the expert—the police surgeon to say how a man has died, the police photographer to fix that last dreadful pose, the finger-print expert. They have their exits and their entrances, they do their part, and go their way. The scene is cleared. The evidence remains to be dealt with.

At ten o'clock next morning Inspector Lamb was engaged in dealing with it. He sat, a massive figure, at Lucas Dale's writing-table. As he flicked over the pages of his notebook, his large, florid face was as nearly expressionless as a face could be. On the opposite side of the table was a slim young man with a pale face and very pale hair worn rather long and slicked very smoothly back. He had a pale blue eye, and an oddly elegant air for a policeman. He was in fact Detective Sergeant Abbott—Christian name Frank, but known among his intimates as Fug, owing to an early passion for hair-oil. It was Inspector Lamb's considered opinion that there were worse young fellows at the Yard, and that in time, and always provided he didn't get above himself, there might be the makings of a good officer in young Abbott. He sat back in his chair and said,

"Get that butler in. I want to take him through his statement."

He picked up a paper from the desk before him and ran his eye over it whilst Abbott went to the nearer door and gave a message to the constable on duty outside.

Raby came in. A thin man with a worried look, rather hollow in the cheek, rather hollow about the eyes, rather white about the gills.

He said, "Yes, sir?" and was invited to sit down.

"Well now, Raby, we're looking to you to give us all the assistance you can."

"Anything I can do, I'm sure."

The man was nervous, but that was only natural.

"Well then, I've got your statement here, and I'd like just to go through it with you. You say that you were crossing the hall at a quarter past six last night, when you heard voices in this room. Now just whereabouts were you when you stood and listened?"

"That's not in my statement. I never said I stood and listened."

Lamb gazed at him impassively.

"You must have done, or you couldn't have heard what was said. What I want to know is how close to the door you were, and which door it was."

Raby swallowed.

"Was it the door you came in by just now?"

"Yes, sir."

"How close were you?"

Raby swallowed again.

"I was bringing some logs along for the fire—"

"Do you generally bring the wood for the fire?"

"No, sir, but Robert was out."

"Oh, yes—Robert is the footman. Just give me that list of the servants, Abbott.... Robert Stack—footman. Where does he go when he's out?"

"Ledcott, sir. His mother lives there."

"The local people have checked up on him," said Abbott. "He was there from four to nine."

Inspector Lamb glanced at the list in his hand.

"The rest of the staff consists of your wife, Mrs. Raby, Esther Coleworthy and Lily Green, housemaids, and Doris Gill, kitchen-maid. None of them were out?"

"No."

Raby showed some relief at getting away from the study door.

"Yes, I see Mrs. Raby says in her statement that the three girls were under her observation during the time between six o'clock and a quarter to seven—when the body was found. They were, she says, in the servants' hall listening to a band programme on the wireless. Now, Raby, we'll just get back to where you were. Which door were you at—this one here behind me, or the one at the other end of the room?"

"It was this one."

Relief had come too soon. They were back at the study door.

"And you were how close to it?"

"Well, I'd come right up to it with the wood, and then I heard them quarrelling, and I didn't like to go in."

"So you stood there and listened. Well now, I'd like you to tell me just what you heard."

"It's in my statement."

"I'd like to have you tell me about it all the same. I'm not trying to catch you, but sometimes a thing comes back to you that you've overlooked."

Raby looked unhappy. Out of the tail of his eye he could see that the young man you would never think was a policeman had got a pencil in his hand and a notebook ready, and the way things were shaping he'd have to stand up in court and swear he had listened at the door. Murder didn't just kill one person, it could kill a man's character too, and where was he going to get another job after being mixed up in a murder case? He took out his handkerchief and wiped his forehead.

"The first thing I heard was Mr. Dale using language."

"What sort of language?"

Raby told him.

"And then I heard the American gentleman say—"

Inspector Lamb took a look at his list.

"Mr. Vincent C. Bell—been stopping here since Thursday. Ever stopped here before?"

"No, sir."

"Ever seen him before?"

"Not before Thursday."

"All right, go on with what you heard him say."

Raby looked apologetic.

"I wouldn't listen in an ordinary way, sir, but the fact is I didn't know whether to go in or not. What with Mr. Dale using language like that, and the American gentleman—"

"Did he use language too?"

"Not exactly. He called Mr. Dale a double-crossing, two-timing skunk."

Abbott's hand came up across his mouth.

"A nice distinction between language and epithet," he murmured.

Inspector Lamb settled himself in his chair.

"And what did Mr. Dale say to that?"

"He swore, sir. And then I thought I'd better not stay, so I came away."

"Now look here, Raby—you say they were swearing and flinging names. We all know there are ways and ways of doing such things. It's not the words that count so much, it's the way a man says them. All this that you say you heard, well, it might have been said chaffing, as you might say, or it might have been said in the way of two people having a difference of opinion and not much in it—if a man's got a habit of using language, it mayn't amount to much—or it might have been said in real deadly earnest, and I want you to tell me which of these three describes what you heard between Mr. Dale and Mr. Bell."

Raby wiped his forehead.

"It was deadly earnest and not a doubt about it."

"You're sure of that?"

"Oh, yes, sir. Both gentlemen were very angry indeed—not a doubt about it."

"Well, go on. What did you do after you left the study door?"

"I went away, but I didn't go farther than the other side of the hall, because I didn't like what I'd heard."

"How long were you on the other side of the hall?"

"A minute or two. And then the study door opened and Mr. Bell came out quick and slammed it behind him, and on through the hall and up the stairs. I don't think he saw me, sir."

"Did you go in and attend to the fire?"

"Yes, sir. Mr. Dale was standing over by the glass door with his back to me. He'd got the door a little bit open. He didn't move or look round. I made up the fire and came out."

"If you came in by this door behind me here, you'd pass the writing-table on your way to the fire. Did you see Mr. Dale's revolver?"

"No, sir."

"You knew he had a revolver, and where he kept it?"

The sweat came out on Raby's forehead. He turned his handkerchief between clammy hands.

"There wasn't any secret about where he kept it. Everyone knew, sir. It was in that drawer on your right—the second drawer."

"Did he keep the drawer locked?"

Raby hesitated, and said,

"Sometimes."

"You've seen it open?"

"Oh, yes, sir."

"Was it open last night?"

"Yes, sir."

"You mean the drawer was open?"

"Yes, sir—it was pulled out."

"Did you see the revolver?"

"No, sir—I wasn't noticing."

"You mean you don't know whether it was there or not?"

"I didn't take any notice one way or the other—I wasn't thinking about it."

Abbott wrote.

Inspector Lamb shifted heavily in his chair. He said in his expressionless voice,

"Are you sure you saw Mr. Dale, and that he was alive when you went in?"

"Oh, yes, sir."

"And when you came out?" Raby looked blank. "He was alive when you came out again? You left him alive in the study?"

Raby looked completely horrified.

"Oh, yes, sir."

"Did you notice what time it was?"

"It was nineteen minutes past six."

"How do you know?"

"By the clock on the study mantelpiece, sir. I noticed it when I had made up the fire."

"And what did you do after that?"

"I went to my pantry until a quarter to seven, when I returned to the study and found that Mr. Dale had been shot. Mr. Dale liked a cocktail at that hour, and I was taking it to him."

Lamb let him go. When the door had closed behind the butler he said,

"What d'you make of him?"

Abbott's pale eyebrows rose.

"He's nervous."

The round brown eyes of Inspector Lamb had a faintly reproachful look.

"That's natural," he said. "You'd be nervous if you'd found your employer murdered and weren't sure whether the police were thinking of putting it on you, let alone having to own up you'd been listening at doors, which isn't the best of manners for a butler."

"Oh, quite—quite."

"Well?"

"Well, that leaves from nineteen minutes past six till a quarter to seven for someone to have come into the study and shot Dale with the revolver which he kept in his writing-table drawer. Everyone in the house seems to have known about it. It doesn't take twenty minutes to shoot a man, wipe the revolver, and melt from the scene. There was plenty of time for our Mr. Vincent Bell to come back and finish his quarrel. I wonder if he did. Are you going to have him in and ask him?"

"I think I'll have the secretary first," said Inspector Lamb.

Chapter Sixteen

MONTY PHIPSON gazed earnestly, first at Inspector Lamb and then at Frank Abbott. He wore an air of horrified interest blended with a desire to be helpful, yet tinged—yes, quite definitely tinged with nervousness. Abbott, staring coolly back, was reminded of a rabbit eyeing a specially delectable piece of lettuce. The nose twitched with appetite, the whiskers twitched with terror. Monty Phipson had in fact no whiskers, but the illusion persisted.

Lamb took him through his statement. He had been upstairs in his room from six o'clock till a quarter to seven. He had seen no one, and he had heard nothing. His room was on the other side of the house. He had written some letters, and then he had played some records over on his gramophone. Just after a quarter to seven the butler came and told him that Mr. Dale had been shot. He at once rang up the police.

"This matter of your not hearing the shot, Mr. Phipson—it seems to me somebody ought to have heard it. Mrs. Raby and the maids had the wireless on. Raby's pantry is next door to the servants' hall. He says there was a band programme and they were getting it pretty loud. There's a baize door and a lot of hall and passage between this and the kitchen wing. And you were playing over gramophone records. When did you start?"

Mr. Phipson removed his glasses, polished them, and replaced them on his nose. A rabbit in pince-nez.

"Oh, well now, Inspector, I shall do my best to be accurate, but I wasn't looking at the time. It was six o'clock when I went to my room—I do know that, because the grandfather clock in the hall was striking as I went upstairs. And then—let me see—I wrote two letters—let us say about ten minutes to each—and addressed the envelopes and stamped them—so that would bring us to between twenty and twenty-five past six. And then I got out a case of records and put on—now, let me see—it was the finale of the Ninth Symphony."

"A loud piece?"

Abbott cocked a pale eyebrow.

"A very loud piece, sir. Orchestra, chorus, four soloists—all going full split. *Joie de vivre* with the lid off—fully choral and *fortissimo*. In fact, very loud. It really might drown the sound of a shot."

"We'll try it out," said Inspector Lamb.

"How many discs did you play?" said Frank Abbott.

Mr. Phipson looked nervously helpful.

"Well, I am not quite sure. There are three discs of the finale, and I put on the first one, and then my mind rather wandered to one of the letters I had written, so I let the record stop. In the end I re-wrote the letter, and I can't really say whether I turned the disc over or put on the next one. I know this must sound very foolish and absent-minded, but I was thinking about my letter, and I am afraid I did not notice what I was doing. In fact, I was not really attending to the music—my mind was on something else."

"On Mr. Dale?" said the Inspector.

"Oh, no, no—not at all."

"Would you care to tell us what you had on your mind?"

Mr. Phipson dropped his glasses and picked them up again.

"Well, really, Inspector, it was a private matter—a very private matter—but if you will regard it as confidential—"

Inspector Lamb gazed at him with a kind of ponderous patience.

"As to that I can't give any undertaking, Mr. Phipson. But a private matter that hadn't anything to do with Mr. Dale's death—well, neither Abbott nor me would mention it."

Mr. Phipson drew an agitated breath.

"It is naturally painful to me to have to take strangers into my confidence, but of course in a murder case I understand nothing is sacred. The letter I have alluded to was to a young lady, and my mind was a good deal disturbed over it. After re-writing it as I have told you I was still not satisfied, and in the end I decided to destroy it. You will now perhaps understand why I have no very accurate recollection of the order in which I played those records."

"Were you still playing them when Raby came to your room?" said Abbott.

A gleam brightened Mr. Phipson's eyes behind the pince-nez.

"Yes—yes—I was playing the last side. I remember that distinctly."

"There are three discs, aren't there?"

"Yes, yes—six sides. Marvellous music!"

"They would take a good twenty minutes to play even if you missed one side of the first disc. And you wrote a letter too."

"I may have missed more than one disc," said Mr. Phipson in a dejected manner. "It is more than probable—in fact, I think I must have done so. With the interval I have already mentioned, I suppose I was playing from about five-and-twenty past—no, no, it would be a little later, wouldn't it—I know the importance of being accurate— shall we say twenty-seven minutes past?" His nose twitched in a worried manner. "I am afraid I find it very difficult to fix the exact time, Inspector, because you see, I cannot be certain how long it took me to write those letters, but perhaps half past six—no, no, I think earlier than that—this is really very difficult—"

Of all witnesses, the nervously conscientious witness is the least dear to the official heart. Interminable delays, small verbal quibblings, acute attacks of conscience over minor details have a very rasping effect upon the temper. Inspector Lamb said,

"We'll leave that for the moment, Mr. Phipson. How long have you been with Mr. Dale?"

"Three years—no, let me see, that is not quite exact—it would have been three years next Thursday."

"But Mr. Dale had not been here for three years."

"Oh, no, Inspector. When I took up my duties he was in London. And then we travelled. He was very fond of travelling. I accompanied him to Egypt and to South Africa. Then about a year ago he bought King's Bourne. Mr. Bourne the late owner had just died. Mr. Dale decided to have the whole place done up, and I was backwards and forwards a great deal seeing to things. Mr. Bourne's widowed sister, Mrs. O'Hara, was living here with her daughter Miss Cathleen O'Hara and her niece Miss Susan Lenox. Mr. Dale wished her to have any furniture that she fancied, and I was to see about that, and about doing up the house she was moving into. It is called the Little House, and it is just at the foot of the garden here. Mr. Dale was most considerate about the whole thing—really most considerate."

"Is that the Miss O'Hara who has been employed as a secretary here?"

A slight flush came into Mr. Phipson's face.

"*Social* secretary—yes. Not, of course, that I couldn't have done all that was necessary in that way, but—well, to speak quite frankly—I suppose I had better speak frankly—"

"Much better," said Inspector Lamb with a sudden dry sound in his voice.

Mr. Phipson looked at him over the top of his pince-nez.

"Well then, I think Mr. Dale was glad to put the employment in her way. Mr. Bourne died in embarrassed circumstances, and there was very little left for the family. And then, of course, there was his feeling for Miss Lenox."

"And what sort of feeling was that?"

Mr. Phipson looked arch.

"Oh, the usual one, Inspector. Mr. Dale made no secret of it. It really was quite obvious from the first, but of course the news of the engagement did come as a surprise to us here in the house—I don't think it can have got very much beyond the immediate household, because he only informed us yesterday."

"Mr. Dale was engaged to Miss Lenox?"

"So he informed us yesterday—let me see—it was just before tea. And of course it was a surprise, because Miss Lenox was engaged to Mr. Carrick."

Lamb put up a monumental hand.

"I'd like to know about this engagement to Mr. Carrick. Who is he?"

Mr. Phipson explained with gusto. Mr. Carrick was the son of the late Dr. Carrick, deceased some two years ago. He had been engaged to Susan Lenox for about that length of time. He was an architect with his way to make. He had done some work on the alterations to King's Bourne.

Mr. Phipson took much longer over it than that, but the Inspector suffered him with patience.

"And when was this engagement broken off?"

Monty Phipson assumed the air of a man of the world.

"As far as my information goes—well, it never was broken off—the lady just changed her mind. Very suddenly, Inspector. Mr. Carrick was certainly down staying at the Little House last Wednesday night, and of course they may have quarrelled then, or they may not. But from certain indications I believe—but perhaps I ought not to indulge in conjecture—"

"I think you had better finish what you were going to say."

"If it will be of any help—I am most anxious to assist you in every possible way. I was going to say that Miss O'Hara was taken ill here on Saturday morning, and that Miss Susan Lenox was here for some time, after which Mr. Dale took them both home in the Daimler. From certain indications of emotional disturbance I am of the opinion that Mr. Dale had at that time proposed and been accepted."

The Inspector slewed round to the table and picked up one of the papers which lay there. He said "Yes—" in a meditative tone and faced round again upon the secretary.

"What do you know about Mr. Vincent Bell?"

Monty Phipson put up a deprecating hand.

"Very little, I assure you—very little indeed."

"As what, Mr. Phipson?"

"Let me see—he arrived here on Thursday morning quite unexpectedly—"

"Mr. Dale didn't expect him?"

"As to that I cannot say, but if you would like me to express an opinion—"

Frank Abbott drew a long breath and permitted himself to gaze at the ceiling.

Lamb said imperturbably, "Let us have your opinion."

Monty Phipson edged a little forward in his chair.

"Well, in my opinion Mr. Dale was taken completely by surprise, and it was not a very pleasant surprise either. Mr. Bell just said he was stopping—and he stopped."

"What sort of terms were they on?"

"Well, I hardly like to say. I naturally feel the responsibility of giving evidence like this, and I am most anxious to be fair. I think I might say that there was a good deal of tension. Mr. Bell's manner was not very tactful. I think he and Mr. Dale had had some business association in the United States. I believe Mr. Dale was engaged in—well, Inspector, in rum running during the prohibition period. If I had not had some idea of this before, I should have guessed as much from Mr. Bell's allusions and hints. Mr. Dale resented them a good deal, and several times I thought there was going to be a quarrel, but Mr. Bell would always laugh it off."

"I see. Well now, Mr. Phipson, how did you and Mr. Dale get along?"

The question, in this homely shape, did not seem to worry Mr. Phipson. He looked conscientious and said,

"Oh, I hope he had no cause to be dissatisfied."

"That's no answer, Mr. Phipson. I don't want to know what you hope. The question is, was he satisfied?"

An air of offence became evident.

"*Really*, Inspector, I am being most careful about my answers. Mr. Dale had no reason to be dissatisfied—no reason at all. If you want to know whether he *was* satisfied, I can only say that he gave me no reason to think otherwise."

The Inspector opened his mouth to speak and shut it again. His right shoulder jerked slightly.

Frank Abbott took up the tale.

"What was Dale like to work for? Easy—considerate—difficult?"

Monty Phipson looked at him coldly.

"My position was an extremely confidential one. Such a position is never without occasional difficulties. I think I may say that Mr. Dale appreciated that."

Abbott's left eyebrow twitched.

"Hang it all, man, you're talking like a book! Did you like Dale? That's what we want to know—did you like him?"

A pale, ugly flush suffused Mr. Phipson's features, particularly the nose which reminded young Abbott so strongly of a rabbit's. He said in a huffy, stuffy voice,

"I was with Mr. Dale for three years. The relations between us were of a perfectly satisfactory nature."

Chapter Seventeen

VINCENT BELL came into the room with a brisk and jaunty air. His eyes went to and fro, his black hair stood up aggressively. He sat down with an air of assurance and addressed himself to Inspector Lamb.

"Well, Captain, what can I do for you?"

"You can answer some questions, Mr. Bell."

"That's all right by me."

Inspector Lamb was being careful. He said,

"You understand that you are not obliged to answer? I'd like to make that clear."

"I'm not obliged to talk, but I can if I like?"

"That's right, Mr. Bell."

"All right, Captain, shoot!"

"Well then, Mr. Bell, perhaps you'll give us an idea of what your business was with Mr. Dale."

"Well, I don't know that it was exactly business."

"But you had had business relations with him."

Vincent Bell's eyes snapped.

"Dale's secretary been talking? Well, I won't deny it."

"Rum running or something of that sort?"

Vincent Bell laughed.

"Something of that sort," he agreed.

"Well, that's nothing to do with us over here, but if you and Mr. Dale came to loggerheads about it—"

Lamb made a suggestive pause.

"Well, I won't say we didn't. But that's not to say I'd take the trouble to come over here and shoot him, because if I'd wanted to put him on the spot I could have done it three years ago without travelling three thousand miles."

Frank Abbott looked up from his shorthand notes.

"But you did come three thousand miles. Why?"

Vincent Bell grinned.

"I'd a notion it might be worth my while. Look here, boys, I'm not holding up on you. The truth is Dale got away with a helluva lot of money that was half of it mine. I was sick, and he collected and walked out on me—thought I was going to die and there would be no questions asked. Well, I didn't die, but what with one thing and another I wasn't in a position to follow him up for a year or two, and then it took a bit of time before I hit his trail."

Inspector Lamb put up a hand.

"You came over here to try and recover a sum of money from Mr. Dale?"

"You can put it like that."

"Did you come over here to threaten him?"

Vincent laughed.

"I came to get my money."

"How did you expect to get it?"

"Not by shooting him. That wouldn't make sense, would it? How much money can you get from a guy with a bullet in his brain? I wanted my money, and the way things are I don't get a cent. I guess that lets me out."

Inspector Lamb leaned forward. He said in a weighty voice,

"You were heard quarrelling with Mr. Dale at a quarter past six. He was shot some time between then and a quarter to seven when the butler found him dead. What have you got to say about that?"

For the moment Mr. Bell hadn't anything to say. There was a noticeable alteration in his colour. He looked here and there, and in the end flung out a hand.

"That puts me in a spot. But I didn't shoot him. You don't shoot a guy because you have a quarrel with him. I wasn't watching the time, but if someone heard us talking at a quarter past six, it wasn't much after that when I quit and went upstairs, and Dale was alive then. I left him right here in this room. He'd his back to me and he was going over to that glass door. We'd both got a bit heated, and I guess he meant to open it. It was found open."

"It was open when he was found," said Lamb, varying the order of the words. "Well, Mr. Bell, what did you do next?"

"I went upstairs to my room, and then I took a bath."

"Can you fix the time you were in the bath?"

Vincent shrugged his shoulders.

"If I'd known Dale was going to be murdered I'd have kept right on looking at my watch and I wouldn't have taken a bath. I'd have gone and sat with that secretary guy so I'd have a nice water-tight alibi. That's the worst of not being the murderer. It's just too bad. All I can tell you is I was out of my bath and part way dressed when Raby gave the alarm, and that was round about a quarter to seven."

"And you didn't hear the shot?"

"I wouldn't have heard twenty shots," said Vincent Bell. "I guess the plumbing in this house is pretty old. When you've got a tap turned on it's bad enough, but when you turn it off—well, it's like the Fourth of July."

"Noises in the pipes?"

"I'll say so."

Inspector Lamb's round brown eyes dwelt upon Vincent Bell. Mr. Bell sustained the look. He even grinned, and said,

"Try them for yourself, Captain."

The Inspector frowned.

"Everyone in this house has got a reason for not having heard that shot. I can believe one or two of them, but I can't believe them all."

Vincent Bell laughed cheerfully.

"Mine's O.K. whatever the others are," he declared.

He went out as briskly as he had come in, and at that moment the telephone bell rang.

Inspector Lamb lifted the receiver and heard an indisputably clerical voice say,

"Is that King's Bourne? Is that Raby?"

"Detective Inspector Lamb speaking."

There was a clerical cough.

"Oh, yes. Good-morning, Inspector. My name is Mickleham—the Reverend Cyril Mickleham—and I am the Vicar of this parish."

"Yes, sir?"

There was another cough.

"Well, Inspector—er—the fact is my wife, Mrs. Mickleham, has some information which I feel it is her duty to—er—place at your disposal. It is very painful to us both, but private feelings must not be allowed to interfere with public duties."

"Well, sir, if Mrs. Mickleham has any information to give us, I shall be glad if she could make it convenient to call here as soon as possible."

"Exactly—there is no time like the present. We can be with you in twenty minutes, if that will be all right."

Lamb hung up and hunched a shoulder.

"Vicar's wife, with evidence—coming along now. We can be trying out Mr. Bell's water-pipes and Mr. Phipson's records."

Chapter Eighteen

THE PIPES amply substantiated Vincent Bell's account of their activities. As soon as any water had been run off there was such a gurgling, banging and groaning as would have camouflaged a royal salute.

Raby deposed to having heard the sounds from his pantry.

"A shocking noise they do make, and no mistake about it, sir. The pipes come down beside my sink, and there are times when they bang so loud you'd think they'd burst. They weren't as bad as that last night, but round about half past six they were at it for a matter of ten minutes or so. There isn't anyone can have a bath in this house without its being known. Very put out about it, Mr. Dale was, and meaning to have the old pipes out and a new lot put in. He only spoke of it yesterday, sir, and said if he went abroad on his honeymoon, it could be done very convenient whilst he was away."

Tests with the records in Mr. Phipson's room went to show that a shot fired in the study could not be heard during any of the louder passages, and that with the door and window shut and the curtains drawn it would be extremely likely to pass unnoticed at any time. In the servants' hall it was quite inaudible, even without a band programme on the wireless.

Lamb led the way back to the study, sat down at the table, and said,

"Carry on, Abbott. What do you make of it?"

Frank Abbott sat on the corner of the table and swung an elegantly trousered leg.

"No one has a motive," he said. "Everyone has lots of opportunity. Nobody has an alibi."

Lamb grunted.

"Bell had it in for him all right."

"I don't fancy Bell, but let's say he had half a motive. Opportunity and alibi as before."

The Inspector grunted again, but this time produced no words. Frank Abbott carried on.

"Opportunity—Raby said he was in the pantry from just after twenty past six to a quarter to seven. We have only his own word for it that he left Dale alive. He could have shot him when he came to make up the fire, *or* he could have come back from the pantry and done it, *or* he could have taken in the cocktail and done it then. Opportunity for Raby practically unlimited. Motive, as already stated, none. Alibi practically non-existent—Mrs. Raby says she called out to him in the pantry somewhere round about half past six and he answered her.

"Now for the secretary. There's no motive so far as we know, and he loses his job. There's no alibi of any sort, kind or description. He says he was playing gramophone records and writing letters. Perhaps he was, perhaps he wasn't. The discs were lying about in his room, and the last one was still on the gramophone—he was playing it when Raby came up. He did write letters. There was one for the post addressed to a firm of sanitary engineers in Ledlington, and there were torn-up pieces of something discreetly affectionate in his waste paper basket. He gets so tangled up when he's trying to be accurate that it's no good trying to trip him—he keeps on doing it himself. I don't know whether you could make head or tail of his times, but I couldn't, and I don't believe he could either. I was left with the feeling that he might have disentangled himself from the Ninth Symphony and his correspondence, hared downstairs shot Dale, and got back in time to listen to the final panegyric of joy. Only why in heaven's name should he shoot him?"

There was no answer.

At this moment the young constable on duty outside the door opened it and ushered in the Vicar, his cheerful rosy face composed as for a funeral, and Mrs. Mickleham who looked as if she had been crying for hours. She still most incredibly resembled a hen, but a hen with dejected and ruffled feathers. Her long neck poked, her hair was in wisps under a crooked hat, her eyelids were red and swollen, the ridge of her bony nose scarlet. She held a pocket handkerchief tightly clasped in a black gloved hand. As she sank into the chair recently vacated by Vincent Bell she pressed the linen to her lips and heaved a heart-broken sigh.

Frank Abbott, having provided the Vicar with a chair, sat down at the far side of the table and opened his notebook. The Vicar cleared his throat.

"My wife is very much distressed, but I have told her that her duty is clear. Perhaps you will allow me to explain. Does the name of Miss Susan Lenox convey anything to you?"

Inspector Lamb picked up a sheet of paper from the table.

"Niece of the late owner of King's Bourne, now resident with her aunt, Mrs. O'Hara, at the Little House, Netherbourne."

"Exactly, Inspector. Miss Lenox is a very charming girl whom I have known since she was quite a child. For the past two years she has been engaged to William Carrick, the son of our late doctor—a very great loss and much respected. William Carrick is an architect by profession, and I have looked forward very pleasantly to marrying these young people as soon as William's circumstances became such as to enable him to support a wife. Imagine my surprise and consternation when I received a visit yesterday afternoon from Mr. Dale, in the course of which he informed me that he and Susan Lenox intended to be married on Thursday, and that he had just been making the necessary arrangements for a licence. His call was for the purpose of asking me to perform the ceremony. I could hardly believe my ears, and I felt that I must communicate as soon as possible with Miss Lenox. I really found it impossible to believe her capable of terminating a two years engagement for the purpose of entering so precipitately into marriage with a stranger. I was deeply concerned, not only as her parish priest but as an old friend."

Inspector Lamb said, "Quite so."

The Vicar put up a hand.

"Permit me to continue. I thought it inadvisable to use the telephone to discuss so confidential a matter. The amount of gossip in a village is deplorable—quite deplorable. I made it the subject of my Lenten sermons last year under such headings as Evil Speaking, Lying, Slandering, etcetera—But I must not digress. I was about to sally forth to the Little House, when I received a very urgent call to a dying parishioner at Ledcott. I therefore asked my wife to go and see Miss Lenox and ascertain the real facts from her. In a way, I felt perhaps that a woman's intuition—"

A smothered sob from Mrs. Mickleham broke the thread of what had begun to sound ominously like a sermon.

Inspector Lamb turned to the afflicted lady.

"Perhaps you would tell us the rest yourself, Mrs. Mickleham."

The hand with the crumpled handkerchief returned to her lap, where it was tightly clasped by its fellow. In the wretched voice of one who has got a most repugnant lesson by heart, she said,

"I went to the Little House and I walked in—we know them so very well that I usually just walk in. There was a light upstairs, but it was dark in the hall. The drawing-room door was ajar, and I knew there was no one there because the room was dark, so I opened the dining-room door and went through to go to the kitchen. Susan does all the cooking, so I thought she might be there—"

"One moment, Mrs. Mickleham—what time was this?"

Mrs. Mickleham sniffed miserably.

"I left the Vicarage at six o'clock, and it takes about twenty minutes."

"And what time was Mr. Dale's visit?"

"He was with me from half past three until ten minutes to four," said the Vicar. "We were expecting a guest to tea, or I would have gone to see Miss Lenox immediately. By the time our guest had gone I had received the urgent summons I told you of. It was then, I think, about a quarter to six."

Inspector Lamb returned to Mrs. Mickleham.

"So you reached the Little House at about twenty past six?"

Mrs. Mickleham caught her breath.

"Oh, I think so—but then I stopped for a moment to ask Mrs. Stock about her little boy with the whooping cough, so it must have been later than that."

"Very well, will you go on? You went through the dining-room to go to the kitchen because you thought Miss Lenox might be there."

"Oh, *yes*," said Mrs. Mickleham. "There was a light under the door and I could hear them talking. I really did not know what to do—whether to go back—but then the Vicar had expressly charged me—"

"What did you do, Mrs. Mickleham?"

"I stood still and tried to make up my mind—"

"One moment—do you know who it was in the kitchen?"

"Oh, yes—it was Susan Lenox and Bill Carrick. And I could not help hearing what he said—he was speaking so loudly. And of course one couldn't be surprised—after being engaged for two years, and the change so *dreadfully* sudden."

The Inspector leaned forward.

"Do you mean that Mr. Carrick and Miss Lenox were quarrelling?"

"Oh, no, no—I don't think so—it wasn't like that at all. Poor Susan kept saying things like 'I must' and 'I've promised', and Bill was saying he wouldn't let her, and things about going up to King's

Bourne and—and having it out with Mr. Dale. And I thought how dreadful if he went up there in the state of mind he was in, so I opened the door and—and—" The tears began to well from Mrs. Mickleham's eyes and her voice failed.

"Come, come, Lucy." The Vicar laid an admonitory hand on her shoulder. "My dear, control yourself. You must tell the Inspector what you heard William say."

"I *can't*."

"You can do your duty, my dear, and I am sure that you will."

Mrs. Mickleham leaned back and closed her reddened eyelids upon the welling tears. She spoke in an exhausted voice.

"He said—oh dear, I heard him say—oh dear, I wish I hadn't, but he said—he said— 'Do you want me to kill him, Susan?' Oh dear! And then he said, 'I think I'm going to.' And I pushed open the door, and as soon as he saw me he pulled away from Susan and rushed out through the scullery."

"Did you see where he went?"

"Oh, no—it was quite dark. But I could hear him running up the garden."

"Would that be the way to King's Bourne?"

"It would be the nearest way," said the Vicar.

"Oh *dear*!" said Mrs. Mickleham.

"What happened after that?"

"Oh, I don't know. Poor Susan looked as if she was going to faint. I tried to explain to her why I had come, but I don't think she was listening to me—she seemed too much distressed. And all at once she ran out through the scullery after Bill, and there didn't seem to be anything to stay for then, so I came away."

"Thank you, Mrs. Mickleham. I suppose you didn't notice the time whilst you were in the kitchen? I should like it a little more exact than we've got it yet."

"Oh, *yes*," said Mrs. Mickleham. "And I always notice a clock. One does if one leads a very busy life. I'm sure I don't know where I should be if I let myself get behind. And the clock is on the dresser— just opposite the door."

"Then you noticed the time as you came in?"

"Oh, *yes*—it was three minutes to the half hour."

"Good," said the Inspector. "Then Mr. Carrick started up the hill to King's Bourne at twenty-seven minutes past six. And how long would it take him to get there? What's the distance?"

"Four hundred yards to the front door," said Mr. Mickleham with a faint air of superiority. "I carry a pedometer—a hobby of mine. I believe I could tell you the exact distance between any two points in my parish."

Lamb's gaze dwelt upon him for a moment and then withdrew.

"Four hundred yards—mostly up hill—he was in a hurry.... Say three and a half minutes. Now how long were you talking to Miss Lenox before she followed Mr. Carrick?"

"I don't know, I'm sure. Oh, yes, I do, because I looked at the clock when she had gone, and I thought I had better not wait."

"And what time was it?"

"Just the half hour—oh, yes." She began to dab her eyes and straighten her hat.

"He'd three minutes start of her, and he'd go quicker. Three minutes start.... Thank you, Mrs. Mickleham."

When they had gone he looked up the number of the Little House and asked for it.

"Can I speak to Miss Susan Lenox?"

"I am Susan Lenox."

"Detective Inspector Lamb speaking from King's Bourne. I should be glad if you would come up here as soon as possible. I think you may be able to give us information which we shall be glad to have. Can you tell me where Mr. Carrick is?"

"He is here."

"I shall be glad to see him too. Can you come up now?"

Susan Lenox said, "Yes."

Chapter Nineteen

"Going to see them together?" said Frank Abbott.

Lamb nodded.

"Queer set-out. Looks like the girl's been playing tricks, throwing a poor man over for a rich one, and the fat in the fire. Yes, we'll see them together. It's how they are together will tell us what we want to know. Here, Abbott, you stand ready by that glass door and let them in that way. I've got a notion that may show us something too."

As they crossed the lower terrace, Susan said,

"I'm going to tell the truth, Bill."

"How much of it?" His tone was grim.

"Not Cathy, or the pearls—I can't."

"All right. They'll want to know why you were going to marry him."

"Bill!"

"He'd been to old Mickleham. It's bound to come out. Of course you could say you didn't know anything about it."

"They wouldn't believe that."

"They might."

"Mrs. Mickleham heard us talking. Oh, Bill—she heard what you said!"

"Do you think she'll tell?"

"Cyril will make her," said Susan with wretched conviction.

"All right, we'll tell the truth. Let's hope we shame the devil."

As they came up the terrace steps they saw Frank Abbott at the open glass door, and he saw them. His light eyes looked them over as he beckoned them in. Not the sort of girl you'd expect. Nice chap. I suppose he did it, poor devil. He shut the door behind them and saw them to their chairs. They were both pale. Bill Carrick steady and composed. Susan fine-drawn, the contours of brow and chin emphasized, lips parted, nostrils taut. Frank Abbott thought, "She'd be lovely with a colour"; and then, "She's lovely now."

Inspector Lamb's ox-like gaze dwelt first on Bill and then on Susan. He had three daughters of his own, and was sometimes put to it to conceal a most obstinate softness of heart where girls were concerned. Miss Susan Lenox appeared to be of the same age as his Margy. He felt it a handicap, frowned portentously, and addressed himself to Bill.

"Mr. Carrick, we have certain information which I will ask you to confirm. Until recently you and Miss Lenox were engaged to be married?"

Bill looked him in the eye.

"Miss Lenox and I have been engaged for two years. We are still engaged."

"Yesterday afternoon Mr. Lucas Dale called upon the Vicar of this parish and asked him to officiate at his marriage to Miss Lenox on Thursday next—"

Susan said quickly and breathlessly,

"It was a dreadful mistake."

"You mean that Mr. Dale was mistaken in thinking that you would marry him?"

Susan became even paler, and said, "No."

"Had you quarrelled with Mr. Carrick, and engaged yourself to Mr. Dale on the rebound, as it were?"

Frank Abbott's hand covered his mouth for a moment. Old Lamb and his "rebound"! Something queer behind all this—something very queer.

Susan said, "No."

"Now, Miss Lenox, you know you needn't answer any of these questions. We're not in court, and there's no charge—" He paused and added "*yet*. But I'll tell you one thing—if you or Mr. Carrick have got your reasons for being afraid of the law, then you'll do best to say no more than you need. But if you've no reason to be afraid of the truth coming out, then the more you help us the more we can help you. We're not out to hound people down, we're out to get at the truth. In trying to get at it we've got to ask all sorts of questions about people's private affairs. It isn't pleasant for you and it isn't pleasant for us, but it's got to be done. Anything you tell us that hasn't got to be used as evidence—well, it'll be as private as if you only knew it yourself. If you don't tell us what we want to know, we're bound to try and find it out, and that means raking round and stirring up the mud. Now are you going to be frank and tell us why you broke off your engagement to Mr. Carrick and when— particularly when?"

Susan had lifted startled eyes to his face. She looked now at Bill. He nodded. She drew a long, difficult breath.

"I'll tell you as much as I can. There wasn't any quarrel. Bill and I—" Her voice faltered, but she went on gallantly. "It's always been Bill and I. Then Mr. Dale came here. He wanted to marry me. I said no. He knew I was engaged to Bill." For a moment her colour flamed. "He said he always got what he wanted. He found a way to threaten someone—I—cared for. Not Bill—it was nothing to do with Bill."

"You say he was blackmailing you?"

Susan drew another long breath.

"I suppose so. I said—I would—do it."

"You agreed to marry him?"

"Yes."

"When was this?"

"Saturday."

"And you wrote to Mr. Carrick. He got the letter on Monday morning and came down to forbid the banns. Is that right?"

Bill said, "Yes."

"When did you get here, Mr. Carrick?"

"Soon after six. I didn't get the letter until late—I'd been out all day."

"Well, you got down here, and you had a scene with Miss Lenox in the kitchen at the Little House. Mrs. Mickleham walked in on the end of it."

"Yes—I left."

"She says you were declaring your intention of going up to King's Bourne and having it out with Mr. Dale, and Miss Lenox was begging you not to go and saying she had promised. Is this correct?"

"Yes."

"She states that she heard you say, 'Do you want me to kill him, Susan? I think I'm going to.' Is this also correct?"

"It was what I was feeling like," said Bill. "I suppose I said it. But I didn't kill him, Inspector. He was dead when I got here."

There was a momentary pause. Lamb looked at him and said,

"You did come here then?"

"Oh, yes, I came. I'll tell you if I may." He glanced at Abbott. "He can take it down. I've nothing to hide—I'd rather say just what happened. I ran out of the house and up the hill as hard as I could go till I got to the second terrace. Then I stopped because I realized that I'd got to pull myself together. Whilst I was standing there I heard the shot. I wasn't sure where the sound came from at first. Then I went on up to the house. I came up the steps at the end of the terrace by the corner of the study. One of those windows in the recess over there was open and the curtain drawn back. I could see the light. I went and looked in—"

"Why did you do that?"

"I don't know. I think I wanted to see if he was there, and if he was alone. I saw his hand and arm stretched out on the floor. I don't know how long I stood there. It was—a shock—because I—had wanted to kill him. I thought about the shot. I thought perhaps he had killed himself. After a bit I went back on to the terrace. The glass door was open—"

"One minute, Mr. Carrick—as you came up the steps on to the terrace the glass door would be in front of you on your left, and the windows of the recess still more to your left and at right angles?"

Bill nodded and said "Yes."

"Very well, when you came up the steps you noticed that the window in the recess was open. Was the glass door open too?"

"I didn't notice it."

"It was nearer to you than the window was—would you not have noticed it?"

"I don't know. I didn't."

"Yet you noticed it at once when you came back. Do you think it possible that it was not open when you came up the steps, though it was open when you came back after looking in at the window?"

"I don't know—I just didn't notice. As soon as I saw the door was open I went in. Do you want me to tell you what I saw?"

"If you please, Mr. Carrick."

"Dale was lying face downwards behind the writing-table. It was his left hand and arm I had seen from the window. The right was doubled up under him. He had been shot through the back of the head. The chair you are sitting in was pushed back, and the second drawer on the right of the table was open. There was no sign of a struggle. There was a revolver lying across the corner of the blotting-pad on this side. I came as far as the end of the table and stood there for a bit. I thought I ought to give the alarm, but I—well, I funked doing it. Then I heard someone on the terrace and went out. It was Susan. When I saw her the only thing I thought about was keeping her out of it. I told her Dale was dead, and I took her back to the Little House. That's all, sir."

"You say there was a revolver on the table. Did you touch it?"

"I didn't touch anything."

"Ever see the revolver before?"

"No."

"Did you know Mr. Dale had a revolver?"

"I don't know—Susan says I must have—she says every-one knew."

Frank Abbott's lips drew together as if he were about to whistle. No sound issued from them, but in his own mind he rendered the opening phrase of Chopin's Funeral March.

Lamb said a thought gruffly,

"Did you know where he kept it?"

"He *didn't*," said Susan—"not till I told him. Oh, he did-n't really!"

Lamb looked at her for quite a long time. Then he said,

"Did you hear the shot, Miss Lenox?"

"Yes."

"Where were you?"

"I had just come out of the orchard. I was clear of the trees."

"We'll have to check the time that takes you—we'll have to check all these times. But I dare say you've got a good idea how long it takes. Was there time for Mr. Carrick to have reached the study before you heard the shot?"

Susan had been very pale. She became paler still. She said in a voice that did not rise above a whisper,

"He was on the terrace. He didn't go—straight—to the house."

"But if he had—was there time?"

She looked at him and did not speak.

"Was there time, Miss Lenox?"

Bill said roughly, "Of course there was! What's the good of beating about the bush? If I'd gone straight on to the house the way I was going I'd have been there when the shot was fired—it's no good making any bones about that. But I didn't go straight, so I wasn't in the house. I was on the second terrace."

"Sure of that, Mr. Carrick?"

"Quite sure."

"Yes.... You said you were pulling yourself together. Were you out of control?"

"I wanted to kill him," said Bill grimly.

Frank Abbott glanced up from his shorthand and murmured something which sounded like "The prisoner conducted his own prosecution". He received a majestic glance from his superior officer and went back to his notes.

Bill's colour rose.

"I didn't kill him—I only wanted to. He was a blackmailing swine, and I had to get Susan clear. I'd got sense enough left to know that it was no good crowding in and offering to beat him up. I'd got to keep my head. That's why I was on the lower terrace and not up at the house when the shot was fired."

Inspector Lamb made no comment. He said,

"Did you touch anything at all while you were in the study?"

"No."

"And you, Miss Lenox?"

"I didn't come in. I didn't come any farther than the middle of the terrace."

Lamb swung round in his chair and picked up a paper from the table. His eyes travelled slowly from the page to Susan's face.

"Were you aware that Mr. Dale made a fresh will yesterday?" he said.

Frank Abbott saw Bill Carrick start. Susan clenched her hands and said,

"Yes."

"Were you aware of the terms of that will?"

She kept her eyes on his face.

"He rang me up and said he had made a will."

"Did he tell you what was in it?"

Susan steadied the very small amount of voice she had left.

"He said—it was the old-fashioned everything-to-my-wife sort. He said—he just wanted me to know—"

The voice failed altogether.

Bill Carrick sprang up.

"She wasn't his wife—she never would have been! The will isn't worth the paper it's written on!"

Inspector Lamb got up too, slowly as befitted a man of his girth.

"The will leaves everything to Miss Susan Lenox in anticipation of marriage. Mr. Duckett of the Market Square, Ledlington, who drew it up, will tell you that it is perfectly valid."

Susan lost the Inspector in a mist. It was a very thick mist, like cotton wool. She stopped trying to compete with it and shut her eyes.

Chapter Ten

"WELL," SAID INSPECTOR LAMB—"and where does this get us?"

Frank Abbott opened his notebook.

"Those times check up pretty well the way we thought. If Susan Lenox started up the hill three minutes after Carrick did, he could easily have reached this study by the time she got to the top of the orchard. Mrs. Mickleham gives us the times they started from the Little House."

"Think he did it?" said Lamb.

Frank Abbott laughed.

"Do you?"

"I'm asking you."

"Hearing the boy his lessons," murmured Frank Abbott. " 'Home-work at the Yard', and 'How to become an Inspector'—I beg your pardon, sir."

"You'll need to one of these days. Tongue trouble—that's what you've got. What do you say about Carrick? That's what I asked you, you know."

"Well, Dale was shot with his own revolver—that's been confirmed. Carrick most obligingly informed us that everyone knew about Dale's revolver, and if he couldn't remember knowing about it himself, that was just too bad and quite his own fault. If you're going to take Susan Lenox's evidence as to the time of the shot, Dale was killed at between one and two minutes after the half hour, and nearer the one than the two. I think we've got to believe her, because if she was going to lie she would produce something that would look a bit better for Carrick. As it stands, he had between four and four and a half minutes to reach the study and shoot Dale. I don't believe he did shoot Dale. Firstly, because no guilty person ever furnished the police with quite so much gratuitous evidence against himself—to my mind he said everything that the murderer wouldn't have said. Secondly, the thing is stiff with inherent improbabilities. He's not only got to reach this room in four and a half minutes, he's got to get hold of the revolver and shoot it off while Dale's back is turned. I can't see how it could possibly have happened. If I was mad enough to kill a chap who had taken my girl I'd want to damn him into heaps before I shot him. If it had been Carrick's own revolver, he might have rushed off with it, got in at the glass door, and shot Dale. But even so I don't see how he was going to get behind him. Anyone sitting at this writing-table has that door in view all the time. And anyhow it wasn't Carrick's revolver, it was Dale's. Suppose he came in and threatened Dale, and Dale got out his revolver—Carrick would have to take it from him. Dale was a powerful man. Do you think he could have got it without a struggle? And if he had got it, was Dale going to turn his back and let himself be shot through the head? And all in four and a half minutes—from the kitchen of the Little House, to Dale dead here on the floor. I say it couldn't be done. And if it couldn't be done, then I say Carrick didn't do it."

"Suppose it was this way," said Lamb—"he didn't come in through that glass door at all, he got into the house some other way and came in by the door the butler used—the one that's behind me now. Dale wouldn't see who it was—he'd think it was the butler or the secretary. But Carrick would see the open drawer, and the revolver lying handy. Then you'd get it this way—Carrick snatches the revolver, Dale pushes back his chair, and Carrick jumps back and shoots him as he gets up. How about that?"

"How did he get into the house? There wasn't a door or a window open on the ground floor except the door and the window in this room. As Dale sat at his table he was facing between the two with the window on his right front and the door on his left front. No one could have come in by either without his seeing them."

"Here's another way then," said Lamb—"the revolver wasn't here at all—Miss Lenox had it. She may have taken it because she was afraid of what might happen when those two met. Raby saw the drawer pulled out, but he didn't see the revolver. We took that to mean that he wasn't noticing, but it may have meant that the revolver wasn't there. Suppose Miss Lenox did take it, and Carrick came on it. They were in the kitchen. One of the dresser drawers would be a likely enough hiding-place. Say he came on it and stuffed it down into the pocket of his coat. He rushes in on Dale and begins to tell him off. He called him a blackmailing swine to us just now. Suppose he let off like that at him—what would Dale do? Push back his chair and turn round to go and ring the bell. And Carrick shoots him. That wouldn't take so long."

Abbott nodded.

"Highly ingenious, but I don't think. Too many ifs and ands. You can ask Susan Lenox."

"You think she'd tell the truth?"

"I don't think she could tell a lie without giving herself away. No practice, and would always be a very poor performer."

"It's a queer set-out," said Lamb.

"As you said to start with. And how true. Here, to agree with Bill Carrick, is a first-class blackmailing swine on the verge of smashing up certainly two, probably three people's lives. Someone removes him in the nick of time—a most praiseworthy act—and it is our unfortunate duty to hunt down this benefactor and get him hanged."

The rosy face of Inspector Lamb became stern. His eyes protruded slightly.

"Now, Abbott, that's enough of that. Fancy ways of talking about it don't make crime into anything except just crime. Murder's murder, and the law is the law. There's a law against the blackmailer for his blackmailing, and there's a law against the murderer for his murdering. It's the law that's got to punish people—not you, or me, or Mr. Carrick, just because we think a man's a bad man. He's got the right to have a judge and a jury on that, and be found guilty or not guilty as the case may be. So don't let me hear any more of that fancy stuff. Too much tongue, my lad—that's what's the matter with you, and some day it's going to get you into trouble."

"*Absit omen,*" murmured Frank Abbott—"I mean, yes, sir."

Lamb grunted.

"Where's the report on those finger-prints? I want to run through it.... Now, let's see how this works in. Raby's prints all over the place—faint. That's what you'd expect.... Very good and fresh on the wood-box and the edge of the hearth. That bears out his statement all right.... Only Dale's own finger-prints on that pulled-out drawer and on the pushed-back chair.... No finger-prints at all on the revolver. Whoever used it wiped it off or wore gloves.... Dale's prints on the handle of the glass door and the latch of the open window.... A print of nearly the whole of Carrick's hand on the window sill. That bears out his statement that he stood there and looked in."

"Then there isn't any possibility that he could have shot Dale in the time."

"Looks that way. Now—let's see—what about the glass door? His statement looked as if it wasn't open when he went along to the window, but it was open when he came back. There are some old faint prints of the footman's, the one person in the house who has an unbreakable alibi, and apart from them nothing but Dale's. If that door was opened after Dale was shot, or pushed wide after being ajar as seems likely from Raby's evidence—he said it was a little bit open—then the person who pushed it open must have carefully avoided leaving prints. That's where I can't fit young Carrick in. Apart from all this time business, I don't see him being so careful about prints—not in the frame of mind he was in. He might have thought to wipe the revolver, but I don't see him bothering with the door. Of course he might just have given it a shove with his shoulder, and off like that. But if he found it wide open, as it was found by Raby at a quarter to seven, well, then he'd have no call to touch it."

"I think he was telling the truth," said Frank Abbott. "I don't know what a jury would think."

Lamb frowned.

"Well, there it is. Now, what about this footmark?" He picked up a piece of paper and stared at the drawing on it. "Fore part of a woman's shoe—size five—no heel mark.... There's a muddy puddle on the path up from the Little House just before you come to the lower terrace. I noticed Miss Lenox went wide of it without looking when we went down with them just now. It's a soft bit of ground— probably always wet after rain. She stepped wide without having to give it a thought. The question is, did she forget about it last night? The shoe that made that mark had been in a puddle all right. If it hadn't rained before we got here, we'd have been able to pick up the prints on the terrace and on the steps. The woman who wore that shoe stood just inside the glass door. That's the only clear print, but there were traces of mud right across to where the body was found. I think she came as near him as that. Perhaps she was wearing gloves. Perhaps she handled the revolver. Perhaps she shot him. Now Miss Lenox says she didn't come into the room—Mr. Carrick says so too."

"Susan Lenox couldn't have shot Dale. She didn't leave the kitchen of the Little House till the half hour, and she heard the shot—" Frank Abbott stopped abruptly.

Lamb wagged a finger at him.

"She heard the shot, and Carrick heard the shot—*and nobody else did*. And it's their times we're taking to argue with. If they're not telling the truth, what happens to your four and a half minutes and Carrick not having time to get here? If they're not telling the truth about where they were when they heard the shot, they had the best part of a quarter of an hour to come and go upon, and either of them could have shot him, or they could both have been in it together—as far as the time was concerned—" Lamb paused, and added, "Miss Lenox takes a shoe that's very much the size of this."

Chapter Twenty-One

The telephone bell rang. Frank Abbott listened, scribbled on a piece of paper, hung up, and pushed the paper over to Inspector Lamb.

"The bank at Ledlington—about those notes. He drew the two hundred in four fifties. These are the numbers."

Lamb picked up a bunch of keys and unlocked the top drawer on the right-hand side of Lucas Dale's writing-table. The contents of the dead man's pockets came into view—a handkerchief, a stub of sealing-wax, a pocket-knife, a green and blue marble, a twist of twine, a pencil, a fountain pen, a snapshot of Susan Lenox in a small brown leather case, a cheque-book on a Ledlington bank, some loose change, and a sealskin wallet with his initials on it in gold.

Lamb took up the cheque-book and flicked over the counterfoils.

"Here we are—the last cheque he drew, dated yesterday—self two hundred pounds. And—" he took up the wallet and opened it—

"here are three of the fifties. This one"—he put a splayed forefinger on the last of Abbott's scribbled numbers—"this one's gone. When I rang up this morning the manager was out. I said they could wait till he came in if it made them any happier, but the clerk I talked to remembered Dale coming in. He said it was after lunch round about a quarter to three. Now the Vicar says it was half past three when Dale came to see him. That means he drove straight from the bank to the Vicarage, and he must have driven fast. Well, he was back here at four o'clock according to Raby. That was when he informed the household of his proposed marriage. Then he had tea. By six o'clock or so he was quarrelling with Mr. Vincent Bell. When, where, and how did he get rid of that fifty-pound note?"

"He might have given it to the Vicar—fee for marriage—donation on occasion of marriage or what not."

"Ring him up and ask him," said Lamb.

But Mr. Mickleham denied any knowledge of a fifty-pound note. The denial was on the verbose side, and the Inspector was frowning before Abbott at length said politely,

"Thank you very much, sir—that was all we wanted to know," and hung up.

"Chatty—very chatty. A citizen's first duty and all that sort of thing, but quite clear that he never saw hair hide or hoof of a banknote. His conversation with Dale was all high moral scruples and such. The sordid question of money never came into it at all."

"Where's that fifty-pound note?" demanded Lamb.

"He may have posted it to someone."

"Well then, he didn't. There was only one letter for the post last night, and that was Mr. Phipson's to the sanitary engineers. Just ring and get hold of Raby, will you?"

Raby looked paler than ever as he came in. He had an unfortunate imagination, and during the time which had elapsed since his previous interrogation he had been engaged with vivid and horrifying pictures of his arrest, trial, and subsequent execution, together with a quite fantastic vision of stout, comfortable Mrs. Raby starving in a garret. It was all terribly plain in his mind, and to say the least of it harrowing. He turned a pale duck's-egg green when Lamb addressed him.

"Come along in and shut the door. Just one or two things I'm not quite clear about. What's the matter with you, man—are you ill?"

Raby mopped a brow to which the cold sweat clung.

"It's the strain, sir. I'm sure anything I can do—"

"Just a few questions. Mr. Dale came home at four o'clock yesterday?"

"Yes, sir."

"And then he told you about his intended marriage, and after that you served tea in here. Who else was present?"

"Mr. Phipson and Mr. Bell."

"When did you clear away?"

"At a quarter past five."

"Were Mr. Bell and Mr. Phipson still here?"

"Yes, sir. They went away whilst I was clearing."

Frank Abbott thought, "He wouldn't have given either of them fifty pounds in the presence of the other. He wouldn't have given it to Bell in the middle of a quarrel." He met Lamb's eyes and saw the same thought there.

The Inspector said, "And after that, as far as you know, Mr. Dale was alone until his quarrel with Mr. Bell. No one called to see him?"

"No one except the lady, sir."

Lamb's hand came down with a thud upon his own solid knee. He said, "The lady!" and Frank Abbott said, "The lady!"

Raby, on the verge of a nervous collapse, echoed them.

"The lady, sir."

"What lady?"

"A Miss Cora de Lisle, sir."

The Inspector flung himself back in his chair.

"Go on, go on, go on!"

"A Miss Cora de Lisle, sir."

Lamb's face became quite astonishingly crimson. Frank Abbott said in his quiet, cultured voice,

"Miss Cora de Lisle—can you tell us anything about her?"

Raby shook his head.

"Not a friend of the family?"

He shook it again.

"Never seen her before?"

Raby looked as if he was going to faint.

"Only Thursday," he gasped.

Frank Abbott got up and clapped him on the shoulder.

"Hold up—we're not going to eat you. You see, any visitor Mr. Dale had yesterday evening may be important. Brace up and tell us all about Miss Cora de Lisle. By the way, how do you come to know her Christian name? She didn't say 'Call me Cora' when you answered the door, I take it?"

Raby revived a little.

"Oh, no, sir—it was on her card. Thursday morning Miss O'Hara rang the bell in here, and when I answered it she was up in the window at her table, and this Miss de Lisle, she was outside leaning in over the window-sill. A very odd-looking person, if I may say so."

"In what way?"

"Wild, sir, and in my opinion a bit under the influence."

"Drunk?" said Lamb.

"Oh, no, sir, I wouldn't go so far as to say that—but she smelled of spirits and had a wild kind of look. Miss O'Hara seemed right down afraid of her, and no wonder. She took out a card and gave it to Miss Cathy, and Miss Cathy gave it to me and asked me to see if Mr. Dale was in."

"And was he?"

"Not to her," said Raby with returning animation. "He took the card and he looked at it very ugly indeed, and he tore it up and said, 'Say I've gone out and you don't know when I'll be back.' Not half vexed she was either."

"And she came back last night?" said Lamb.

"A little before half past five. And the minute I opened the door she walked past me into the hall, and she said, 'It's no good your saying Mr. Dale's not at home, because I know he is. I've come here to see him and I'm going to see him, so it'll save me a whole lot of trouble if you just take me along, because if you don't, I'm going into every room, and if you try and put me out I'll scream the house down—and Lucas won't like that'. She called him by his name to me just like that, as bold as you please."

"And was she still under the influence?"

"Rather more so, I should say. So I went along to the study, and I'd hardly said her name before she came pushing past me and as good as shut the door in my face. I waited about in the hall in case I was wanted, and I could hear them going at it hammer and tongs. And then presently they quieted down a bit, and Mr. Dale rang the bell for me to show her out. She looked a deal better pleased than when she came in, which was something. I showed her out of the front door and locked up after her, and Mr. Dale came out to me in the hall and said, 'If that lady ever comes here again, I'm not at home, and you won't be either if you let her in'—meaning, as I took it, that I'd get the sack if she ever got past me again."

"And why didn't you mention this before?"

Raby paled again.

"Mr. Dale told me not to. He said, 'You keep your mouth shut about all this'. And I didn't think it could have anything to do with the murder, seeing I locked up after her well before six o'clock."

"She gave you her card," said Frank Abbott. "Was there any address on it?"

"Theatre Royal, Ledlington," said Raby with relief at being asked anything so easy.

Chapter Twenty-Two

"THAT'S CATHY'S TRAY," said Susan. "I'm taking it up. Aunt Milly's coming down. Just keep an eye on that saucepan and don't let it boil over."

Bill put his arms round her, pulled her up close, and kissed her hard.

"You're fagged to death. Someone ought to be carrying trays up for you."

"Oh, Bill!" Susan actually laughed.

"It's nothing to laugh about. I'm worried sick about you, and if you go about looking like that, old what's-his-name Lamb will feel quite sure you're consumed with inward guilt."

"I'll put on some colour. Do you think that will really convince him that I'm innocent?"

"I should think it would make him quite sure you're not. What you've got to do is go and lie down directly after lunch and get a spot of sleep."

The sleepless hours of three dreadful nights rose up before Susan's eyes. He felt her shudder.

"I couldn't. Take me out in Ted's car. I suppose they'll let us go."

"The last ride together."

"Don't! It might be. I can't laugh about it. I want to have it."

"All right, you shall."

She stepped back and went to take up the tray.

"It's lovely Cathy being so much better, isn't it? She's eating a proper meal, and she's going to get up to tea." She came back to him and dropped her voice. "Bill—when I told her—she said, 'Then I shall get well'. That was strange—wasn't it? And I was so afraid of telling her."

Bill frowned.

"I don't think it was strange at all. He threatened her—he blackmailed you—she collapsed. Wouldn't you expect her to be relieved at hearing he was out of the way for good?"

Susan shook her head.

"No, I wouldn't—not Cathy."

She went up with the tray.

Mrs. O'Hara came down to lunch and talked with a kind of plaintive brightness about how nice it was to see the sun, and if it went on being so mild she might begin to think about going out, only of course spring weather was very, very treacherous, and perhaps it would be wiser not to run any risks. "You see, if I were to be ill, it would throw altogether too much upon Susan, my dear Bill. I sometimes think she has too much to do as it is— Really, my dear, you are very pale to-day, and you are eating nothing, positively nothing. It is just what I have been saying—this unfortunate turn of Cathy's—the minute anyone cannot come down to meals it means trays—and every tray means twice up and down these very awkward stairs—really quite incessant. So we can't be too thankful that Cathy is so much better. She says she is getting up as soon as she has had her lunch, but I told her she had much better rest quietly until tea-time, as I intend to do. And I think you should do so too, Susan. There is nothing like a little rest in the afternoon for helping to pass the day."

Susan got up and began to change the plates.

"Bill and I are going out," she said.

As she went through into the kitchen, Mrs. O'Hara's voice followed her.

"Oh, my dear—do you think you should? Villages do notice everything so much."

Susan came back with the pudding.

"What is there to notice, Aunt Milly?"

"Bill and you, my dear."

Susan's colour burned, and faded. Bill said,

"The village ought to be accustomed to us by now."

Mrs. O'Hara looked from one to the other in a deprecating manner.

"Well, it all depends whether they think you are still engaged, or whether they think that Susan was engaged to Mr. Dale, because if they do they wouldn't expect to see you going about together before the funeral."

Bill set his jaw.

"Look here, Aunt Milly, Susan and I have been engaged for two years. If there's any stupid nonsense going round about her being engaged to Dale it's got to be contradicted, and the best way of contradicting it will be for us to go about together just as we've always done."

Mrs. O'Hara ate her pudding thoughtfully.

"I don't know if you are right—but the village will be sure to talk whatever you do, so perhaps it doesn't matter. Old Nurse used to say—the one Laura and I had when we were children—she used to say, 'Don't you worry about what folks say. It's all emptiness anyway, and when they're talking about you they're giving another poor soul a rest'. A little more pudding, dear. You make this very well. Now I do hope the police haven't got hold of any idea that you were engaged to Mr. Dale, because of course if they have they must think it most strange that he should have committed suicide."

Susan pushed her chair back, and Bill said "Suicide!" in a loud, surprised voice.

Mrs. O'Hara removed an orange pip from her mouth in a perfectly ladylike manner.

"Is there a hole in your strainer, my dear? The flavour is excellent, but there ought not to be pips—I might have swallowed one."

"Dale didn't commit suicide," said Bill Carrick.

Mrs. O'Hara looked pained.

"My dear Bill, of course he did."

"I'm afraid he didn't. He was murdered."

Mrs. O'Hara shook her head.

"The Press is so dreadfully sensational nowadays. I shall open the door to no one while you are out. In fact I should not do so in any case, as I shall be resting."

Susan sat back in her chair and took no part. Bill said with restrained violence,

"It isn't the Press—it's the police. It's the medical evidence. He couldn't possibly have committed suicide."

"My dear Bill, spare me! I prefer to think that he committed suicide. That is quite bad enough without having to believe that we have a murderer in our midst. And now I think I will go up and sit with Cathy for half an hour before I have my rest."

Bill picked up the handkerchief she had dropped, shut the door after her, and groaned.

"She prefers to think he committed suicide, so he did. What a mind! No, that's wrong—she hasn't got a mind. If she wants anything, it's that way as far as she's concerned. Last, lingering, horrible results of the feudal system. You see, in their heyday, if they wanted anything they could just make it so. And it went to their heads. When the power was gone they put up a social camouflage and pretended they'd still got it. Would your Uncle James have admitted to a living soul that he was broke to the wide, and that he'd nothing to leave but debts and mortgages? Did he tell his own sister? You know he didn't. He preferred to believe that it wasn't true, just as Aunt Milly prefers to believe there hasn't been a murder. They just can't bring themselves to believe that they haven't the power to control events."

Susan raised her eyes with a lost look.

"I wish I could pretend, Bill," she said.

Chapter Twenty-Three

FRANK ABBOTT opened the rusty iron gate of 17 Gladstone Villas and walked up a narrow path whose red and blue tiles were in the last stages of dirt and dilapidation. The little square patch of front garden contained a decayed-looking holly tree and half a dozen bushes of golden privet. These had perhaps been intended to form a hedge, but it was obviously years since they had been clipped.

Gladstone Villas lie on the lower side of Ledlington Market Square, a neighbourhood not highly esteemed. No. 17 was inhabited by Mrs. Clancy, who let to the less affluent members of theatrical touring companies. Enquiries at the Theatre Royal had brought Abbott to her door. He rang a bell whose brass had long forgotten how to shine, and had to ring it again. He was just going to try his luck at the back door, when the sound of slow advancing footsteps halted him and the door swung in. Mrs. Clancy stood revealed, a vast and shapeless person with a sacking apron tied on over an old red flannel dressing-gown. Her face streamed with heat, and her wild grey hair stood out all round it in tangles which rather reminded him of the privet. Out of all this wreck a pair of very bright blue eyes twinkled at him.

"Is it Miss de Lisle? Well then, she'll be in her dishabill like meself, and neither of us expecting a foine young man. Wait you a minute." She stepped back to a dark ascending stair and called up it in a rich, sonorous voice, "Miss de Lisle me dear, here's a visitor for ye. Will you be after seeing him?"

There was some faint response which Abbott did not catch. He thought a door had opened. Mrs. Clancy swung round on him.

"Up with ye—and it's the second door on the left."

The second door on the left was standing open. Abbott came to it, and was aware of Miss de Lisle in the middle of the room. He said, "May I come in?" and saw her big black eyes change from apprehension to surprise. She nodded.

"Who are you? What do you want?"

Abbott shut the door. The room was a bed-sitting-room, ill furnished, ill kept, and at the moment littered with Miss de Lisle's possessions—stockings and an old pair of tights on the bed rail; a crushed mass of crimson satin slipping to the floor; across the bed the old black cloth coat and the hat with the scarlet feather in which she had come to King's Bourne—as described by Raby; on the pillow shoes very down at heel, a spangled scarf, a disintegrating pair of stays, a moulting feather wrap.

His eyes came back to the owner of this sordid hotchpotch. Like Mrs. Clancy she wore a dressing-gown. It had once been costly. The silk was frayed and stained. Something dark had been spilt all down the front. The vivid orange colour still flattered the dark skin, the great eyes, and the falling masses of black hair. On the road Cora de Lisle might come very near to looking like a tramp, but in this strange garish garment she was a handsome, haggard creature who must once have been beautiful. She stood clutching her wrap about her and swaying on her feet. The chair from which she had risen was drawn up to a small, hot fire. On a gimcrack table in the angle stood a bottle of brandy and a tumbler.

"What do you want?" said Miss de Lisle.

Frank Abbott came forward.

She looked at the card he offered her and said in a stumbling voice,

"What's all this? I've not done anything." Then, with a sudden flare of anger, "I haven't done *anything*! He can't put the police on me! I tell you he gave it to me! And what's that got to do with the police? I don't wonder you're called busies—busy with everybody else's business, and no more use than a sick headache if you lose your purse or have your pocket picked! I tell you he—" She broke off suddenly and said in a different tone, "What do you want?"

Frank Abbott used his pleasantest voice.

"I just want to ask you a few questions. Even if you did lose a purse and we were too stupid to find it for you, I'm quite sure you would do all you could to help the police. We do our best, you know, and people are mostly very kind about helping us. But won't you sit down? I don't want to keep you standing."

She went back to her chair, arranging her draperies, thrusting out a foot in an old tinsel slipper, laying her left hand along the arm of the chair to display a large gaudy ring which caught the light and turned it ruby-red. She threw back her head against a crimson cushion and said,

"If you've come from Lucas, I haven't got anything to say to you. He gave me the money freely, and there's an end of it."

"The fifty-pound note, Miss de Lisle?"

She laughed.

"Is he going to say I stole it? He'd better not try that on with me! He gave it me, I tell you, and wrote on the back so I could change it. And why shouldn't he? Isn't he rolling in money—and don't I deserve something for putting up with him for five years?" She laughed on a deep, harsh note. "I could tell his Miss Susan Lenox a thing or two, and see if she'd marry him then."

Abbott was leaning against the mantelpiece. His elbow had to find room between a broken china candlestick and a bright blue vase encrusted with gilding. He said quietly,

"When did you see Mr. Dale last?"

She threw him an exasperated look.

"What are you trying to do—trip me up and then make out I've said a lot of things that never entered my head?"

"No, I'm not trying to trip you up. I'm only asking you when you last saw Mr. Dale, and you needn't answer if you don't want to."

Exasperation changed to suspicion.

"Who says I don't want to answer? I'm sure I've got nothing to hide—not like some people I could name that'd be in Queer Street if I was to open my mouth. Well, what do you want to know?"

"Just when you last saw Mr. Dale."

She pushed back her hair with the hand that wore the ring.

"We were here for the week. Thursday I went over and he was out, or said he was—and mind you he knew I was coming, because I wrote. And all I saw was a girl that looked as if she thought I was going to bite her—Miss Cathleen O'Hara. And you'd expect a girl with a name like that to have a bit more spirit. Monday I went over again—that was yesterday. I had to push my way past the butler, or I wouldn't have got in then. I meant to see Lucas if I had to wait all night."

"What time was this?"

She stared.

"I got the bus to the village—got in about five, if you want to know, and had something at the Crown and Magpie just to get my courage up—that's a queer sort of a name, isn't it? I suppose it might have been half past five when I got up to the house."

"Wasn't that going to make you a bit late for the theatre if you were playing last night?"

She looked away.

"Well then, I wasn't. If you must know, I'd got the sack. The show had cleared out. That's why I had to see Lucas."

"And you saw him, and he gave you a fifty-pound note?"

Her look came back, angry and direct.

"Any business of yours if he did?"

"Well, I'm afraid it is. When did you leave Mr. Dale?"

She sat up with a hand on either arm of the chair.

"Look here, what's all this? Do you keep your watch in your hand all the time you go visiting? Because I don't, and I never heard of anyone else that did either."

"I just thought you might have some idea," said Abbott mildly.

She seemed mollified.

"I suppose I was there for the best part of twenty minutes. I'd a bus to catch, and I know I had to hurry."

"The six o'clock bus from the Crown and Magpie?"

"That would be it."

"And did you catch it?"

She turned a full, bold stare upon him.

"Trying to catch me out, dear? Well then, you can't? I could have caught it if I'd wanted to. But I didn't want to—see? And why? Because a nice young man came along with his car and gave me a lift. And you can put that in your pipe and smoke it, Mr. Busy from Scotland Yard!"

"You didn't go back to King's Bourne, did you?"

Her eyes brightened uneasily.

"No, I didn't."

"Are you quite sure?"

"Of course I'm sure. What'd I go back for? I'd got my fifty pounds, hadn't I?"

"Had you?"

The dark colour rushed into her face. He thought of Cleopatra and Semiramis.

"What do you mean? What do you mean? What do you mean?" Her voice ran up to a scream and broke. She got to her feet and stood there shaking—was it with rage? "What's all this about? You'll tell me what you mean or you'll get out! Do you hear?"

Frank Abbott straightened up.

"I've been listening with the greatest interest, Miss de Lisle. Now I'm going to ask you to listen to me. You got into Netherbourne at about five o'clock, and you went into the Crown and Magpie and had a double brandy."

"And what if I did? I told you, didn't I?"

Abbott nodded.

"You did—and now I'm telling you. You went up to King's Bourne and had your talk with Mr. Dale, and came away at about ten minutes to six. And then you went back to the Crown and Magpie and had another double brandy, and missed the bus. You didn't tell me that bit—did you?"

She looked darkly sullen.

"I told you I missed the bus."

Frank Abbott said, "Well—" and saw her colour rise. She bit her lip and did not speak. He thought, "Why doesn't she throw me out—why hasn't she thrown me out long ago? She's angry all right, but she's less angry than afraid. She's dropped the pretence that I've come from Dale. I think she knows he's dead. If the news reached her in any ordinary way, why should she pretend she doesn't know? If she really doesn't know, why should she have answered a single one of my questions—unless the fifty pounds was blackmail? It might be that. I think she knows he's dead, and knows it in a way that she can't or won't own up to. She knows something—*something*—"

He let the silence go on until the room was heavy with it. Then he said so quietly that the silence broke without jarring.

"When you came out of the Crown and Magpie, which way did you go?"

She frowned and tapped with her foot on the floor.

"Come, Miss de Lisle, the landlord remembers your coming in at five o'clock, and again at just after six. It's all downhill from King's Bourne, so it didn't take you so long to come back as it took you to go. And you had your double brandy and 'took it off quick and out again', and he didn't see which way you went. The bus was gone when you got there. Now what did you do when you left the Crown and Magpie?"

She looked down at her tapping foot.

"I told you I got a lift."

"What sort of car was it, Miss de Lisle?"

He got an angry stare.

"I don't know one from another."

He smiled.

"Big car—little car—tourer—sports model? Red—blue—green—black—grey?"

She said with a kind of goaded energy,

"It was dark. Do you think I can see in the dark? I didn't give a damn what sort of car it was. I wanted to get back here."

"Very natural. But you haven't told me which way you turned when you came out of the Crown and Magpie."

The air became charged with furious suspicion. He could almost see her thinking, "Perhaps someone saw me—perhaps they didn't. Better be on the safe side." She said,

"I turned to the right."

"To go back to King's Bourne?"

"No!" She almost shouted the word at him.

"Well, you wouldn't get to Ledlington that way—would you? Wrong direction, I'm afraid."

"Don't you ever take a wrong turning in a place you don't know?"

"I might after two double brandies."

Cora de Lisle whirled round, snatched the large bright blue vase from the mantelpiece, and hurled it at his head. That it smashed against the wall instead of in his face was due to quickness of eye and some proficiency in boxing. He side-stepped neatly and received with calm the flood of vituperation which followed the vase. When angry tears supervened he said,

"That was unpardonable of me. I really do apologize. Why did you go back to King's Bourne, Miss de Lisle?"

She stopped midway in a sob and glared at him.

"I didn't, I tell you—I didn't! Are you trying to make out that it was me—" The loud voice failed. The hand with the ring came up across her mouth. She bit upon the knuckles. Her eyes were sick with fear.

There was a jagged pause.

"Yes?" said Frank Abbott. "You were going to say—"

"I wasn't." The words came in a desperate whisper.

"I think you were. I think you knew last night that Lucas Dale had been shot."

Her hand fell from her lips. The knuckles were bleeding.

"I—didn't—"

He thought, "She did know it. It's no surprise—no shock." He said,

"When did you hear?"

"I don't know—someone told me—"

"Who?"

"I don't—know—"

"You knew last night—you knew when you were at King's Bourne. If you shot him—I won't ask you to incriminate yourself. But if you didn't—if you didn't—don't you see how important your evidence is going to be?"

Her face went grey. She stood back.

"You listen to me, young man. What had I got to shoot Lucas for? If I'd been that sort I'd have shot him fifteen years ago, not now. I was married to him for five years. If I'd been the killing sort I'd have killed him then. I didn't. I ran away from him, and he'd the nerve to divorce me—*him!* And all I wanted was to get quit of him. I haven't seen him since, and I wouldn't have seen him now, only I'm done—finished—out. Can't keep my jobs—can't get them—can't stand it all like I used to. And he'd got all that money. Well, I touched him for fifty pounds, and I'd have gone on touching him. If he'd married his Miss Susan Lenox, it would have paid him to keep me quiet—see? Now perhaps you can tell me why I should shoot Lucas."

Abbott walked over to the window. He stood looking down at the untidy yellow privet. Then he turned round and said,

"It would have been very stupid. People are stupid sometimes. By the way, Miss de Lisle, I see this was a variety show you were with. They left on Sunday. What sort of turn did you put on?"

She stared without answering.

"Are you going to tell me?" He paused. "Is there any reason why you shouldn't tell me?... Well, perhaps I can tell you. I think you were billed as Miss Cora de Lisle, the famous female sharpshooter. That's right, isn't it?"

Chapter Twenty-Four

BILL CARRICK and Susan Lenox drove in the pale sunlight. It had been fine all the morning. It was fine still, but there was an east wind blowing and no warmth anywhere. They went by crooked lanes between bare hedgerows, and then up through a cutting, where tree roots propped the banks, to an open heathy common. Right in the middle of it Bill drove off the road on to a flat sandy place and stopped the car. A solitary motor-bicycle went by and disappeared behind a clump of rowans and gorse bushes a couple of hundred yards away. Susan watched it out of sight. She frowned a little and said,

"He's been behind us all the way."

Bill said, "Yes."

She looked at him with startled eyes.

"I can't hear his engine."

Bill said, "No—he's stopped." Then he laughed. "I wonder what he would have done if there hadn't been a clump of trees."

"Do you mean he's following us? *Bill!*"

He sat round against the side of the car and faced her.

"Of course he is. I expect he's been told to be discreet. He won't do anything more than follow us unless he thinks I'm going to do a bunk. It must be very reassuring for him to see us sitting here in a nice open place like this—very calming. And as he's well out of earshot, we can afford to be calm about it too."

"You mean he's a policeman?"

"Undoubtedly. Look here, Susan, we've got to face this. I'm under suspicion. Old Lamb isn't going to risk my cutting loose. Of course I'd be a fool to do it, but if I'd really shot Dale I expect I should be so rattled by now that I might be ready for any fool trick. Ever since he saw us this morning I've been wondering why he hasn't had me arrested, but now I think it's because he's got me on a string and if I bolt I'll be giving myself away."

Her hands clenched upon one another, straining.

"Bill—*don't!*"

He leaned forward and put his hand down hard over hers.

"I've got to. Look here, my dear, we've got to talk this out and know where we are, and we've got this chance to do it—we may not get another. That's why I brought you here. I picked a place where we shan't be interrupted. We don't want Cathy, or Aunt Milly, or the police, or Mrs. Mickleham getting themselves mixed up with this conversation—it's between you and me. And the thing we start off with is this—are you quite sure in your own mind that I didn't shoot Dale?"

Their looks shocked together and held. A heavenly certainty sank deep into Susan's mind. She said,

"Quite sure."

He nodded.

"That's all right then, because I didn't. But if you'd had any sort of doubt about it, everything was going to be a lot harder for both of us. The next thing is this—how much can you stand? Because it's going to be fairly tough."

Susan said, "I don't know—I don't think I can stand much more."

She felt the hard strength of the hand that was over hers.

"You've got to. Do you hear? You've got to! Cathy's a crumpler, but you're not. If she'd stood up to Dale and told him to go to blazes, we shouldn't be in this mess. That's what crumpling does. It doesn't let you out, and it lets everyone else in. Now are you going to crumple?"

The colour ran up into her cheeks like two bright burning flames. She shook her head.

"You're not that sort. Now, my girl, we're up against it. It'll be all right in the end, but before we get there you're going to want every bit of toughness you can get together, because, short of finding the fellow who did shoot Dale, they're bound to arrest me. They may just keep me on a string till the inquest—and I suppose that'll be Thursday or Friday—but that's the most we can expect. There isn't any jury in the world that wouldn't bring in a verdict against me, with the motive they'll think I had and Mrs. Mickleham's evidence to ram it home. You see, it's exactly the sort of thing a jury understands—motive—threat—opportunity. He took my girl. I said I'd kill him. And I did. It's as easy as pie, and they'll simply eat it."

The little bright flames flickered away. They left the fine skin colourless. The dark blue eyes were steady.

"If you look at it, it won't frighten you so much. You've got to look at it, because as far as I can see it's bound to happen. When you've got used to the idea it won't frighten you. You see, I didn't do it, and someone else did. All we want is time to find out who that someone was, and there'll be plenty of time. Do you see?"

Susan said "Yes" with a break in her voice. She pulled her hands away and sat back. "Bill, it's crazy—you *couldn't* have done it. You had only just time to reach the study. How could anyone believe he would have let you rush right in and get his revolver and then turn round and let you shoot him from behind? It's nonsense. There simply wasn't time before I heard the shot."

His mouth twisted.

"My poor child, do you suppose they're going to believe you?"

"What do you mean?"

He said, "Wake up, Susan! If no one except you and me heard that shot, the bottom drops right out of all that about there not being time. If no one heard it except us, we could fix the time to suit ourselves, couldn't we? And he wasn't found until a quarter to seven. That's what we're up against."

A shiver ran lightly over her. She said very quietly,

"I see."

Her voice stopped as if she could not keep that quiet tone. When she went on again it was dry and strained.

"Someone else must have heard it."

"If they did they're not telling. Besides, who was there to hear it? It's too far for the village, and no one in the house seems to have heard anything, from what I gather." He gave a sudden short laugh. "I expect it would surprise old Lamb if he knew what a lot the village knows. Isn't it tomorrow you have Mrs. Green? You'll get it all from her."

"I wish there was anything to get," said Susan.

He came nearer and slipped an arm round her, pulling her up against his shoulder.

"There may be. It's too soon to tell. Do you know—" his voice had a tinge of astonishment—"do you know, it hadn't happened this time yesterday. It seems incredible, but this time twenty-four hours ago I'd just got your letter and was pinching Ted's car."

"Won't he want it?"

"If he does he'll just have to. As a matter of fact he only uses it at week-ends, and—" He stopped abruptly. A horrid picture of prison walls was black in front of him. The inquest would be before the week-end. Ted Walters would get his car back in plenty of time.

Chapter Twenty-Five

ABOUT THE MIDDLE of that Tuesday afternoon Inspector Lamb walked down through the garden and round to the front door of the Little House, where he first rang the bell and about a minute later rapped sharply with the heavy, old-fashioned knocker. When the sound had died away he heard a light, hesitating footstep and the door was opened. A young girl stood there looking up at him in a shy, questioning manner. She was very light and small—rather a plain little thing in a brown jumper and skirt, and hair that put him in mind of brown thistledown. She was paler than he liked to see any young thing, and she had dark saucers under her eyes which had no business to be there. He asked for Miss Susan Lenox, and she said, "Oh, she's out," which was no news at all to Inspector Lamb. He smiled benevolently and inquired if he was speaking to Miss O'Hara, because if so, "I would be very glad if I might have a few words with you. I dare say you can guess who I am—Detective Inspector Lamb."

"I've been ill—" said Cathy in a faint, doubtful voice.

He nodded.

"I know that. I won't bother you more than I can help."

"Susan is out, and my mother is resting. We could come into the drawing-room—"

Her eyes searched his face and found something kindly and dependable there. She led the way into the crowded room, installed him in a big arm-chair on one side of the fire, and sat looking very small and frail on the edge of another chair on the opposite side of the hearth.

"It's all so dreadful, isn't it?" she said, and it came to him with a shock of surprise that of all the people he had interviewed in connection with the death of Lucas Dale she was the least nervous. In point of fact she was not nervous at all. She was looking at him, and speaking to him with quite visible relief.

He gave that nod of his again.

"Yes, it's dreadful—bad enough anyhow, but worse until it's cleared up. When a thing like this happens the people who haven't had a hand in it have got to get together and help to clear it up. It's everybody's duty to do that. You won't be frightened or upset if I ask you some questions?"

Cathy shook her head.

"Oh, no—you're very kind."

He smiled at her.

"Well, I don't want to make you ill again. First of all I want to ask you about a visitor you had up at King's Bourne on Thursday morning. A woman came and wanted to see Mr. Dale, didn't she?"

"Oh, yes—Miss de Lisle. She frightened me."

"Now why did she do that?"

Cathy gave him her shy little smile.

"I expect because I'm stupid. I *am* stupid about people, you know."

"Well, I suppose there was something that frightened you. Suppose you tell me what it was."

He saw her shrink.

"I thought—perhaps—she had been drinking—"

"Anything else?"

"She was odd and—and rough. She asked questions about Susan, and—and she seemed angry with Mr. Dale. She was leaning in through the window, and I didn't like that very much."

He beamed encouragingly.

"You're doing fine. Now do you think you could tell me the whole thing just as it happened from start to finish—what she looked like—what she said?"

A little colour came into Cathy's face. She said, "I'll try," and gave him a meticulously accurate account of all that had passed on the Thursday morning which seemed so much more than five days ago. When she had finished he asked her if she remembered how Miss de Lisle was dressed.

"Oh, yes, of course I do. I was sorry for her because she looked so shabby. She had on an old black coat with some fur, and a scarlet and orange handkerchief up at her neck, and a black hat with a scarlet feather."

"And you are sure she said she had been Mr. Dale's wife?"

"Oh, yes. And she was. He told Susan about her."

"I see. Well now, Miss O'Hara, I'm afraid I've got to ask you what happened on Saturday. That was when you were taken ill, wasn't it?"

She met his eyes with a confiding, troubled look.

"Yes—it was dreadful."

"Well, you mustn't let it make you ill again, because it's all over. You have been Mr. Dale's secretary for about four months, haven't you?"

"Yes."

"What was he like to work for?"

Cathy's eyes filled with tears.

"He was very kind—until—until Saturday—"

"And what happened then?"

Cathy rubbed her hand across her eyes like a child.

"He thought I'd done something dreadful. I hadn't really."

"What did he think you'd done?"

"Taken some of his pearls—" The words hardly reached him.

He made a clicking sound with his tongue.

"That was bad."

Two little tears ran down her cheeks. She nodded miserably.

"He sent for Susan and made her look in my bag, and the pearls were there."

He clicked again.

"That was very bad. How did they get there?"

Cathy caught her breath.

"Is it very wicked to think that perhaps he put them there?"

Inspector Lamb said, "I don't know about *wicked*. Is that what you think?"

"Sometimes."

Lamb grunted.

"What happened after that?"

"I fainted. After a bit they were talking. I could hear them, but I couldn't move. It was dreadful. He said if Susan didn't promise to marry him he would ring up the police and say I had stolen the pearls. I fainted again."

Lamb gave her a long considering look.

"Where were you yesterday evening between five and seven, Miss O'Hara?"

She answered him at once.

"I was in bed. I've only just got up. I was ill."

"Which way does your bedroom window look—back, or front?"

She said, "Back."

"And your mother's window?"

"Her room is over the drawing-room. It looks out both ways."

"You and she were alone in the house?"

"Yes—if Susan and Bill were out."

"You know Mr. Dale was shot. Do you know if your mother heard anything?"

"I'm sure she didn't. She would have said."

"She was in her bedroom between five and seven?"

"Oh, yes. She's an invalid, you know. She has to rest a great deal. Her window would be shut. I'm sure she didn't hear anything, but I can ask her."

Lamb said, "Presently. What about you? If your window looks towards King's Bourne, you might have heard the shot. Did you?"

She said, "I don't know—" Her voice was puzzled and distressed.

"How do you mean, you don't know?"

"I heard—a shot. I don't know—if it was that shot—"

Lamb spoke quickly.

"What time was it?"

"I don't know. I was asleep—and I woke up. There was a shot. It was very faint. I don't know what time it was—it was quite dark."

"Did you hear anyone else moving in the house? Your cousin? Mr. Carrick? Mrs. Mickleham—she was in the house round about half past six—did you hear her come or go? That would help to fix the time."

"I didn't hear anyone," said Cathy. "I went to sleep again."

Chapter Twenty-Six

MRS. O'HARA did not come down until Inspector Lamb had gone back up the garden to King's Bourne. When she had settled herself cosily on the sofa with a Shetland shawl about her shoulders and her own especial rug to cover her feet, she showed quite an interest in his visit. It appeared that she had seen him go.

"And of course, Cathy darling, you ought to have let me know he was here, because I would have made the effort and come down."

Cathy was on her knees attending to the fire. She put a small piece of coal where it would encourage the somewhat weakly flame and said without turning round,

"How did you know it was the Inspector, Mummy?"

"Darling, you've just told me."

"But the way you said it—it sounded as if you knew who it was when you saw him out of the window."

"And so I did. There is something about a policeman's back—I think I should know one anywhere, even in quite plain clothes. And, as I said, darling, I would have made the effort and come down, because I don't think you're really up to these official interviews— and I do hope he didn't upset you in any way."

Cathy put on another piece of coal, balancing it carefully and sitting back on her heels to observe the effect.

"He was rather a pet, Mummy. I'm so glad it was him and not the young one."

"Abbott," said Mrs. O'Hara—"that's the name. Mrs. Green has been telling me about him—she ran in before lunch. She says he is a perfect gentleman and Lily admires him very much. She'd just been up to see Lily. And do you know, darling, I can't help wondering whether he is the son of Francis Abbott who used to be one of my dancing partners the year I came out, because Lily Green told her mother his name was Frank—"

"Mummy, there must be thousands of Abbotts."

Mrs. O'Hara shook her head.

"Oh, no, darling, not as many as that—and I just wondered— that's all. Of course, before the war a policeman wouldn't have been the son of anyone you danced with, but nowadays people do these things, so there's really nothing at all impossible about it. And I should have thought you would rather have talked to someone like that—"

"Well, I wouldn't. He's got eyes like bits of ice, and the sort of pale manner that makes you feel pale too."

Mrs. O'Hara produced her knitting from the bag which housed it and began to knit in a fitful manner.

"Of course, darling, I can't really see why the Inspector should have wanted to see you at all. If you were ill in bed, how could you possibly know anything about poor Mr. Dale's suicide?"

Cathy got up from her knees and turned round, dusting her hands.

"Mummy, I wish you wouldn't."

"Wish I wouldn't what, darling?" Mrs. O'Hara's tone was an absent one. She counted under her breath. "Three, four, five, six—knit one, slip one—knit two together—oh dear, I'm afraid I've got this wrong—"

"Mummy!"

"What is it, darling?"

"I wish you wouldn't go on saying he committed suicide, because he didn't, and you'll really only make people talk. It's quite bad enough without making it any worse."

Mrs. O'Hara looked a mild reproach.

"Cathy—*darling*—I don't think you ought to say a thing like that! I should have thought anyone could see how much better it was for it to be suicide. But we won't argue about it. You know, Dr. Carrick always used to say it was no good arguing with me—I remember being quite flattered by the way he said it. 'It's no good arguing with you', he said, and he had quite a twinkle in his eye—'no good at all, for I have to keep my feet on the ground, and you're off on a pair of wings somewhere up in Cloud-cuckoo land'. Such a charming expression, I thought, but then he was such a very charming man—darling, I think I've dropped a stitch—if you would just pick it up for me—"

Cathy retrieved the stitch in silence. As she handed the knitting back she directed a soft imploring look at her mother. Mrs. O'Hara patted her hand.

"Darling little Cathy," she said—"I'm glad the Inspector was nice to you. And now we won't talk about it any more, shall we?"

Cathy ran out of the room. Her eyes were full of tears, and she was afraid that if they once began to fall, she would not be able to stop them, and she was afraid of what she might say. Her heart was full to bursting with love, and fear, and anxiety. As she went through the hall, the knocker beat a little fierce rat-tat. She peeped through one of the long glass slits that looked into the porch, saw Lydia Hammond standing there tapping an impatient foot, and let her in.

When the door was shut Lydia took hold of her.

"Cathy—you poor little thing! You know I've been in town for the week-end with the Walters. I stayed an extra day—only just got back for lunch. My dear, what's been happening—and where's Susan?"

"She's out with Bill." The tears had begun to run down Cathy's face.

Lydia marched her into the dining-room.

"First I'll tell you what I've heard, and then you can tell me how much of it's lies. Look here, Cathy, I give you fair warning, if you faint I shall pinch you. I've got to know what's happened. Here, sit down. Now I'll begin. I hadn't heard a word till I got home for lunch—I never read in a train. Well—then there were the parents, too shocked, too restrained—a most painful tragedy, and the less said about it the better. Maddening. Of course I got the real dope from old Lizzie. She's got six cousins and a sister-in-law in the village, so she could tell me what they are saying there. But, Cathy, it can't be true. Do you know, they're saying that Susan had thrown Bill over for Lucas Dale, and that Bill shot him with his own revolver. I told Lizzie it was wicked nonsense, but when I was coming along I met Mrs. Mickleham, and she burst into tears right in the middle of the road and said she felt like a murderess because she heard Bill say he was going to kill Lucas Dale and her husband made her go and tell the police."

Cathy was turning paler and paler. She got to her feet with difficulty and stood holding on to the edge of the dining-table.

"I can't tell you anything, Lydia," she said. "And I think, if you don't mind, I'll go and lie down, because I haven't been very well. Mummy's in the drawing-room."

It was no use. Lydia knew when she was beat. If you pressed Cathy too hard, she would faint on you. She said crossly,

"I've a good mind to pinch you. Can you get upstairs?"

"I think so."

It ended in Lydia helping her up and depositing her on her bed. She made a little face at her from the door and tripped down-stairs again.

Mrs. O'Hara was delighted to see her. They were old cronies. With a pouffe pulled up beside the sofa, Lydia settled herself and said,

"How dreadful!"

"Yes, indeed. But of course it might have been worse. We must all try and look on the bright side, my dear. I'm sure I don't know where I should be if I hadn't learned to do that."

"But, Mrs. O'Hara, they're saying that Susan was engaged to him."

The knitting-needles clicked gently.

"Well, my dear, it would have been worse if they had been married. I was a widow at nineteen myself, and I could not bear to think of dear Susan having such a tragic experience."

"But Mrs. O'Hara, she *wasn't* engaged to him—*was* she?"

The knitting revolved. Mrs. O'Hara began another row.

"Well, my dear, I really can't tell you. It was quite natural of course that he should have fallen in love with her, because Susan is a most charming girl and very like her mother, my dear sister Laura, who was considered by everyone to be the most charming girl of the season. We were presented together of course, and everyone admired her so much."

"And you too," said Lydia. "What's the good of being modest? You were the lovely Bourne twins, and you made a sensation at Court—you know you did."

Mrs. O'Hara bridled.

"It's a long time ago. And Cathy hasn't my looks, though she's a dear child, but I think Susan is just as beautiful as Laura was, and I'd like her to have a happier life. I don't think she would really have been happy with Mr. Dale."

Lydia was of those who rush in where others fear to tread. Her eyes sparkled, and she said in a tone of warm interest,

"Do you know, sometimes I think you're fonder of Susan than you are of Cathy."

Milly O'Hara flushed suddenly into the likeness of her own youth. She said,

"Lydia!" And then, "Not fonder—you mustn't say that—because Cathy is my own child. But Susan is Laura's—"

"And you loved Laura better than yourself, so you love Susan better than Cathy, and I was right." Lydia's voice was soft and teasing.

She got a smile and a shake of the head.

"You mustn't say that to Cathy—and it wouldn't be true either. My dear, will you give me my drops? I forgot to take them when I came down. The little bottle behind the clock, and you know where to get a glass. Two tablespoons of water—and let the tap run, because it is really very nasty if it is lukewarm."

Lydia came back with the glass, and watched Mrs. O'Hara while she sipped.

"Aren't you going to tell me anything? Cathy wouldn't, but I thought you would, because we've always been friends, and I simply rushed down here the moment I heard."

Mrs. O'Hara sipped.

"There is really nothing to tell."

Lydia shook her head mournfully.

"You're shutting me right out. You can't—you really can't! Do you know that people are saying Bill did it?"

"People will say anything," said Mrs. O'Hara, setting down the empty glass.

"They don't really disapprove, you know. In a way, Lizzie says, they rather admire him for it because Mr. Dale had taken his girl. Mrs. O'Hara, I'll die if you don't tell me. Was Susan engaged to him—*was* she? Because the very last time I saw her we were talking about it, and I told her she'd be a perfect fool to let such a chance go by—King's Bourne and all that money, and anyone could see he was simply frightfully in love with her. And I said she might go on waiting years and years for Bill, and then find out he didn't want to marry her after all. A cousin of Freddy's was engaged like that for nine years, and when he got his promotion, and she'd got her trousseau, he told her he didn't think he could go on with it, and he went off and married a frightful widow who'd come home on the same boat. So it just shows!"

Mrs. O'Hara's needles clicked.

"I don't think Bill would do that. Of course he is not really what one would have called a match for her in the old days—no money, and no particular family, though of course Dr. Carrick was very much respected and those things don't count in the way they used to—"

Lydia leaned forward.

"Did Bill shoot him?"

"My dear Lydia!" Mrs. O'Hara looked very much shocked.

"Oh," said Lydia, "he might have. And that's what people are saying. They remember about his throwing the tramp into the pond, and the time he threw a croquet ball at Roger. Lizzie was talking about that. It got him on the temple, and he didn't come round for half an hour. We all thought he was dead. Cathy went and hid in the stable loft, and Susan and I cried ourselves sick, but Bill just stood there as white as a sheet and never said a word."

"My dear, he was only eight years old."

"But it *shows*," said Lydia. "He never did know what he was doing when he got into a temper. He *might* have shot Mr. Dale."

Mrs. O'Hara shook her head.

"All these speculations are very foolish. In my opinion Mr. Dale committed suicide. I am very much annoyed with Mrs. Mickleham for starting all these stories—a clergyman's wife should be more careful. You will oblige me by contradicting everything you hear. Susan and Bill have been engaged for two years, they are still engaged, and there is no quarrel between them. Bill is to design a house for a Mr. Gilbert Garnish who sells pickles, and he and Susan are planning to get married immediately. As I said, there was a time when I should not have considered him a suitable match for her, but they love each other very much, and they will be happy. I want Susan to be happy. And now, my dear, we will change the subject. What news have you of your husband and of Roger?"

Chapter Twenty-Seven

MRS. GREEN "obliged" Mrs. O'Hara on Wednesdays. She came at nine and scrubbed, cleaned, and polished vigorously until half past twelve. Whilst her hands moved her tongue was not idle. If there was anyone in the room, she talked. If she was alone, she lifted a strong unbridled soprano and sang. On this particular Wednesday she was naturally a good deal uplifted by the fact that her daughter Lily was almost certain to be called as a witness at the forthcoming inquest.

"Not that she's got anything to tell, Miss Susan. And of course I can't be too thankful it wasn't her that found him. Lily's always been what you might call easy upset, and you can say what you like, it's an upsetting thing for a girl to come in as it might be to draw the curtains and find a man with the back of his head shot off. Lily, she managed to slip down last night while Mrs. Raby was having forty winks, which she *do*, and she said to me as I might be speaking to you now, 'Mum', she said, 'if they'd have arst me to clean up after it, I couldn't have done it'. That's what she said, and I don't blame her."

Susan sat down rather suddenly on one of the kitchen chairs.

"*Please*, Mrs. Green—"

Mrs. Green turned round from scrubbing the dresser and patted her on the shoulder with a fat, damp hand.

"There, my dear—don't you take on. Lily's just the same—turned as white as a sheet when I arst her whether she'd seen him." She went back to her scrubbing. "And I told her straight, 'It's all very well to say Oh, Mum! and start looking like a drop of yesterday's skim milk, but you'll have to see all sorts before you're through, same as I've done, and no good making a mealy mouth over it either. Births and deaths is things we've all got to see'."

"But not murder," Susan said in a strained, breathless voice.

Mrs. Green looked quickly over her shoulder and away. She was a fresh, upstanding woman with a lot of yellow hair and a big rosy face. She had seen Susan christened, and had seen her nearly every day since then. She considered that she could say anything she chose within the bounds of reason, and she was so full of curiosity and kindly feeling that the reasonable bounds were going to be pushed as far as possible. Because what she wanted to know was whether William Cole was telling lies when he said he had heard Mr. Dale asking the Vicar to marry him and Miss Susan this very Thursday, and she didn't mean to stir a foot out of the Little House until she did know. William might be gardener up at the Vicarage, and he might be walking out with Lily—and she'd no objections to that—but that wasn't to say she was going to take everything he said for gospel. And he might say what he liked, Miss Susan wasn't the kind to play fast and loose, because that was a thing you couldn't hide, no matter how hard you tried—not from all the other women anyhow. Men, of course, were shocking easy deceived for all they thought themselves so clever, and a great temptation it was for the women that had to live with them. But a woman couldn't deceive the other women, no matter how hard she tried. And Miss Susan hadn't any cause to try, because she wasn't that sort.

She picked up her pail and walked to the other end of the dresser. Susan looked after her. She saw broad shoulders, a strong neck, a large bun of yellow hair. She thought, "She knows what people are saying. Everyone will talk to her because of Lily. She'll know what's being said up at the house, and she'll know what's being said in the village—she'll know whether anyone heard that shot. If it only weren't so difficult to talk about it. But I've got to—it's for Bill. We *must* find someone else who heard the shot. I've got to make her talk."

Even at that moment she could have laughed at the thought, because the difficulty was to stop Mrs. Green talking. But she was kind, and Susan had known her all her life.

Mrs. Green moved her pail again, and started on the kitchen floor. Susan took hold of her courage and began.

"Mrs. Green—what are they saying about it in the village and—up at the house? I—I can't ask anyone else."

Mrs. Green sat back on her heels with the scrubbing-brush in her hand.

"And who should you ask if it wasn't me?" she said in a voice of warm interest and kindness. "And I wouldn't have spoke of it if you hadn't brought it up, though it went to my heart to see you looking the way you do. But since you have brought it up, well then, what I say is, don't you take any notice of what's been said and they'll stop taking notice of you."

This was not very encouraging.

"But I want to know what is being said."

"Well, as to that," said Mrs. Green, dropping her brush back into the bucket and getting off her heels into a position better suited to gossip—"as to that, you might say it was a bit of all sorts. There's some says it was a tramp—him having those pearls in the house which is a thing that gets about. And what's the sense of it, is what I've always said—and him a bachelor gentleman with no one to show them off. So some says it was a tramp, or burglars from London which comes to the same thing and a deal pleasanter than having to think that it's anyone local. But up at the house Lily says they're strong for thinking it was the 'Merican gentleman on account of the way Mr. Raby and Robert Stack can say that he and Mr. Dale were going on. Most uncomfortable Mr. Raby said it was from the very first minute he come into the house—what you might call hinting and passing the sort of remarks you don't pass, not without you want to make yourself as right down unpleasant as you can, short of coming plump out with it. All the way through lunch and dinner it'd go on, Lily says, and Robert Stack coming out of the dining-room with a grin on his face, and Mr. Raby as vexed as vexed. Lily says it was easy to see how nervous it made Mr. Phipson. He's not one that'd like being mixed up in quarrels, and Lily says he was going about like a cat on hot bricks. They were all thinking it'd come to a real old-fashioned row between Mr. Dale and the 'Merican gentleman, because Mr. Dale wasn't the sort to put up with a lot of that kind of thing. But nobody thought it'd come to murder."

Susan let out a deep breath which made an "Oh!"

Mrs. Green nodded vigorously.

"And well you may say so, Miss Susan. Quarrelling's what we've all done in our time, and no harm meant and none taken if it don't go on too long, which we was brought up to kiss and be friends before sundown, and a very good rule too. But murder—that's a regular unnatural thing. Mr. Raby says the 'Merican gentleman couldn't adone it along of being in his bath, and him in his pantry where he could hear the pipes thumping. But Lily says to me, 'Why, mum', she says, 'that's all nonsense. The pipes thumping don't go for no more than what someone's been running the taps upstairs. Bath water running don't mean the 'Merican gentleman was in it having his bath'. That's what Lily says. Nothing to stop him turning on the taps and coming down and shooting Mr. Dale and up the stairs to the bathroom—that's what Lily says. Her and William Cole had the best part of a quarrel over it because he said she'd no call to say it and 'ud be getting herself into trouble with the police if she didn't look out."

"What does William think?" said Susan.

Mrs. Green was well away. Just a little prod now and then and she would cover the whole range of Netherbourne opinion. But for some reason this particular prod seemed to fail of its effect. Mrs. Green reddened to the roots of her yellow hair. She said with energy,

"William's nothing to go by. He may be gardener at the Vicarage, but that don't say he's got any more sense than he was made with, and so I told him."

Susan was invaded by a dreadful sense of chill. *Gardener at the Vicarage....* She said,

"You'd better tell me—it doesn't matter—"

Mrs. Green tossed her head.

"Well then, my dear, he's got hold of a pack of rubbish about you and Mr. Dale—said he heard him fixing up with Vicar to marry you on this very Thursday that'll be tomorrow. And he says if he was Mr. Bill he'd do the same as what he says Mr. Bill done—shoot the life out of anyone that tried to take his girl. Lily come over as white as a sheet, and I took and told him to mind his tongue. 'Lily won't marry no murderers', I said—'not while I'm her mother', I said.

'And it's late enough and you'd better be getting along', I said—'and you needn't wait for Lily, because I'll be walking up the road with her myself'."

Susan leaned her forehead upon her hand and said,

"Is it only William—does anyone else think that about Bill?"

"They're a pack of fools!" said Mrs. Green hotly. "Though mind you, they're not blaming him—only one here and there. But I'll say, and I'll stick to it, Mr. Bill never did no such thing—did he, my dear?"

Susan lifted her head.

"No, he didn't do it. But if the police think he did—" Her voice failed.

Mrs. Green regarded her with compassion.

"William, he says it was Mrs. Mickleham that put the police on to Mr. Bill—says she ought to have her neck wrung for it for a cackling old hen. Seems he's working round the house putting in wallflower, and what with the Vicarage windows always open the way they are—and how anyone can abear the draughts passes me—well, what people says with those open windows they can't complain if it's heard. Crying something dreadful Mrs. Mickleham was, William said—and Vicar telling her she only done her duty. Seems she heard Mr. Bill say he was going to kill Mr. Dale, and Vicar made her tell the police, and now she's fit to cry her eyes out. William says it fair sickens him the way he's got to listen to them going on about it. He says he don't suppose he'll ever fancy wallflowers again, the way he's had to plant them and listen to Vicar going on about a citizen's duty. Right down irreligious he talked, and I told him I wouldn't have it in my house, and if Lily was what I brought her up to be she wouldn't have it in hers neither. And he give me a look and says, 'It'll be my house', and out he goes and bangs the door, and Lily she sets down and cries."

"Bill didn't do it," said Susan. "He wouldn't do a thing like that. He was angry, and he said what Mrs. Mickleham heard him say, but—oh, he didn't do it, Mrs. Green! The dreadful thing is that no one seems to have heard the shot except Bill and me. If we could only find someone else who heard it and knew what time it was, it would help Bill. Mrs. Green, if there was anyone who did hear it, you'd tell me, wouldn't you? I know people don't like getting mixed up in this sort of thing, but if you did come to hear anything, you *would* tell me?"

Mrs. Green nodded emphatically.

"And willing, my dear. Not that I can think of anyone that'd be likely to hear a shot round about that sort of time. People aren't so fond of having their windows open as Vicar and Mrs. Mickleham, and most of them with the wireless on as like as not, same as the girls up at King's Bourne, and a good loud band programme it was too. I like something more refined myself, but it's surprising the people that are partial to a band. And you can't hear nothing else when it's on—that's sure enough."

Chapter Twenty-Eight

FRANK ABBOTT walked up and down the study and discoursed on Miss Cora de Lisle.

"She knows more than she has told, I'll swear to that. The longer I think it over, the odder it all looks. I tell you she began by pretending that Dale had sent me over to get back her precious fifty-pound note. But she didn't keep that up. She knew he was dead all right, and she was scared stiff. Of course she must have known that the note would be traced." He laughed. "It was quite obvious that she'd spent some of it on brandy already. She'd a bottle and glass beside her when I came in. Now you know, she doesn't look to me like a regular soak. I should say she was the sort that goes to it for ginger or for consolation. She'd had some when she came to see Dale at twelve o'clock in the day. Well, if she habitually drank at that hour she wouldn't have got even the fifth-rate job she's just been sacked from. She's the sort that breaks out, not the sort that does it all the time. Well, on Monday she'd got the sack, and the company had gone on and left her high and dry, so she was desperate. Suppose it happened this way. She goes over to King's Bourne—and we know she had a good stiff drink to take her there.

She got in past Raby, and she got fifty pounds out of Dale. We know that, and we know she came back to the Crown and Magpie and had another double brandy just after the six o'clock bus had gone. After that, she says, a nice young man gave her a lift back to Ledlington and she doesn't know him or his car from Adam. Now suppose she didn't get that lift, or at least not then. Suppose the double brandy put it into her head that it was a pity to go away back to Ledlington with one fifty-pound note when Lucas Dale had three more of them in his pocket-book—she'd have seen them, as likely as not when he took out the one he gave her."

"That's supposing," said Inspector Lamb in a particularly stolid voice.

"I said so, didn't I? More coming. Suppose she goes round the house the way she did when she saw Cathy O'Hara—she leaned in at the window and talked to her, you know. Well, we know that window was open on Monday evening. She looks in and sees that Dale is alone. She sees too that the glass door to the terrace is ajar, and she goes round there and walks in. After that—anything. Cora rather drunk and possibly quite abusive. Dale, who had just been touched for fifty pounds, certainly very angry. He may have got out the pistol to frighten her and have put it down on the table. She may have snatched it. He wouldn't be really on his guard with a woman— and a woman who had been his wife. No one will ever know just the way it went—if it went that way. In the end he's not taking any more. He goes to ring the bell, and she shoots him as he turns."

Lamb pursed his lips.

"Too much imagination—that's your trouble," he said. "If she came here to get those fifty-pound notes, why did she go away without them?"

"Because she was scared out of her life. She'd lost control and killed him. The only thought she'd have in the world would be to get away before anyone came—get rid of the revolver and run. And if we find the nice young man who gave her that lift, I think we'll find it was nearer seven than six when he picked her up. Meanwhile I'd like to know whether they've been able to dig up anything about her record at the Yard."

Lamb nodded.

"There was a call just now."

"Well, have they got anything?" A keen look had displaced Frank Abbott's usual air of languor.

"Depends on what you call anything," said Inspector Lamb.

"What was it?"

Lamb regarded him composedly.

"All worked up about this, aren't you—set on making out it was this Cora de Lisle because young Carrick's one of your own sort and you like his girl."

Frank Abbott whitened.

"You haven't got any right to say that, Inspector." Lamb sat back, filling his chair.

"Well, I'm saying it all the same, my lad—and something else that you can put to it and keep. You can't go looking for a criminal and say, 'This is a chap I like, so he didn't do it and I've got to find someone else', or, 'This chap turns my insides, so he'll do'. And no need to look at me like that, young Abbott. When I've got something to say I'm going to say it. See? What we're looking for every time is facts—lots of potty little facts that you wouldn't give a damn for if you took them one by one, but when you add them up they make something. You can't shirk facts, and you can't bend them. You've got to take 'em as they come and see what they add up to. Perhaps it's the answer you'd like it to be, and perhaps it isn't. That's not my business nor yours. And here's a little fact about Miss Cora de Lisle. She was in a bit of trouble two years ago over a shooting act at the Old George at Hoxton. There was another girl, and she got hurt. It wasn't serious, and there wasn't enough evidence to show that it wasn't just the sort of accident that does happen once in a way in these turns, but it seems there had been a quarrel, and if Miss de Lisle wasn't drunk she was as near it as makes no matter, and the girl who was hurt went about saying some pretty nasty things. There's your fact, Frank, and you can put it away with the others."

"Thank you, sir." Face and voice were both respectfully non-committal.

Lamb looked at him pretty straight and said,

"I wonder. But you will some day, if you don't now. Now here's a job for you. Go down to the Little House and measure the women's shoes. We haven't fixed anyone up with that footprint yet. Pity you couldn't get one of Cora de Lisle's whilst you were about it."

Frank Abbott half closed his eyes and called up the picture of an impatient foot in a shabby tinsel shoe.

"Long—narrow—a good deal arched—about nine inches—I'd say she took a five."

"And what would you guess Miss Lenox?"

"Oh, hers will be a five. Foot a bit wider than the other, but of course she was wearing a country shoe, and Cora had on a gimcrack evening slipper."

"When she came here on Thursday morning she had on a pair of old black strap shoes, a good deal trodden over—Miss O'Hara's description, and she doesn't miss much, I should say. Her own feet are too small," he added hastily.

"Unless she was wearing Susan's shoes."

Lamb turned his shoulder.

"Get along down to it! And be on the look out for any sign of clay on a shoe. There's clay where that puddle is—that's why it holds the wet—and I haven't noticed it anywhere else about the place. To my mind, whoever made the foot-mark had been into that puddle, so you keep a bright look out for traces of clay."

Chapter Twenty-Nine

THE BELLS of the Little House rang in the kitchen. Mrs. Green looked over her shoulder and saw that it was the front door bell which had just rung. She looked at Susan, who was mixing batter, and Susan nodded.

"If you don't mind, Mrs. Green—"

Mrs. Green said, "Well, I've just about finished that floor," and got up. She wiped her hands on her apron and walked through the dining-room and hall at a leisurely pace, humming Jerusalem the Golden as she went.

The sight of the elegant young man on the doorstep gave her what she afterwards described to Lily as a turn. " 'Is Miss Lenox at home?' that's what he said, and, 'Can I see her? I'm Detective Sergeant Abbott'. As if I didn't know that, with you describing him to me, let alone me seeing him with my own eyes coming out of the Crown and Magpie after he'd been talking to Mr. Pipe. So I left him in the hall, which is good enough for detectives whether they're got up to look like gentry or not, and went and told Miss Susan. And she put her batter to the one side, which if it was me I wouldn't have minded keeping him waiting a bit, and washed her hands under the tap and out she went to him. And what do you suppose he wanted? Well there, I'd better tell you, for you'd never guess—every blessed pair of shoes in the house. And the way he looked them over, if he'd taken a magnifying glass to them I wouldn't have been surprised."

Susan, accompanying Frank Abbott on his round of inspection, began by wondering what he could possibly want with their shoes, and ended with the conviction that the answer was a very frightening one. She met his first demand with incredulity.

"You want to see our shoes?"

"If you don't mind, Miss Lenox."

Of course this was the merest form, because, however much she minded, it would make no difference to this polite and inexorable young man.

She took him upstairs to Cathy's room first. Cathy had gone down to the village, so there would be one pair of shoes unaccounted for, but when he had looked at the others, from the little silver slippers to the brogues which looked as if they had been made for a child, Detective Sergeant Abbott didn't seem to think it mattered about the missing pair.

"Your cousin has a very small foot. I suppose she takes a four."

"A small four. These"—Susan touched the silver slippers—"these are only three and a half."

He appeared to lose interest after that, and she took him along the passage to Mrs. O'Hara's door, where she knocked.

Mrs. O'Hara said "Come in" in her plaintive voice, and Susan opened the door.

Frank Abbott, not at all embarrassed, entered a bedroom which contained more furniture than he could have believed possible. The room was of a fair size, running through the house from front to back, but the suite of mahogany furniture imported from King's Bourne stood around the walls in gloomy, towering masses and reduced the floor space to a minimum. There was a four-poster bed with a canopy. There was a vast wardrobe. There were chests of drawers, a double wash-stand with a marble top, two bedside tables, a large dressing-table, a pier glass, and various chairs. An elderly but still handsome carpet covered the floor and disappeared beneath the furniture. There was no colour-scheme. The curtains, of a nondescript brocade, were quite unrelated to the bed furnishings, which were of an uninteresting blue, or to the carpet, which was passing from its original crimson and green to a dull rose and grey.

Mrs. O'Hara, in a mauve dressing-gown, occupied a massive easy chair upholstered in one of those Victorian tapestries which were designed not to show the dirt. After some forty years of wear the stuff was still intact, but all traces of pattern were now submerged in a general olive gloom. It had not occurred to the generation which had evolved all this solid, deep-toned mahogany, or to Mrs. O'Hara who had inherited it, that its warm red-brown might be repeated, heightened, illustrated by a whole range of beautiful shades from chestnut and terra cotta through rosy gold to golden rose.

Mrs. O'Hara smiled graciously upon Frank Abbott, and appeared to find nothing unusual in his request to be allowed to see her shoes.

"Really, it is quite like Cinderella," she remarked. She looked complacently at the toe of her small black velvet slipper. "Do you want me to take this pair off? Susan my dear—"

"They look very nice where they are," said Frank Abbott, gravely.

His eye glanced along the row of shoes which Susan had produced from the wardrobe—brocade, glacé, suede, satin, all with an arched instep, a high heel, and an appearance of extreme fragility. Size four again, and not one that could possibly have made that footprint on the study carpet. He looked up quickly at Susan and said,

"What about outdoor shoes?"

She detached the thin pair of glacé kid and pushed them forward an inch, kneeling on the faded carpet and not looking at him.

"I'm afraid she hasn't got any."

Mrs. O'Hara allowed the smile of a brave invalid to relax her pretty, pale lips.

"You see, I never go out—at least not during the winter—and not in the summer unless it is quite warm and dry, and that is so very seldom. And I hardly walk at all. My health is not what I should like it to be, I am sorry to say."

Frank Abbott had seen all he wanted to, but he lingered for some social minutes, making sympathetic conversation, agreeing that the season was a mild one compared with last year, and picking up and restoring a ball of wool, a spare knitting-needle, and a small embroidered handkerchief. After which he made his farewells with address and followed Susan back along the passage to her own room.

She stopped in the doorway and said with sudden energy,

"What are you looking for, Mr. Abbott?"

His face remained expressionless even when he smiled. It was a smile that said nothing, and his eyes were cold. He murmured, "Sergeant", and left the question unanswered.

She repeated it.

"What are you looking for?"

"I don't quite know. I'm looking at shoes under orders from my superior officer. May I look at yours?"

She set them out as she had done the others—two pairs of brown walking-shoes, one a little heavier than the other, a pair of dark blue house shoes, an old brown pair, some evening slippers.

He ran his eye down the line and picked up the heavy walking-shoes. These were the right size, the right shape. He turned them about and about. They were clean and polished. There was no clay on them, no sign that the left foot—the print was a left-foot print—had trodden in a puddle of clay on Monday night. He wondered if it had.

"When did you wear these last, Miss Lenox?"

"Yesterday. I've been wearing them every day."

He put them down and picked up the lighter pair.

"And when did you last wear these?"

Susan said, "I don't know."

He was turning them in his hand.

"Have you had them on today?"

"Oh, no."

"Yesterday?"

She shook her head.

"No—I've been wearing the others. They're thicker."

"Did you wear this pair on Monday?"

Monday was so far away that she had to force her thoughts back to it. She had not been out all day on Monday until she ran out through the scullery to follow Bill up the garden way to King's Bourne. She touched the old brown house shoes.

"No—these are what I was wearing on Monday."

"All day?"

"All day."

"You didn't stop to change them before following Mr. Carrick up the garden?"

The thought of her agony of haste left her dumb. She shook her head.

"You were in too great a hurry?"

"Yes."

"Why?"

She was silent.

"You were afraid of what Mr. Carrick might do?"

She lifted her eyes to his and said,

"He didn't shoot him—he really didn't."

Frank Abbott was inclined to believe her. Old Lamb would say that it was because the dark blue eyes which were looking straight into his were quite unreasonably easy to look at. But it wasn't that at all. She might have had the handsomest eyes in the world and he could still have believed her to have a guilty knowledge. No, it was something else—a kind of simplicity.

He withdrew an appraising gaze, diverting it to the pair of shoes in his hand. They had not the polish of the thicker pair. He discarded the right shoe and turned the other one over. It had been worn and wiped, not cleaned or polished. Rather roughly wiped too, for where the upper joined the sole there was a muddy smear and a caking of what looked uncommonly like clay. He frowned at it and said,

"I am afraid I must ask you to let me take this pair."

Susan frowned too.

"What do you mean? Why should you take them? What do you want them for?"

"You can't make a guess?"

"Of course I can't."

He said, looking past her,

"This shoe stepped in a puddle. I think it was that puddle half way up the hill. It stepped in it, and it came out sticky with clay, and after that—after that, Miss Lenox, it stepped on the study floor up at King's Bourne and left a print there."

It was at this moment that Mrs. Green, unable to bear the dull solitude of the kitchen any longer, looked round the open door and saw, as she told Lily afterwards, "every drip and drab of colour go clean out of Miss Susan's face".

Chapter Thirty

Mr. Montague Phipson walked down the garden in the direction of the Little House. He wore a worried and preoccupied air. Everything was really very difficult, very difficult indeed. The atmosphere of gloom and officialdom pervading the house—the impending inquest—the impending funeral—the extreme uncertainty of his own position—and nothing, literally nothing, sacred from the prying activities of the police. He had reason to believe that even the fragments of his torn-up letter to Evangeline Bates had been abstracted from the waste-paper basket in his room and carefully pieced together. In the circumstances he could not be too thankful that he had not in any way committed himself. It was just a warm letter of friendship, no more, but that correspondence even of a platonic nature should be subjected to the scrutiny of the police was a most disturbing occurrence. And as if all this were not enough, there was the continued presence in the house of Mr. Vincent Bell, a person so uncongenial that prolonged association with him would at any time have been a trial. In the present delicate situation Mr. Bell's jaunty air, his cheerful voice, his frank admission that he considered Mr. Dale no particular loss to a world which he had very successfully exploited, was extremely distasteful.

Mr. Phipson had ventured to express this view to Inspector Lamb that very morning. He had seen his opportunity and had nerved himself to take it. The Inspector, a stolid person, had gazed at him with eyes which really had a most extraordinary resemblance to bull's-eyes—the round, old-fashioned, peppermint-flavoured kind—and said,

"Well, I expect you'll be getting rid of him as soon as the inquest is over, Mr. Phipson. Moving on yourself too, I dare say?"

Not a very helpful way of putting it—not tactful. But of course one didn't expect tact from the police. He had responded with dignity that he really could not say what his plans might be, but that if, as he understood, Mr. Duckett the solicitor and Miss Lenox were the executors under Mr. Dale's will, they would probably be glad of his assistance in settling up the estate.

He thought the Inspector's manner rather off-hand as he inquired how he knew that Mr. Duckett and Miss Lenox were the executors, and he was rather pleased with the dignity of his own reply.

"In my capacity as Mr. Dale's confidential secretary, would you consider it strange that I should have prepared a rough draft embodying the points which Mr. Dale desired should be incorporated in the will?"

The Inspector's reply was still more off-hand.

"In the circumstances, very strange indeed."

He had downed him though, he had downed him, because he had been able to produce the draft, and neither the Inspector nor anyone else was to know that it was a copy of Mr. Dale's own notes.

And why not? And why not, if you please? A secretary who was conversant at all points with his employer's business was in a position of considerable strategic importance. There were times when knowledge became a very valuable thing. Mr. Phipson rather thought that this was one of those times.

He walked slowly down the orchard path between the apple, pear and plum trees which would be sheeted with pink and white blossom in another two months time. He went round the house to the front door, knocked, and was pleased when Susan herself opened it. They had not met since the day when she had talked with Lucas Dale in the rose garden. That was Thursday—the day Lucas Dale had proposed to her—the day Vincent Bell had arrived—the day that all this horrible business had begun. It was not quite a week ago, but it felt like years. Susan looked at him across the gap and felt dizzy.

But Mr. Phipson was quite at his ease. He said, "May I come in?" and when she moved away from the door and they were in the hall he led the way to the drawing-room and made the careful little speech which he had prepared.

"May I offer my condolences, Miss Lenox, and, if you will accept them, my services?"

Susan stopped feeling dizzy, and could have laughed. What a ridiculous little man he was, with his dignity and his absurd stilted speeches. They had been meeting continually for months, but they were still Miss Lenox and Mr. Phipson, though he called Cathy by her name. Susan and Cathy and Bill had always called him Fibs behind his back. Cathy said he crept and crawled, and Bill said he was like one of those pale, flat, jointed insects which you turn up under a stone. If he only knew—She said as quickly as possible,

"It's frightful—isn't it? It was nice of you to come."

She supposed this was a call. They sat down, Susan in one corner of the sofa, Montague Phipson in the other. He gazed, cleared his throat, and said,

"I wished to lose no time in offering you my services."

Susan hesitated.

"That's very kind of you."

He shook his head.

"I am entirely at your disposal."

Susan thought, "If Fibs is going to propose to me, I shall scream." She said in a controlled voice,

"It sounds very kind, but I don't really know what you mean." And then she had a panic, because if he was thinking of proposing, she didn't want to know what he meant, and he would be certain to think she did.

Mr. Phipson looked atrociously solemn and important. If he had belonged to an earlier generation he would have addressed Susan as "My dear young lady".

"When I said I was at your service, I was alluding to the trying and protracted business of settling so large an estate as Mr. Dale's. You will certainly require assistance, and I think you will agree that there is no one so well qualified as myself." He shifted his pince-nez and gazed at her through the lenses. "Without any failure of modesty, I think I can say that."

Well, he wasn't proposing. But this was almost as bad, because if it meant anything at all, it meant that he knew about Lucas Dale's will. She winced from the thought and said,

"I don't know what you mean."

His gaze sharpened, shifted, and then came back to dwell upon her with a certain quality of reproach.

"You don't really mean that, Miss Lenox."

The colour of anger came to Susan's face.

"I think you had better explain."

Mr. Phipson desired nothing better.

"Certainly, Miss Lenox. As you are probably aware, I was a good deal in Mr. Dale's confidence, and I am naturally aware that he made a new will on the very day of his death. I am also aware of the terms of that will. Mr. Duckett and yourself are the executors, and you are the sole legatee. I naturally assume—"

Without waiting to hear what Mr. Phipson assumed, Susan broke in vehemently.

"It's all a dreadful mistake! The will should never have been made!"

"But it was made, Miss Lenox. I believe it is perfectly in order, and that Mr. Duckett will be coming to see you about it as soon as this very painful business of the inquest is over. I understand it is to take place on Friday, and—"

Susan broke in again.

"Mr. Phipson, all this has nothing to do with me—that will has nothing to do with me. Mr. Dale made a dreadful mistake. I couldn't possibly take anything."

Mr. Phipson's mouth fell open, his pince-nez fell off. He considered that his ears must have deceived him. He could not possibly have heard a penniless young woman assert that she intended to refuse a fortune. Things like that didn't happen. As he replaced his glasses he fully intended to ensure that this rule held good.

"You are the sole legatee," he repeated.

"Not if I won't!"

"My *dear* Miss Lenox!"

Susan's eyes were dark with indignant distress. A bright colour burned in her cheeks.

"Nothing would induce me to take a penny of it!"

"That," said Mr. Phipson, "is nonsense."

"I don't think so. I couldn't possibly take it."

"I hope you will change your mind."

Someone else had said that to her—someone else—Lucas Dale—on the far side of the gap that had opened so suddenly between Monday and all the time that went before. Lucas Dale had said it when he had asked her to marry him. And she had said no—and she had changed her mind—or had it changed for her. The words put a chill upon her angry mood. She said, "No," and he repeated them.

"I hope you will. I can't tell you just what the estate is worth—Mr. Duckett will be able to do that—but there is at least four hundred thousand pounds invested in this country, and the American holdings come to as much again or more."

The cold and the anger had fused. Susan felt an icy rage. She said in a level voice,

"It has nothing to do with me. Please stop talking about it, Mr. Phipson."

"Oh, but I am afraid I can't—I can't do that. You see, Miss Lenox, it is very important indeed that you should accept this bequest." He leaned forward a little. "If you will allow me—"

Susan said, "No."

She heard him make a small, vexed sound, and wondered at his pertinacity. It appeared that he was not at all prepared to let the subject drop.

"If you please, Miss Lenox, I would just like to clarify the position. There is this large fortune which is actually and legally yours. If you refuse it, what happens to it? There are no relatives—I have heard Mr. Dale say he had not a relation in the world. It will revert to the Crown."

"I don't care what happens to it," said Susan bluntly.

Mr. Phipson looked a good deal shocked.

"But it is your duty to care, Miss Lenox. Consider for a moment. Mr. Dale in leaving everything to you placed a very great responsibility upon your shoulders. There were bequests which he should have made—which he might have made if he had taken a little more time to consider. I happen to know that he intended to consider these bequests at leisure after his marriage."

Susan said steadily, "It was all a mistake. I should never have married him. That is why I can't take the money."

Inconceivable folly—really quite inconceivable. He made the same vexed sound again.

"I hope you will hear me out. You are, if I may say so, in the position of a trustee. If you refuse, those people who would have received bequests will lose their money. Your aunt, Mrs. O'Hara, is one of them. Cathy is another. He intended to provide for them, but had not decided on the exact amounts. If you refuse, you will deprive them of the benefits he intended."

Susan flared.

"If he intended it, why didn't he do it? And how do you know what he intended?"

Mr. Phipson looked so smug that she could have slapped him.

"I was more in his confidence than you seem to think. You must understand that this will was in the nature of a gesture. He wished, I think, to impress you, to be able to come to you and say, 'Look at this—I have left you everything.' He did tell you that—didn't he?"

The anger died out of Susan, the cold stayed. Yes, Lucas Dale had done that. She remained silent.

Mr. Phipson said, "I see he did. It was a gesture. No one would really leave so large a fortune to a single person and make no provision for those who had served him. He intended to make a new will in the immediate future. Naturally, he could have had no idea that for him there was to be no future."

Susan shuddered. The words called up a picture of Lucas Dale as she had last seen him—a dominant, vital figure, proud, handsome, sure of his power to take what he wanted from life. No, he hadn't expected to die almost before the ink on that will was dry.

Mr. Phipson went on speaking.

"You see now what I meant when I said that you were in the position of a trustee towards those people who would have received bequests under the will he intended to make."

Susan felt as if the room had grown smaller, as if the walls were closing in. The crowding furniture stood about her and Montague Phipson and closed them in. She was too near him. It was like being in a trap. She had been in a trap from which Dale's death had released her. She saw the will now mainly as another trap, closing down. With a vehement revulsion she cried,

"Who are these people—besides Cathy and Aunt Milly? How do I know that he wanted to leave them anything? And how do you know? What has it got to do with you?"

She had a feeling that the room shook. And then that some violent clash had shaken her. And then that it was her own anger—because she wasn't used to being angry like this. It couldn't have anything to do with Fibs, because he was looking at her quite mildly through his thick lenses and saying,

"There was Mrs. O'Hara, and Cathy—I told you that. And a sum for Mr. Vincent Bell, though he had, I believe, not quite made up his mind about that. Some provision for a woman who had been his wife, a Miss de Lisle—I suppose you knew that he had been married. Money bequests to any servants who might have been with him for more than a year. And—well, I have no reason to conceal it—a substantial recognition of my own services."

Something in Susan's mind gave a small mocking laugh and said, "Now we're getting there!" There was a glint of satire behind the deep blue of the eyes she turned upon him.

"I see." She got up rather quickly. "I can't take the money. I don't think we'd better go on discussing it, because it's no use. I can't take it."

Mr. Phipson got up too. He fumbled in a pocket and brought out a large square envelope which he held towards her without speaking. Susan took it, lifted the flap, which was not fastened down, and drew out something small in a wrapping of tissue paper. She looked at it doubtfully.

"What is this?"

Mr. Phipson took it from her, opened it, and displayed in the middle of a tissue paper square a small, fine linen handkerchief. An initial S was visible upon one of the up-turned corners.

He said, "I think this is yours," and watched her colour fade.

"I don't know—"

"I am sure you do. Even I know that it is one of a set Cathy gave you at Christmas. I have watched her embroidering the initials."

She put out her hand to take it, and he went back a step.

"You don't ask me where I found it."

"Does it matter?"

"It matters very much. Or shall I say that it would matter very much if Inspector Lamb were to know where I found it? There is no need for him to know."

Susan looked at him. One of those jointed insects that you turn up under a big stone—pale, brittle, and faintly repulsive, but quite, quite harmless. Fibs—just how harmless was Fibs? They had always laughed at him—

She said firmly, "Where did you find it?"

Mr. Phipson said, "Ah!"

"Where did you find it?"

"You don't know?"

"I shouldn't ask you if I did."

"You didn't miss it?"

"Why should I?"

Mr. Phipson said, "True—you would not necessarily know where you had dropped it."

"Where did I drop it?" said Susan, and wondered why her lips should feel so stiff.

He looked at her—pale—brittle—faintly unpleasant.

"You dropped it when Mr. Dale was shot. It was found beside his body."

Susan looked back at him. He was still there, but she could not see him, because the air had thickened between them—thickened and grown dark. She moved away from him, a step at a time, very carefully, until she touched the sofa. She sat down, leaned back into the corner, and heard him say,

"I am afraid that was a shock. Would you like me to fetch you a glass of water?"

She heard herself say "No."

"Are you sure? I will wait until you are quite yourself again."

Susan shut her eyes and called up all the strength and courage she possessed. The darkness passed from her eyes and from her mind. She said in quite a clear, steady voice,

"It was horrible to hear you say that. But I don't know what you mean. I never went into the room. My handkerchief couldn't have been there."

Mr. Phipson cleared his throat.

"Miss Lenox, this is waste of time. Consider whether it would not be better to be frank with me. You are doubtless aware that Raby found Mr. Dale at a quarter to seven. He did not wait to make any examination, but rushed upstairs to fetch me in a state of horror and distress. We entered the room together, and as I bent over the body I saw this handkerchief lying crumpled up near the feet. I do not know whether Raby noticed it or not—I do not think that he did. He was groaning aloud and averting his head. I recognized the handkerchief at once and put it in my pocket. If I were not your friend, would I have run this considerable risk? Had you not better be frank with me and let me help you?"

Susan said, "I couldn't have dropped it. I wasn't there."

"Somebody dropped it," said Mr. Phipson. "Cathy gave you the handkerchiefs. Perhaps she picked it up—perhaps she dropped it."

Susan said, "She was ill—Cathy was ill."

"Somebody dropped that handkerchief," said Mr. Phipson.

There was a long silence. Susan looked down into her lap and saw the knuckles whiten where one hand clasped the other. She thought quick and clear, "I didn't drop it. Somebody dropped it. Somebody wore my shoes. Cathy? Aunt Milly? *Impossible*." Was it impossible? She had come to the place where possible and impossible met, mixed, parted, and came together again like the reflections in broken water. She could not tell real from unreal, unreal from real. Two things emerged with clarity—the handkerchief, and Fibs who had brought it to her. Now just why had he brought it? And why had he spoken about the will first—the will and Lucas Dale's intention of recognizing his secretary's valuable services? She thought Mr. Montague Phipson looked upon her as the heir to that intention. She thought he was there to drive a bargain. She thought she was to make Lucas Dale's intention good. She wondered if it had ever existed, and what she was going to do about it. Suppose she snatched the handkerchief out of his hand and went straight up the hill to Inspector Lamb. Cathy—Aunt Milly—she couldn't do that. She didn't know what she could do.

She lifted her head and said, "Why?"

"Why, Miss Lenox?"

Susan spread out her hands.

"All this—the will—the handkerchief. What is it all about—what does it mean—what do you want?"

He smiled a polite and formal smile.

"I want to help you, Miss Lenox. I am your friend. I should like to know that we are to work together in friendly association. I am—" He cleared his throat again. "Frankly, Miss Lenox, I am without any resources to fall back upon. Mr. Dale's death has been a great blow to me. If I could feel assured of a continuance of my present salary and something on account of the legacy which Mr. Dale intended me to have—"

The sheer impudence of it took Susan's breath away. She came to her feet with the strength of anger.

"Mr. Phipson!"

He said, "Careful, Miss Lenox—I really do advise you to be careful. Once I have laid this evidence before the police there will be no turning back."

Susan caught her breath, caught back the words which that breath should have carried. She could hold them now, but once spoken they would be beyond recall. And if she made this man her enemy, what would be the end of it? She didn't know. No one could possibly tell. With a very great effort she forced her voice to a quiet tone.

"Mr. Phipson, I don't know what to say. You must give me a little time."

He echoed her words with a difference.

"A little time? Oh, certainly, Miss Lenox, but it would really have to be a little time. I will call again tomorrow."

Chapter Thirty

SUSAN SHUT the front door behind Montague Phipson and stood there leaning against it. The solid, old-fashioned brass door-knob was cold in her hand. She didn't know how long it was before she straightened herself and turned. She was not faint. Faintness would have been a relief. She went slowly through the hall and up the stair to where her door faced Cathy's across the narrow passage.

Cathy's door was ajar, and Susan could hear her moving. With sudden energy she pushed open the door and went in, shutting it behind her. Cathy, on her knees before a pulled-out drawer, looked round and showed a startled face. She was still exceedingly pale, and her eyes had smudges under them. She said rather quickly,

"I was turning out this drawer."

Susan sat down on the bed. She was so tired that it would be easy just to sit here—pull up the pillows and lean back—leave unsaid the things she had come here to say. It would be easy, but she couldn't do it—she had to go on.

She said, "Cathy—"

"Yes?"

"Cathy, are you all right again?"

"Yes—I am, really—you needn't worry about me."

Susan shook her head. There was more to worry about than Cathy's health. She said,

"Then I want to ask you about Saturday. I want to know how much you heard."

Cathy bent over a little pile of underclothes. Her hand shook as she picked them up one by one and laid them back in the drawer. She said,

"I fainted."

"Yes, I know you did, but you didn't go on fainting. Mr. Dale and I were talking. I want to know how much you heard."

Cathy looked over her shoulder. It was an involuntary frightened movement.

"Please—don't let's talk about it."

"Do you suppose I want to talk about it? I've got to. I've got to know how much you heard."

Cathy began to tremble. She had been kneeling. She got up and came towards the bed.

"Oh, Susan, I wouldn't have let you do it—I wouldn't really."

"Then you did hear what he said."

Cathy sank down at the foot of the bed. She had a defenceless look which went to Susan's heart. She said in a whispering voice,

"I couldn't let you do it, could I—even if he sent me to prison."

Susan looked at her and wondered. Was it Cathy? Could it have been Cathy? In anything except a nightmare the answer would be "No". But they had got far from daylight and its ways, and in a dream like this any impossible thing might wear a possible shape. She said,

"You heard everything. You knew I was going to marry him."

Cathy drooped against the bed foot. Her hands plucked at one another.

"I couldn't have let you do it. Oh, Susan, I *couldn't*!"

"What could you have done?" said Susan wearily. Then, with sudden energy, "Cathy, what *did* you do?"

Cathy sat up.

"I don't know what you mean."

"Look here, you've got to tell me—I've got to know. We're all groping round in the dark, and I can't bear it any longer. If one of us did it, I've got to know who it was. No—don't say anything yet—you've got to listen. Mr. Abbott came here yesterday evening and looked at all our shoes. Someone left a muddy foot-mark on the study floor. My brown shoe fits it. Cathy, I cleaned those shoes on Friday, and I haven't worn them since. I cleaned them and I polished them, and I haven't worn them since. But somebody has. When I turned them out for Mr. Abbott to see, they had been worn, and wiped—not cleaned or polished. And the left one had trodden in clay—you can see the mark quite plainly. That's what he was looking for—a shoe that had stepped in that clayey puddle up the garden and then made that footprint on the study floor."

"Anyone might step in that puddle—I'm always doing it." Cathy's voice came quick and frightened.

"I don't—ever. Besides I wasn't wearing the shoes—I haven't worn them since Friday. But somebody wore them. Somebody wore them, and trod in that puddle, and made the foot-mark on the study floor, and dropped one of my handkerchiefs by Mr. Dale's body. And I've got to know who it was."

Cathy said "Your handkerchief?" in a trembling voice.

"One of the set you gave me for Christmas, with my initial. Fibs has got it."

The colour came faintly to Cathy's face.

"I thought you meant the police!" She got the last word out with a gasp. "He won't tell them, will he? He—oh, we've laughed at him, but we've always been quite friends—he won't tell."

Susan bit her lip—hard.

"Not if I make it worth his while not to. Fibs has his price. I'm to take Mr. Dale's money and pay him the legacy which he thinks he ought to have, and then I can have my handkerchief again, and he'll forget he ever saw it."

"He said that?"

"No, he didn't say it, but that's what he meant. It was all most beautifully wrapped up, but that's what he meant. And that's why

I've got to know who wore my shoes, because if it was you or—or Aunt Milly, I can't just tell him to go and drown himself."

Cathy broke in with surprising energy.

"Susan, you're mad! No, darling, I don't mean that of course—but you're not well—it's all the strain. Only you mustn't drag Mummy into it. Why, if it wasn't so serious, we should laugh at the idea of her going out on a cold, damp night, when she hasn't been out of the house for months. Just think what you're saying. And, darling, do lie down and have a rest. You've been doing far, far too much, and it's all my miserable selfish fault."

Susan's eyes burned blue. She looked at Cathy and said,

"They think Bill did it—they'll arrest him any time now. They'll think I was there—they'll arrest me too. Don't you see I've got to know where we are? If one of us did it, I've got to know who it was. I can't let them arrest Bill—I *can't*."

There was a silence. Then Cathy said in a small, shaking voice,

"If they knew that someone else had worn your shoes, would it stop them arresting Bill?"

Susan threw out her hands.

"I don't know—I think it would. I can't really think at all, but if someone else was there it means someone else might have shot Mr. Dale, or—no, I didn't mean that, but they might have seen something or heard something—oh, don't you see, if there was anyone else there at all, it would make things better for Bill."

Cathy made a wringing motion with her hands and said,

"I didn't shoot him."

Susan found herself on her feet without any notion of how she had got there. She was on her feet. She had Cathy by the shoulders and she was saying,

"Was it you? Did you wear my shoes? Did you—*did* you?"

"I didn't shoot him."

"But you wore my shoes—you went up to King's Bourne."

"Yes—" The word was practically inaudible.

"Why?"

"To tell him—to tell him—you couldn't—marry him."

"What happened—*Cathy*—"

"He was dead—" It was just a sighing whisper.

"What did you do?"

"I went in—and I looked at him—then I came away—"

"Did you hear the shot? Did you see anyone?"

Cathy shook her head.

"I didn't see anyone."

"But you heard the shot—you must have heard the shot."

Cathy shook her head again. It was the same mournful gesture.

"I didn't hear anything at all."

Chapter Thirty-Two

"THAT'S WHAT she says."

Susan and Bill were in the drawing-room, standing close together at the French window which opened upon the garden. Two steps led down to a paved place where Mrs. O'Hara sometimes sat in very hot weather. Beyond the paving there was a border with snowdrops and crocuses just pushing up through the dark soil. And beyond the border and a little to the left the ground began to rise and the path went up the hill to King's Bourne.

"She must have heard the shot," said Bill. "And I don't see why she didn't bump into us either going or coming, unless—" He stopped on the word, took Susan by the shoulder, and pulled her round so that they faced each other. "Look here—did Cathy shoot him?"

It marked the distance they had travelled that Susan made no real protest. She said in a tired voice,

"Oh, no—she couldn't—not Cathy."

Bill frowned deeply.

"I don't know—I don't think you can cut it out like that. She'd had a bad shock—she was in a queer state—she'd heard him blackmailing you. By her own account of it she woke up and felt she had to tell him that she wouldn't let you marry him. She didn't dress. That shows that she wasn't normal. She took a coat and your shoes. Now why did she take your shoes? They must have simply slopped about on her feet."

"I don't know. Hers may have been downstairs. I suppose she was dazed."

He gave an emphatic nod.

"There you are. She was dazed. She went up there with the idea that she'd got to stop him marrying you. She wouldn't have shot him if she had been herself. But that's the whole point—she wasn't herself. Suppose she went up there and he wouldn't listen to her—laughed at her—perhaps threatened her—"

All Susan's colour was gone. She said "No" in a kind of horrified whisper.

"It's no good saying 'No'. It might have been that way, and if she had run out on to the terrace at once she could have got away before I got there—I don't know—"

Susan shook her head.

"You've forgotten about the glass door. It was shut, or nearly shut, when you came up the steps and went along to the side window. It must have been, or you would have noticed it, because the first thing you did notice when you came back was that the glass door was open. Someone must have opened it in the time between your leaving the terrace and coming back again."

He said, "I had forgotten. But if someone opened that door— why, then it fits. Don't you see how it fits? Cathy was there between the curtain and the door. She may have seen me look in at the window, and when I turned away she pushed the door and ran out. If she went down the far steps she wouldn't meet you."

Susan said "No" again, and this time her voice was strong. "It couldn't have been Cathy—I can't believe it. Don't you see it's all wrong? He wouldn't have got that pistol out to frighten Cathy— he had plenty of other things to frighten her with. And you can't believe that Cathy went right round the table and got the pistol out, and then got behind him and shot him while he just sat there and did nothing. It doesn't begin to make sense. No, I think she came up after we had gone and saw him lying there. There was plenty of time for her to come and go before Raby found him at a quarter to seven. And that would explain why she didn't hear the shot. She mightn't have heard it if she was still in her room—the windows were shut— Aunt Milly didn't hear anything—" Her voice trailed away.

She said suddenly and sharply,

"That doesn't help you. Oh, Bill, it doesn't help you at all."

"No." He laughed. "We had our exits and our entrances, hadn't we? They might have been timed. Perhaps the counsel for the prosecution will take hold of that—I shouldn't wonder. Anyhow the moral dilemma is off. We haven't got to make up our minds to be noble and let me be hanged in order to save Cathy, because so far as I'm concerned I don't see that her story makes a pennorth of difference. She may have been there before me, or she may have been there after me, but unless she's going to say she did it, this story of hers is neither here nor there, and she'd better keep her mouth shut. Rub that into her good and hard. There's absolutely no sense in dragging her in—absolutely none. What you can do is to press her just as hard as you can about whether she was behind the curtain when I looked in at the window. You can just see the window from that door."

"Then you could see the door from the window."

"I suppose I could. Yes, of course I could. And the curtain was drawn—yes, I'm sure about that. She must have been there. Press her as hard as you can."

Susan shook her head.

"It's no good—she says the same thing every time. She stood just inside the door and saw him lying on the floor. She went right up to him and saw that he was dead. She must have dropped my handkerchief then. She was dreadfully frightened and she ran away. She says she came down the near steps. If she was behind the curtains when you were looking in at the window she would have passed me going down the garden. No, it wasn't Cathy behind that curtain. If there was anyone there, it wasn't Cathy, and we've got to find out who it was."

He made a sudden movement. His voice was heavy with discouragement.

"Susan, it's no use—we're trying to make bricks without straw. The curtain was drawn, and there isn't a scrap of proof that there was anyone behind it."

"The door," said Susan urgently—"the door! It wasn't open when you passed it to go to the window, but it was open when you came back. Someone opened it."

"I don't know—I couldn't swear to all that about the door. I've thought about it till I can't think straight. It didn't amount to more than an impression. You go over and over a thing like that until you don't know what you thought at the time. The fact is you don't notice things because you don't know they're going to be important. They just slide by you with the thousand and one other things which you're not particularly noticing all day long. They're part of a pattern, and you notice the pattern, but you just don't notice the details. And then quite suddenly one of those details is so important that you've got to remember it, and you can't. That's where I am. It's a matter of life and death about that door, and for the life of me I can't remember. It was too unimportant at the time, and it's too important now. I can't get it into focus, and the more I try the less certain I am about anything. By the time it comes to standing up and being cross-examined I shan't be able to open my mouth without getting tied into knots. And if you get down to rock bottom, there's no more in it than this—I didn't actually notice whether the door was open when I went past to the window."

"But you *would* have noticed."

"Would I? I don't know. You see that's what we come back to every time—I don't know."

Susan caught him by the arm.

"Wait! Bill, when you came back and found the door was open and went in, was the curtain still drawn?"

"I think so. Yes, it was. I remember I had to pull it back before I could see into the room. And that would account for my not noticing whether the door was open. If the curtain had been pulled back,

I should have seen the light. I did see the light from the window. That's why I went there—I thought I would look in and see if he was alone. But there wasn't any light from the door—I'm quite sure about that. It may have been open all the time."

Silence came down between them. There was no more to be said. Presently he threw up his head and laughed.

"I took my shadow a good deal farther than he wanted to go this morning. He's that young Lane from Ledcott, and he's much better on a motor-bike than he was up the Quarry hill on his own flat feet. He may get his own back by arresting me, but I can give him points and a beating when it comes to a rough climb. I took him up through the gorse, and he wasn't loving me much."

"I wondered where you were."

He laughed again.

"I found a flat, sandy place and roughed out a pretty good plan for old Gilbert Garnish. I expect Lane thought I was crazy, but he didn't mind having a rest. I came down the steep side over the rock, and I believe he had thoughts about suicide. Anyhow he'll have taken off the best part of half a stone, and that's all to the good. Actually, I've had a brain-wave about the Garnish affair—" He stopped suddenly, put his arms round her, and said with suspicious lightness, "I'm afraid I'll get the sack if I'm arrested—and it's a pity, because it was coming out a treat."

Susan said "Don't!" in a muffled voice, and all at once she was holding him as he was holding her, and they were kissing with a desperate, straining passion—with blinding tears. Their world had broken round them and there was no protection anywhere, no safety and no help. The only happiness and comfort they could know was in this embrace which might be their last.

They clung together without words.

Chapter Thirty-Three

LILY GREEN had her afternoon and evening out on Wednesday. Since William Cole would not be free until after five, she would put in a little gossip with Annie Gill or Florrie Pipe and then come home to tea. Mrs. Green had an old cottage right on the village street. It was picturesque, insanitary, and quite destitute of modern conveniences. Mrs. Green still pumped water from a well in the back garden, and everything else was to match. The rooms were dark, the floors uneven, the bedroom ceilings sloped to catch an unwary head. But when Lily came into the kitchen there was a nice clear fire with some buttered toast on the hob, and an excellent currant cake of Mrs. Green's baking on the table, which was covered with a bright checked table-cloth. A well trimmed wall-lamp diffused a warm yellow light and a perceptible odour of paraffin. On the dresser, and only used upon state occasions, was the pink-flowered china tea-set which had been a wedding present from Mrs. O'Hara's mother. There was also a figure of Red Riding Hood stroking an affectionate wolf, a King George V jubilee mug, two copper candlesticks, and a Dick Turpin in a blue coat and sprigged waistcoat on his famous mare Black Bess. He had very long black moustaches and rode in a peculiar manner with both hands on the same side of the mare's neck.

Mrs. Green gave Lily a hearty kiss and began at once to make the tea and to tell her all about Detective Sergeant Abbott and the shoes.

"And I thought Miss Susan was agoing to faint. There wasn't a drip nor a drab of colour in her face. 'Miss Lenox' he said, 'that shoe is the one that stepped in the old clay puddle going up the garden way. It stepped in and it stepped out', he said, 'and after that it made a print on the study floor. And I must take the shoes away with me', he said. And there was poor Miss Susan as white as a bit of sugar icing."

Lily Green put three lumps of sugar in her tea. She was just what her mother must have been at twenty-two, and a very pretty girl—nice skin, nice hair, nice eyes, and a pleasantly rounded figure. She leaned an elbow on the table and dropped her voice.

"It's right enough about that footprint," she said. "Mr. Raby, he saw it, and I heard him tell his wife. They put one of the big chairs right over it so as it shouldn't be trod on till the London police came down. But whatever makes them pick on Miss Susan? There's plenty of others might have trod in a puddle besides her. What about that Miss de Lisle that pushed her way in past Mr. Raby? She came up from the Magpie, didn't she, and there's clay down there. Why couldn't she have made the mark on the floor?"

Mrs. Green looked thoughtful. She munched buttered toast. Then she said,

"There wouldn't be enough clay left on her shoes to mark a floor by the time she'd come all the way round by the road from the Magpie."

"Nor there wouldn't," said Lily. She looked doubtfully at the hot toast. "I don't know that I ought to, Mum—I'm putting on."

Mrs. Green laughed her jolly laugh.

"And I've put on, so what's the odds? You don't want to be one of the break-in-half-as-soon-as-look-at-them kind, do you? William'll have a word to say about it if you do. Men don't like bones, and that's a fact. They like something they can get their arm around."

Lily laughed and frowned.

"If William goes on the way he's been going he won't put his arm round my waist. Thinks himself a sheikh, I wouldn't wonder, the way he carries on. I'm not to say this, and I'm not to say that, and I'm not so much as to breathe a word about—" She pulled herself up with a noticeable jerk and buried her face in her cup of tea.

Mrs. Green took another piece of buttered toast and said firmly, "About what?"

Lily finished her tea and pushed up her cup for more.

"I suppose we'll all be getting our notice," she said. "I told William I'd look for a place the other side of Ledlington if he went on like he's been going—and what do you think he had the nerve to say?"

Mrs. Green put three lumps of sugar into Lily's cup.

"They've got the nerve to say anything, Ducks. What *did* he say?"

Lily tossed her head.

"Said I needn't expect he'd come over there to walk out with me, and there were plenty hereabouts would be pleased to have his company."

"I hope you didn't give in to him," said Mrs. Green in a shocked voice. "Time enough when you're married. There's ways you can get your own back then, but a girl that lets her young man right down tread on her before they've been to church together, well, she'd better stay an old maid and make the best of it, because she'll be trod as flat as any worm, and no good putting the blame on him. Men are made that way, and if you ask for it you'll get it. So you mind and keep your end up, Lily, and don't go giving in to William any more than what's right." She changed her tone suddenly. "What's all this that he won't let you talk about?"

Lily took the last piece of buttered toast and bit into it with a fine row of even teeth.

"Nothing," she said with her mouth full.

"Now, Lily—" Mrs. Green settled herself back in her chair and put a hand on either knee—"now, Lily, what are you a-keeping back?"

"Nothing."

"Oh, yes, you are. And if William Cole's going to set you on telling lies to your own mother—"

Lily's shoulder jerked pettishly.

" 'Tisn't nothing," she said, "only—"

"Only what?"

"Reelly, Mum—how you do go on! You don't want to be drawn in any more than what William does."

"Drawn into what?" said Mrs. Green with some asperity.

"Nothing."

Mrs. Green leaned forward and took the cup from her hand.

"Don't you answer me like that, Lily! What's all this about? If it's something about Mr. Dale's murder, William Cole or no William Cole you'll tell me this directly minute. Shuffling and hinting is what I'd whip any child for—and when you *was* a child I didn't have to. Open as the day you was, like anyone ought to be that hasn't got things to hide, and if William Cole is going to make you tell lies to your own mother, it's the last time he comes inside my house, and that's a fact!"

Lily jerked again.

"I'd as soon tell you as not. It was William said we oughtn't to get drawn in." She relaxed suddenly into a giggle. "And do you know what was at the bottom of it, I do believe? He's jealous—that's what he is. Thinks I'll have to go into court, and be a witness, and have my photo in the papers. It wouldn't be half exciting, would it, Mum? And I wouldn't mind reelly, not if it wasn't for William. The Inspector's ever so nice, and that Sergeant Abbott, well, he might be a real gentleman, so I wouldn't mind it myself, but William 'ud be fit to cut my throat."

"Don't you talk that way," said Mrs. Green in a shocked voice. "And you stop shallying about and tell me plain what it is you've been hiding up."

Lily leaned across the table and dropped her voice.

" 'Tisn't anything, only—well, I suppose it might be something. You see, it was this way—and look here, Mum, don't you go telling anyone, because Mr. and Mrs. Raby they've told the police and swore to it that us girls were all in along of Mrs. Raby listening to the wireless between six and a quarter to seven."

"And weren't you?" said Mrs. Green.

Lily giggled.

"Esther and Doris were there all right, but I wasn't. Mrs. Raby, she's only got to set down and listen to a band programme and it sends her off as sound as sound, so as soon as I see she was off I ran out by the back door into the yard."

"Whatever for?" said Mrs. Green.

Lily giggled again.

"Go on, Mum! What does a girl run out for? I'll bet you did it yourself."

"William?" said Mrs. Green in a disapproving voice.

"Well, we'd had a bit of a tiff Sunday night, so I thought he'd be round. It reelly was a tiff, Mum, and I wouldn't make it up, nor let him kiss me nor nothing, so I made sure he'd be round. He carries on, you know, Mum, but he's awful in love with me. Sometimes I wish he wasn't quite so much. It's bad enough when I don't mean anything, but if I was reelly to throw him over I do believe he'd do something desperate, he's that jealous. You know, he didn't half like me being in service with a single gentleman—"

Mrs. Green's bright blue eyes very nearly popped right out of her head.

"Lily! You're not going to tell me it was William that shot Mr. Dale?"

Lily had quite a prolonged fit of the giggles.

"I'd like him to hear you say so! Why, Mum, whatever put that into your head?"

Mrs. Green was justly annoyed. Her colour had deepened considerably, and her voice was sharp.

"Now, Lily, that's enough. You tell me right out what you know about Mr. Dale being shot. And if there's any more beating about the bush—"

Lily dropped to a confidential note.

"Well, William was there like I thought he'd be, and we made it up—not all at once, because I wouldn't after the way he carried on Sunday. I was ever so cold and haughty at first—I reelly was, Mum—but after a bit I give in."

Mrs. Green sniffed.

"And always will!" she said.

Lily took no notice.

"Well, he got me to walk a bit of the way with him. I knew Mrs. Raby'd be safe till seven, so I was going to. We come round the corner of the house, and round the front to go down the drive. I said I'd go as far as the gate, when all of a sudden we heard a shot. I said, 'What's that?' and William said, 'It's nothing to do with us'. But I ran as far as the corner of the house and looked round—"

"Which corner?" said Mrs. Green.

"Where the shot came from," said Lily. "And I looked along, and there was one of the study windows open and the light shining out, and I hadn't hardly seen it before someone came running past."

"Lily!"

Lily nodded.

"Reelly, Mum. You know there's a bit of paving runs all along that side of the house between the terrace and the front drive. Well, that's where she come, right along the side of the house as quick as a rabbit, and past where I was and down the drive, running all the way. And William said it was none of our business and we wasn't to get drawn in, and that's what he's gone on saying ever since. Rough as rough he was—took me by the arm and ran me along back to the yard and told me to keep my mouth shut and never let on we'd heard the shot nor seen anyone."

Mrs. Green put her elbows on the table and propped her shaking chin upon her hands.

"Oh, lord!" she said. "Lily, what did you see?"

Lily leaned close.

"I saw her as plain as plain where she crossed the study window. The light was on over Miss Cathy's table and it shone right out."

Mrs. Green shut her eyes for a moment. Everything inside her was shaking. She said in a whisper,

"Who was it—who was it, Lily? Who was it?"

"I didn't know then, but I know now."

Mrs. Green took a long breath and sat back. She picked up the corner of her overall and wiped her forehead and chin.

"What's the matter, Mum?"

"It come over me," said Mrs. Green. "Who was it you saw?"

"She'd on a black coat, and a black hat with some sort of a red feather in it—I saw it in the light. A tall, gipsy-looking woman—and I didn't know who she was then, but it was this Miss Cora de Lisle all right, the one that was Mr. Dale's wife and got in to see him earlier on, and Mr. Raby—"

Mrs. Green let out the breath she had been holding with a noisy gasp.

Lily stared.

"Why, Mum, what's come to you?"

Mrs. Green fanned herself with the saucer belonging to her teacup.

"If ever anyone had a turn!" she said.

Lily went on staring.

"Why, whoever did you think I'd seen?"

"Never you mind what I thought. But you shouldn't give anyone a turn like that. It all comes of hinting instead of saying bang out what you mean. You're sure it was her you saw—that Miss de Lisle?"

"Sure as I'm here," said Lily.

"Then the first minute you've finished your tea you'll put on your hat and up to the house and tell the police."

Chapter Thirty-Four

"WELL, WE'RE ABOUT through here," said Inspector Lamb. He pushed his chair a little way back from the writing-table which had been Lucas Dale's.

He looked round the study as he spoke. With the curtains drawn and a bright fire blazing, the fine proportions and rich but sober colouring of the room were apparent—the deep-toned Persian rugs, dark shining parquet, chairs covered in maroon leather, walls lined with books, a wide and welcoming hearth. Inspector Lamb approved it with a nod.

"All the same," he said, "you've got to be brought up to this kind of house before you can feel at home in it. It's too big for me. Eight rooms—I don't go above that—not for comfort. Four downstairs and four up, and none of them so big you've got to spend a fortune getting them warm—that's my limit. And as far as my own tastes go, eight's too many. Six is all I want, and enough for anyone, with families the size they run nowadays. And that's a funny thing, you know, Abbott—when families ran twelve and fourteen there wasn't half the accommodation for them there is now, when it's one here, and two there, and none at all round the corner. I was one of nine, and I've got three—and that's quite a big family these days."

Frank Abbott made no comment. He was stacking papers back into a pulled-out drawer.

Lamb pushed his chair a little farther.

"I don't know that I ever went through so much stuff and knew so little about a man at the end of it. Nothing but business from beginning to end, and beyond the fact that he seems to have sailed as near the wind as makes no difference, and that by hook or by crook he'd got together a pretty big pile, we don't know much more about him than we did when we began."

Without lifting his light eyes Frank Abbott said,

"It was chiefly by crook, I imagine."

"He might as well not have had a private life. Not a personal letter, or a souvenir—none of the kind of things people hoard. Well, I don't know how it strikes you, but the way it gets me is that any private life he had was the sort he'd be careful to keep private."

Frank Abbott nodded rather abstractedly. His hands were busy with the papers. Behind a particularly impassive face his thoughts were busy too. Something wrong about this case—something wrong. Inquest on Friday, 10.30 sharp at the Magpie, and an absolute cast-iron certainty that the result would he wilful murder against William Carrick. Not so certain about the girl. Footprint undoubtedly made by her shoe. Arguable that her story was substantially true. She said she hadn't been into the room. The footprint gave her the lie there. But it was only just inside the glass door. She might have stepped in—met Bill Carrick—and hardly realized—A cold gleam of sarcasm lit his thought. The girl was probably an accessory after the fact. In the light of that cold gleam he told himself that the probability would have been a certainty if Susan Lenox had not been what she was.

"What I can't make up my mind about," said Inspector Lamb, "is whether to wait for the inquest or not. It's tricky giving him the chance to bolt."

"He won't," said Frank Abbott. "No chance of getting away, and a dead certainty that he'd be putting the rope round his neck. He might as well confess as bolt—comes to the same thing with a jury."

Lamb wagged his head.

"That's all very well for a theory. People don't act on theory when they've done a murder. It's astonishing how often a criminal does the very last thing he ought to do—the very thing that's going to give him away. He's like a cat up a tree with a dog barking at the foot of it. If the cat stayed put it'd be all right. But it doesn't—it gets rattled and jumps. I've seen it dozens of times—jumps right down in front of the dog and gets caught. And that's your criminal to a T—he can't let well alone. He's committed a crime, and he'll commit another to cover the first one up, or he'll lose his nerve and bolt. All things considered, I think we'd better have Carrick under lock and key—I'd be easier in my mind."

"I'm not easy in mine."

Lamb looked at him, his large face rosy and expressionless.

"You've got a bee in your bonnet, Frank. Better get rid of it. What's the matter with arresting Carrick?"

Frank Abbott was silent. Lamb drummed with his hand on his knee.

"I asked you a question, my lad."

He got a cold, respectful stare.

"I beg your pardon, sir."

"I said, 'What's the matter with arresting Carrick?' "

"If I knew the answer to that, we'd be getting somewhere."

"Do you call that an answer?"

"Hardly. But I can't give you a better—" He paused, and said with a complete change of manner, "I thought Carrick was speaking the truth—that's all."

It was at this moment that Lily Green opened the door and stood hesitating upon the threshold. She was still in her outdoor things, and her face, between the fur collar of a brown winter coat and the small brown felt hat, looked pale and frightened. Actually, she was not so frightened as she looked. Thirty-six hours of fairly

close contact had robbed the London police of their terror, and
William or no William, if there was any way of getting her photo in
the papers, she meant to do it. Something to talk about for the rest
of her life—that's what it would be.

She came in a step, and Frank Abbott saw her and said,

"What is it? Do you want anything?"

Lily poured it all out.

"Ever so nice they were to me, Mum," she told Mrs. Green later
on that evening. "I said right away that you'd made me come. And
they wanted to know about you, so I said how you obliged Mrs.
O'Hara, and you couldn't bear to see Miss Susan the way she was.
And of course I said when it was put that way I could see it wasn't
hardly right for me to hold my tongue and let Mr. Bill be got into
trouble when I'd seen that Miss de Lisle with my own eyes not half a
minute after the shot went off. Well, they couldn't have been nicer—
made me sit down, and Mr. Abbott, he wrote it all out. He writes
beautiful, and very near as quick as if it was shorthand, and every
word as plain as print. I had to read it over and sign my name. And
they pulled the curtain back and opened the window by Miss Cathy's
table same as it was Monday night, and the Inspector he said was
I sure I could see enough to recognize anyone running along the
side of the house by the light coming from the window. So I spoke
right up and said, 'Well, I didn't recognize her, because I'd never
seen her before, but I saw her quite plain, and I could recognize
her now'. Mr. Abbott, he took up a newspaper he'd got there with a
lot of headlines, and he held it up and kept on walking away from
me. And they wanted to know how far off I could see the headlines,
and I could see them right away across the room. So then they took
me outside, and I was to run along past the window like I'd seen
Miss de Lisle whilst they went on to the front drive where William
and me were. Well, then I ran past, and they could see my face all
right, like I told them I could see hers. And they praised me ever
so, only of course they said I did ought to have mentioned it before,
so I told them about William being that jealous I didn't like to go
against him but you'd made me own up. And they said quite right,

and the Inspector said not to take any notice of William, because a girl ought to listen to her mother when she'd got a good one like he could see I had. And he said I've to go to the inquest—half past ten Friday morning at the Magpie. And they both said it'd all be in the papers, and photographs too."

Mrs. Green gazed admiringly at Lily's pretty, flushed face.

"What about William?" she said.

"I just don't care," said Lily Green.

In the study the two men looked at one another. Lily, pleased and excited, got to her feet.

"You'll have to swear to all this at the inquest," said Inspector Lamb.

"Oh, yes, sir."

Frank Abbott turned from the table and went over to the alcove. The wind blew in through the open window. He passed Cathy's table, pulled the casement to, and drew the wine-coloured curtain across it. The room settled back into its air of rich security.

And then, just as he turned, he caught the faintest of faint sounds. He thought it was the click of a latch. He thought the click came from the door on the far side of the room. It took him a moment to come round the table and cross to it. When he reached the door and opened it there was no one there.

The straight passage ran through to the hall, with the second study door opening upon it to the right. The stair to the bedroom floor ran up a dozen feet away, light, and bare, and empty. There was a door to the left and a door beyond the stair, one shut, the other ajar. He opened first one and then the other—a cold, small room like a waiting-room—the main hall of the house. No one in either place—no one at all.

As he stood looking into the hall, Raby crossed from a room on the other side. He had not met anyone or seen anyone—he had been making up the dining-room fire, he said.

Frank Abbott's light eyes went over him. He said,

"Isn't that Robert's work?"

With a vaguely nervous gesture Raby said, "Yes." And then, rather haltingly, "Robert—Robert has just stepped out to the post."

Chapter Thirty-Five

CORA DE LISLE was packing. She had been packing, or trying to pack, for the best part of an hour, ever since the front gate had creaked and clanged to behind Mrs. Clancy. Not that there was such a dreadful hurry. Mrs. Clancy had gone to the pictures, and it would be three hours good before she was back again. As long as Cora was gone by then, everything would be all right. But she ought to have gone yesterday. She ought to have gone right away on the Tuesday morning. She'd have had to change the fifty-pound note anyhow. But that was all right. She'd got Lucas Dale's signature to show, and they'd made no trouble about it. Of course they hadn't heard about Lucas being dead then, but her going there and changing the note and showing what Lucas had written—well, that was all to the good, because it looked as if she didn't know anything either. And whatever it looked like, she had to have the money. But when she'd got it—that's where she'd made her mistake. She ought to have been out of Ledlington and off back to London just as quick as the train could take her. Nowhere in the world so easy as London if you wanted to be out of the way for a bit, and with fifty pounds she could have stayed quiet till everything had blown over.

Her hands shook as she tried to fold the orange negligée. She ought to have gone right away, but the feel of the money, that's what had done her down—the feel of it, and the thought of what it would buy. Not the brandy, but what the brandy would do for her. She just hadn't been able to resist it, though she'd known at the time that she ought to be getting away.

The orange negligée dropped from her shaking hands. She picked it up, crammed it in anyhow, and threw the tinsel shoes in after it. She ought to have gone yesterday before the detective came. She would have gone too if she'd been herself, but with that awful cold shaking in her, how was she going to pack, and get to the train, and start looking for somewhere to hide at the other end? No, not *hide*—somewhere where she could be quiet and make the fifty pounds last a good long time. Things blow over, and out of sight is out of mind. She wondered if old Mrs. Isaacs would take her in....

Stupid to go on shaking like this—not like her either, but her nerves weren't what they used to be. Some would say it was the brandy—but you'd got to have something, hadn't you? Where she'd made her mistake was going back. She'd got away with fifty pounds, and she ought to have let it go at that. It was when she was having that last drink in the Crown and Magpie that it had come over her what a fool she was to let Lucas off with fifty pounds when she might just as well have had a hundred out of him, or a hundred and fifty. It wasn't as if she hadn't seen the other notes. He had had the four of them out, and she had been fool enough to let herself be fobbed off with one. By the time she had finished the brandy she had made up her mind to go back. It would be worth more than a hundred pounds to Lucas if he could stop her mouth. There were things she could tell Miss Susan Lenox that he wouldn't want her to hear.

Well then, she had gone back—

She stood there fumbling with the half-packed clothes. It wouldn't be so bad if she didn't keep on hearing the shot. And Lucas lying there—just his hand and his arm—that was all you could see from the window. But it was Lucas all right. When you've been married to a man you don't forget even if you've come to hate him. Lucas Dale's hand—with the ring on it which she'd seen when he took out the notes—there hadn't been any money for rings in the old days. Lucas Dale's hand and arm, and Lucas lying dead—and as like as not they'd try and make out she'd done it. And she'd lost her head, run on to the terrace, and then back again the way she'd come, all along by the side of the house and almost into someone there at the corner. That's what frightened her. There'd been someone there, and it might have been the one that shot Lucas, or it mightn't. She couldn't tell whether it was man or woman—and hadn't wanted to then. Hadn't wanted anything except to get away.

She turned from the shabby, half-filled suit-case, poured out a stiff tot of brandy, and gulped it down. There wasn't much left. She could put the rest into the empty eau-de-Cologne bottle and have it in her handbag so that she could have a nip in the train. She wouldn't be getting any more until she was safe in Mrs. Isaac's back room. Then she could have all she wanted—enough to stop the fear and the horrible cold shaking. She tilted the two bottles together, heard them rattle with the shaking of her hands, and saw half the brandy spill and waste itself, running down in a yellow trickle over the edge of the chest of drawers and dripping on to the littered floor. Her lipstick had dropped. She couldn't be bothered to pick it up. Very little of the brandy went where it had been meant to go, but she screwed down what there was and slipped the eau-de-Cologne bottle inside a battered handbag. For the moment she felt better. The spirits she had swallowed gave her warmth and confidence, but she had been nipping all day, and with each return to the brandy bottle she became less able to co-ordinate her thoughts or to fix them upon what she had to do. Yet at the back of everything there was a fear which drove her.

The suit-case filled slowly. If she put in a shoe she would forget its fellow, spend muddled time looking for it, and come upon it by chance already stuffed in under a huddle of torn underclothes. Once she found that she had packed the skirt which she must wear to travel in. Tugging to get it out, she spilled half the contents of the case. She put the skirt on without noticing that she was wearing one already.

It was while she was struggling to fasten the belt that she heard a motor-bicycle come chugging up the street. She heard it stop, and after that the squeak and clang of the gate. Oh, well, if it was anyone for Mrs. Clancy, she was out and there was an end of it. Curiously enough, she did not think that it might be anyone for herself. The brandy swam in her head, and it never crossed her fuddled mind that it might be the police.

The man who had ridden the motor-bicycle knocked on the front door. He wore a leather cap and goggles, and a loose waterproof coat. He looked through the goggles and observed that the parlour was in darkness—the room above it too. Well, people who lived in Gladstone Villas would be more apt to be found at the back of the house.

He went round to the back and found all dark below, but a lighted window overhead. He tried the door and found it locked. He kicked his foot against the mat and, feeling underneath it, came upon a key. He used it, wiped it, and put it back again. There was a glove on his hand as he turned the handle and went in with the faint beam of an electric torch to show him the way.

When he had come soft-foot up the stair to where a thread of light showed beneath a closed door he switched off the torch and put it in his pocket. Then he opened the door and went in.

Miss de Lisle was on her knees in the corner beyond the fireplace. The recess had been fitted with pegs and screened by a dingy curtain. She was stretching forward to reach a forgotten pair of shoes, when she heard footsteps behind her. It was the last thing she heard. There was no time to turn. Her drugged mind moved slowly. There was no time to be afraid. She did not even cry out.

The man laid the poker back upon the hearth and went quickly and noiselessly down the stair and out of the house. Nobody saw him come or go. The motor-bicycle chugged and receded. There was no sound in the house.

Chapter Thirty-Six

THE CAR TURNED in to Gladstone Villas and stopped at No. 17. Inspector Lamb got out. Frank Abbott, who had been driving, followed him. The gate creaked and the door-knocker sounded, the silence of the house was jarred by the shrill tinkle of an electric bell.

Presently the two men went round to the back, as the motor-cyclist had done. Like him they saw the lighted bedroom window, and like him they presently found the back door key, but not until they had rapped and called, and been answered only by the silence.

As they came up the stair, the silence warned them. No house with a lighted window should be as still as this.

Frank Abbott led the way to the second door on the left, knocked upon it, and, answered only by that warning silence, threw it suddenly open. The smell of spilled brandy hung upon the close air. There was a half-packed suit-case on the bed, an untidy muddle everywhere—a coat hanging over a chair, a hat on the chest of drawers beside the empty brandy bottle. And, face downwards in the corner beyond the fireplace, Miss Cora de Lisle with the back of her head smashed in. The poker which had quite obviously been used to smash it had been laid tidily back upon the hearth.

Inspector Lamb stopped to feel for a non-existent pulse. The wrist he touched was limp and warm. He straightened up, his rosy face hard and set.

"It's only just happened—she's warm. Cut round to the station and tell them—and hurry."

Frank Abbott hurried, and as he went, and made his report, and came again, and the whole machinery which waits on murder clanked into action, his thoughts raced and swirled. When the Ledlington Inspector and his men had trooped into the little crowded room he touched Inspector Lamb on the arm.

"If I could speak to you, sir—" His tone was urgent.

Lamb said, "Presently." But the urgency of the tone stayed with him, and in what he himself would have called 'half no time' he came out upon the narrow landing and said,

"Well, what is it?"

"We've got to get back, sir—leave them to it and get back. The murderer came from King's Bourne, and if we go straight back we'll have a decent chance of getting him."

"King's Bourne?"

Frank Abbott's face was more nearly eager than the Inspector had ever seen it.

"Yes—yes! There isn't a minute to lose! Let the locals get on with the photographs and the fingerprints this end, but we've got to get back. There's something I didn't tell you—I didn't think it important then. But we must get back. I'll tell you as we go."

Inspector Lamb gazed imperturbably. Something about this case seemed to have stirred young Frank right up. It wouldn't do him any harm either. In a slow and ruminating voice he remarked that if that was the way of it, he would just have a word with Inspector Grey, and Frank had better be starting the car.

They cleared the narrow exit from Gladstone Villas and came out by this way and that to the comparative quiet of a long road running between ribbon edgings of small twinkling houses and their attendant lampposts to the dark, silent country beyond.

Frank Abbott began to speak, taking up his own last words and repeating them as if there had been no interval of sound, silence and suspense.

"There's something I didn't tell you—I didn't think it important. When I went to shut the window in the study after we'd finished with that girl, the door clicked—the far door, not the one behind you. I think there was someone there with the door ajar. I think he had been there most of the time listening, and when I shut the window the door clicked to. He may have shut it, or it may have shut itself because he wasn't there any more to hold it. You saw me go out of the room. I went through to the hall, and saw Raby coming out of the dining-room. He said he'd been making up the fire, and I said, 'Where's Robert?' " Frank Abbott paused and went on again. The break and the even repetition which followed were curiously mechanical—the needle lifted from a gramophone record and set down again to reproduce a phrase. "I said, 'Where's Robert?' And he said, 'Robert's just stepped out to the post'."

"Robert?" The Inspector's bulk shifted. His large face turned. "Here, what's this? Sounds nonsense to me."

"We met a motor-cyclist a little way back from here as we came in. Remember?"

"What's that got to do with it?"

"Robert's got a motor-bicycle. Did you know?"

"What's that—a motor-bike? Are you sure?"

"Oh, quite. I saw it this morning. He keeps it in one of those sheds round the yard. The Doris girl told me all about it. Robert's grandmother left him a legacy, and he bought an aged Douglas. He's got a girl over at Ledcott, Mary Leeson by name, and he can get over in ten minutes any time. Seems to me we've got to reconsider the question of Robert's alibi. He was having his birthday party at Ledcott on Monday evening, and I'm beginning to wonder if he didn't slip away for half an hour and murder Lucas Dale. Ledcott's only two miles. Give him half an hour, and he and the Douglas could have done it on their heads."

"Letting your imagination run away with you, aren't you, Frank?"

"Perhaps—I don't know. I want to get back and see if that bike has been out, and what Robert's alibi is this time."

"Motive," said Lamb—"what's your imagination got to say about that? Unless you're plain homicidal you've got to have a motive. And what motive would Robert have for murdering Cora de Lisle?"

"None, unless he was the murderer of Lucas Dale—and we don't know what motive he might have for that. But I've never been so sure about anything in all my life as I am that Dale's murderer stood eavesdropping by the study door whilst Lily Green made her statement. He heard that she had seen Cora de Lisle by the open study window just after the shot was fired. We took it to mean that she had murdered Dale, but if that was so, she wouldn't have been murdered herself. She wasn't killed for the balance of the fifty-pound note, because it was there in her handbag. No, she was murdered because Dale's murderer stood at the study door and heard that she had been, or might have been, a witness of his crime. The window was open, the curtain was drawn back, and a moment after the shot was fired Lily saw Cora de Lisle by that open window. Dale's murderer couldn't risk what she might have seen. He got away before we did—say ten minutes start and no regard for the speed limit. He had the luck to find the house empty, and he silenced her. They're wasting their time looking for fingerprints. There won't be any—he's a cunning devil."

"Robert?" said Inspector Lamb in his solid voice.

The mechanical precision deserted Frank Abbott. He said uncertainly,

"I don't know—"

Chapter Thirty-Seven

THEY PICKED UP a young constable in Netherbourne, and sat silent in front whilst he sat silent behind until they reached the house. The yard was dark. Beyond it vague light from blinded windows, and very faintly the rhythmic throb of dance music from the wireless in the servants' hall.

Frank Abbott's torch sent a sharp beam into the dark. He led the way to a shed on the left, flung the door open, and let the beam come to rest upon a motor-bicycle. With Lamb still on the threshold, he swung round.

"Only just off the road—the engine's hot, and look at those tyres."

The Inspector looked, took the torch from his hand, and turned it about. From a nail on the wall depended a motor helmet and goggles. He put down a hand to feel the engine, gave Abbott back his torch, and walked out of the shed.

"We'll need to see Robert," he said. "Now you and me, we'll go along to the front door and ring for Raby. And you, Gill, I'd like you to go in this way. Ring the back door bell and say I'm expecting you. If Robert Stack is there, tell him I want to see him and bring him along to the study. Got that?"

The young constable said, "Yes, sir."

Waiting on the front door step for Raby, neither of the two men spoke. Through the dragging silence came at last the sound of footsteps, a key turning, and the grinding of the bolt. King's Bourne kept its approach well guarded on this side at least. But if the enemy was within the gate—

The door swung in. With Frank Abbott's thought unfinished they passed into the hall.

Lamb said, "Robert in yet?" and at Raby's half surprised, "Oh, yes, sir," he added, "Send him through to the study. I want to see him."

Raby was apologetic.

"I'm afraid the fire's been let down, sir. I didn't understand that you would be coming back."

"It doesn't matter—just leave it. Send Robert along. Here, just a minute—when did he come in?"

"Ten minutes ago, or a quarter of an hour, sir—I couldn't say for certain."

Though the fire had died, the study was still warm. Order and sober beauty sprang into view as the light came on. There was a strong contrast with the room they had left in Ledlington, yet the two rooms were held together by the dreadful link of murder. Frank Abbott went to the fireplace and stood looking down at the sunk ash upon the hearth. A charred log still smouldered. He pushed it with his foot, and a stray spark or two flew up.

The Inspector took his accustomed seat, and almost at once Robert Stack came in—a thin young man with dark eyes and a sallow complexion. He looked nervously about the room, and started slightly as the door was closed behind him by Gill.

Abbott straightened up and walked over to the table. His light eyes scanned the pale face, the thin, rather ungainly figure. How much nerve did you have to have to commit two murders in three days? It occurred to him that Robert did not look as if he would have the nerve to kill a rabbit. But then murderers never did look like murderers. They had the outward shape and aspect of the ordinary man. Only within there lurked the thing which set them apart.

Lamb allowed the silence to become menacing before he said,

"You have been out?"

"Yes, sir."

"When did you go?"

"Round about a quarter to six, sir. Mr. Raby gave me leave."

"And you came in when?"

"Not very long ago, sir."

"How long ago?"

"Matter of ten minutes or a quarter of an hour."

"You went out on your motor-cycle?"

Robert's eyes shifted.

"Oh, no, sir."

Lamb leaned forward, an impending bulk, his red face not good-natured any more but threatening.

"You've had your bicycle out." He used Abbott's words unconsciously. "It's only just off the road—the engine's hot."

Robert looked terrified.

"Oh, no, sir—indeed I never. Indeed, sir, you've got it wrong."

Lamb kept his eyes on the agitated face, but he leaned back in his chair and said,

"All right, go on—tell your own story."

Robert didn't seem to have any story to tell. He twisted his hands and repeated nervously,

"I just stepped out. Mr. Raby gave me leave."

Frank Abbott helped him out.

"Where did you go?"

"Down to the village."

"See anyone?"

"No, sir."

Lamb came in again.

"Why did you go down into the village?"

Robert's pallor became suffused with an ugly flush. His Adam's apple slid up and down as he gulped and said,

"I just stepped out."

Lamb brought the flat of his hand down sharply upon a massive knee.

"Look here, my lad, if you can give an account of yourself you'd better do it. If you can't, well, it'll be the worse for you. You're not bound to incriminate yourself, and I'm bound to tell you that anything you say may be used against you. But if you've got a reasonable explanation to give and you don't give it, well, you'll only have yourself to thank for what you get."

Robert cast a harried glance about him. The ugly colour deepened under the damp skin.

"I don't know what you've got against me. You can ask Mr. Raby—he gave me leave."

"What for?"

"It wasn't for anything as it turned out. They'd gone in shopping to Ledlington."

"Oh, that's your story—you went to see someone. Who was it?"

"It was Mary Leeson."

"Yes? Mary Leeson—who is Mary Leeson?"

"From Ledcott—and she's staying with her aunt Mrs. Pipe, so Mr. Raby gave me leave to step out, but when I got down there the house was all shut up."

"So you took your motor-bike and went off after them—is that it?"

"No, sir, I didn't—I never went near it. I just waited, thinking they'd be home any time."

"Who do you mean by they?"

"Mary and her aunt Mrs. Pipe, sir."

"And how did you know they had gone to Ledlington?"

Robert swallowed desperately.

"Well, sir, they said so. Mary said she'd be going in with her aunt shopping, but they meant to be back for tea, so I waited."

"And when did they come?"

The Adam's apple shot up and down.

"They didn't come, sir. They must have missed the bus, and I dursn't wait any longer, so I come away."

Inspector Lamb heaved himself out of his chair and went to the door. He had a word with Gill and came back.

"All right," he said, "you can go. If I want you again I'll send for you."

He watched him out of the door, slewed round, and said,

"Well—what do you make of that?"

There was no expression at all in Frank Abbott's face as he said,

"Someone had that motor-bike out."

Lamb nodded.

"I wonder whether Mr. Carrick has an alibi this time."

"Carrick?"

"Carrick," said the Inspector.

"But he couldn't have known—it must have been someone in the house. The girl had hardly finished her statement. How could Carrick possibly know that she had heard the shot and seen the de Lisle woman by the study window? He couldn't have known—there isn't any possible way. The girl had only just told her mother."

"And her mother works for Mrs. O'Hara. She works for Mrs. O'Hara, and she was so concerned about Miss Susan Lenox and Mr. Bill Carrick that she made her daughter own up to having seen Miss de Lisle—flat in face of the daughter's jealous young man. Well then, she didn't come up here with Lily, did she? Do you suppose she stayed at home and washed up the tea things? There isn't the woman born that'd stay at home with a bit of news like she'd just got from Lily, and if she didn't come up here with her, it's because she'd got somewhere better to go. I say she took her news over to Mrs. O'Hara. And I say Mr. Carrick had it before we did, and didn't waste the time over it that we did either. Why, he knows the place and everyone in it like the back of his hand. Do you suppose he didn't know that Robert had a motor-bike, and where he kept it? What had he got to do but walk up the garden and ride the bike over to Ledlington and back? There was the helmet and goggles ready to his hand—a disguise you can't beat."

"And what about Lane? He's supposed to be keeping an eye on him."

Lamb frowned.

"That's where I blame myself—Carrick ought to have been under arrest. Lane couldn't be both sides of the house at once. I say there wasn't anything to stop Carrick going up the garden in the dark and taking that bike. There's one thing—he'll think he's been too clever to be suspected. I'll just check up on Mr. Bell and the secretary, and then we'll get going."

There was a sameness, it appeared, about the accounts which Mr. Phipson and Mr. Bell had to give of themselves. Mr. Phipson had been in his room engaged in the peaceful pursuit of reading the *Times* and writing half a dozen letters. He actually had them in his hand stamped for the post as he entered the study. He had been out in the afternoon, but not since tea—"Oh, no, certainly not," though he proposed walking down to the village with his letters so as to get a breath of air before dinner. Secretarial work though of great interest induced, he feared, somewhat sedentary habits. If the Inspector did not require his presence, he really would appreciate the opportunity of getting a little fresh air. . . . The Inspector preferred that no one should leave the house for the moment? "Oh, certainly, certainly. My letters are not really of great importance—they can very well wait."

So much for Mr. Phipson.

Mr. Vincent Bell, with a lamentable lack of originality, had once more been having a bath.

Lamb's eyebrows went up. Abbott restrained a smile. He said, "Quite a lot of people do, you know, before dinner."

"Seems a funny time to me," said Lamb.

Vincent Bell laughed.

"Well, you see, I'm a very methodical man, and I've got my habits. I go out walking round about six o'clock, and then I come in and have a bath and a change. Some folk don't like walking in the dark, but I do, so there it is. I missed my walk on Monday because I was talking to Dale, but every other night I've been here I've gone out and walked, and come back and taken a bath. You can ask Raby—he can tell you he's heard the noise those pipes make."

Inspector Lamb looked glum. Vincent Bell laughed again.

"I haven't got any alibi. But say, Captain, why do I have to have one? Monday night Dale was getting himself bumped off. Naturally, you want to know what everyone in the house was doing. That's O.K., but what's all this getting busy over when I went for a walk, or whether I had a bath tonight? Dale's dead, isn't he? Do I have to have someone around to give me an alibi every place I go? What's the big idea?"

"Do you ride a motor-bicycle, Mr. Bell?"

Vincent's eyes sharpened.

"Not if I can get an automobile," he said.

"Did you ride one tonight?"

The sharp gaze became a wary one?

"I told you I went walking."

"Where did you go? Did you meet anyone?"

"Now let me see—I went down the drive and turned to the left, and up a hill, and around and about. And I didn't what you'd call meet anyone. There was a car or two, and a petting party going on by a field gate, but they wouldn't be taking any interest in me."

"You didn't ride a motor-bicycle into Ledlington and pay a call on Miss Cora de Lisle?"

Vincent Bell whistled.

"That dame! What would I be wanting to pay a call on her for?"

"I don't know. Did you know her?"

"No, I didn't. I saw her go away the morning she came here to see Dale. He talked about her afterwards—said she was poison and he was well quit of her—said she'd do him a mischief if she could, but he'd see to it she didn't."

"You ought to have told us all that before," said Lamb quickly.

Vincent said, "Oh, well—" and then, "It was just Dale's way of talking. I don't suppose she'd a thing to do with it—looked kind of down and out to me. And that's where Dale was foolish. He'd money to burn—why couldn't he pay her alimony and keep her quiet? He didn't give her a cent—of course she was sore." As he talked, his eyes went from Lamb to Abbott.

Frank Abbott said,

"Did you see her tonight?"

"I never saw her at all but the once she was over here."

"You didn't go into Ledlington this evening?"

"No, I didn't. And I'm asking you again what's all this about?" He pushed back his chair and got up, his eyes bright and intent.

"Ledlington—and a motor-bicycle—and Cora de Lisle—and an alibi—what's it all about? Looks to me as if something had happened to Cora de Lisle. Is that what you're getting at?"

Inspector Lamb said sharply, "What makes you think that, Mr. Bell?"

"Wouldn't anyone think of it, Captain?"

Lamb looked at him hard and said, "Cora de Lisle probably saw Dale shot. Somebody knocked her on the head round about half past six this evening in Ledlington."

"And you think it might have been me?"

"It was someone who was afraid she might be going to give him away," said Inspector Lamb.

Chapter Thirty-Eight

SOME TIME LATER Vincent Bell came into the inner hall. Mr. Montague Phipson was setting his watch by the grandfather clock. He turned about and came to meet him.

"This is a very strange affair," he said with a mixture of nervousness and formality in his manner. An onlooker might have thought that, much as Mr. Phipson disliked his present company, he yet considered it in the circumstances to be better than no company at all. "Perhaps if I might have a word with you—" He opened the drawing-room door as he spoke and put on all the lights.

The candles in their gilt sconces lit up the old-ivory panelling, the polished floor, the dim lovely colours of the Persian rugs, the graceful Adam mantelpiece, and the long, straight folds of blue which curtained the four tall windows.

Mr. Phipson shut the door and came into the middle of the room. He thought it had a dead feeling. It was warm because of the central heating installed by Lucas Dale, but no fire had been lighted here for the past two days, and the air felt dead. He cleared his throat, straightened his pince-nez, and repeated the words which he had used in the hall.

"This is a very strange affair. I really cannot make it out. Why should the Inspector ask us all these questions? I have been in my room all the evening, but why does he want to know where I have been? It seems to me extremely intrusive. Are we to account for every moment of our time?"

Vincent surveyed him with a twinkle in his eye.

"Well, that's how I put it to him myself."

"And what did he say to that? Did he tell you why they were asking all these questions? I am sure I am most willing to assist the police in the execution of their duties, but I think we are entitled to an explanation."

"Oh, there's an explanation all right," said Vincent Bell rather soberly. "There's been another murder—that's what."

"Another murder!" Mr. Phipson's voice was shrill with horror.

"Cora de Lisle," said Vincent Bell.

Mr. Phipson had to retrieve his glasses. They slipped from his nose and hung dangling. He put them on crooked, and said in a shaking voice,

"Miss de Lisle?"

"Knocked on the head in Ledlington at half past six this evening— that's what the Inspector says. And that's why they want to know what you and I were doing between six and seven, Sonny boy."

Mr. Phipson disregarded the insult.

"Murder!" he said. "But why? Why should anyone have murdered her?"

He got a shrewd glance.

"Old Lamb seems to think she knew more than was good for her—seems to think she knew who bumped Dale off. Say, did he ask you if you rode a motor-bicycle? Because that's what he asked me—seemed to think the guy who bumped her off took a ride to Ledlington on a motor-bicycle."

Mr. Phipson's face expressed horror.

"No—oh, no—he didn't ask me that."

"And do you ride a motor-bicycle?" said Vincent Bell. It didn't seem likely, but it amused him to see the little man wince and wriggle.

"No—oh, no—oh, certainly not."

"Then you're in luck."

Mr. Phipson dropped his glasses again. He did not put them on immediately, but let them dangle while he blinked at Vincent with his near-sighted eyes.

"Oh, dear me—what a terrible thing! Do you mean to say that the unfortunate woman has actually been murdered?"

"That seems to be the idea, Sonny boy."

"Don't call me that!"

Vincent Bell dropped his tone of badinage.

"Quit acting like it then. The woman's been killed, and they want to know who killed her. There's something behind this motor-bicycle stuff. Who's got one here?"

Mr. Phipson took out a silk pocket-handkerchief and began to polish his glasses.

"Robert—" he said in a meditative tone. "He keeps it in the yard."

"I suppose old Lamb is wise to that? I shouldn't pick Robert for a killer myself."

Mr. Phipson replaced his pince-nez and answered the first part of this remark.

"I don't know—it might be one's duty—" He moved a little nearer the door. "Oh, dear me—how very upsetting! My window looks out upon the yard. I'm really very much afraid that it may be my duty to let the police know that I heard the motor-bicycle go out—now, let me see, when would it have been? I had just finished drafting an advertisement for the *Times*—I have, naturally, to seek re-employment—and I think—yes, I am sure it was about six o'clock. Did you hear anything?"

"No—I was out at six." Vincent spoke carelessly and without thought. It was not until he noticed a most peculiar expression on Mr. Phipson's face that he realized the possible implications of what he had just said.

"Oh, dear me," said Montague Phipson—"you went out at six. How very unfortunate—for you—and perhaps for Miss de Lisle."

Vincent glared.

"What do you mean by that? If it's your idea of a wisecrack, you'll be doing it once too often!"

Mr. Phipson reached the door and stood ready to open it.

"You had better be careful. If you threaten me, I shall not hesitate to call for help, and it will then be my clear duty to inform the police that not only did I hear that motor-bicycle start up just after six o'clock, but that I went and looked out of my window, and to the best of my belief it was not Robert who was taking it out. The yard was dark of course, but I have very good night sight— short-sighted people not uncommonly have—and I am prepared to swear that the rider was a smaller man than Robert. You," said Mr. Phipson gently, "are a smaller man than Robert."

Vincent Bell said something vigorously unprintable. Then he was controlled again.

"What sort of fool story is this?" he inquired in a hard voice of rage.

Mr. Phipson clutched the door handle. At the slightest threat of violence he would turn it and call for help. He said so between chattering teeth.

"If you attack me, I shall feel no further hesitation."

"So you're hesitating, are you?"

"In certain circumstances," said Mr. Phipson cautiously, "I might feel that it was not my business."

"Meaning?"

"I think I must leave that to you."

Vincent Bell made a movement which was almost immediately checked. He might be tempted, but he did not mean to fall. It would hardly help to clear him if he were found wringing this little rat's neck. He plunged his hands deep in his pockets and said,

"Blackmail?"

"Oh, I wouldn't call it that," said Mr. Phipson mildly.

"The police would."

"But they won't have the chance. It would be most unfortunate for you if they did, because it would be only your word against mine, and I should still have heard and seen that motor-bicycle."

Vincent Bell stood quite still and looked him over.

"Poison—aren't you? With all this bumping off going on, it's a plain pity nobody thought about you."

"I shall call for help," said Mr. Phipson hurriedly.

"You needn't bother. How much do you want?"

Mr. Phipson heaved a sigh of relief. Violence was always so regrettable, and there had already been far too much of it.

"Well, you have to consider that I may be out of a job for some time. When you used an extremely regrettable word just now, I think you perhaps failed to take into consideration the fact that compensation is not unusual where prospects have been impaired or forfeited."

"So I killed Dale, and I'm to compensate you for the loss of your job. Is that it?"

"You might put it that way. It would, of course, be perfectly clear to the police that the person who killed Miss de Lisle would be the person who shot Mr. Dale. I think reasonable compensation for my loss of employment is—er—not unreasonable."

"And what do you call reasonable compensation?"

"A thousand pounds," said Mr. Phipson with a slight tremor in his voice.

Chapter Thirty-Nine

INSPECTOR LAMB had been quite right about Mrs. Green. Torn between a desire to accompany Lily to King's Bourne and an urge to be the first to convey such exciting news to the Little House, she decided after a brief struggle upon the latter course. At King's Bourne she would have had to play second fiddle to Lily—she might not even have been admitted to the study whilst Lily made her statement— but at the Little House she would have the field all to herself. She had carried many pieces of news in her time, but never anything so exciting as this. She put on her Sunday hat and coat, and after a heartening contest with William Cole, who had arrived to find Lily gone and was consequently in the worst of tempers, she slammed and locked her front door and stepped across the village street.

The Little House was only a couple of hundred yards away, yet Mrs. Green arrived there quite out of breath with excitement and hurry. Susan, opening the door to her knock, wondered what could possibly have happened. Then, with a sickening leap of the heart, she began to be afraid.

"Oh, Mrs. Green, what is it?"

"Miss Susan my dear, I had to come and tell you."

Susan caught at the newel-post of the stair.

"Bill?" she said with lips that barely moved.

"Now, my dear, don't you take on. I wouldn't have hurried myself like I have if I'd been bringing you bad news—stands to reason I wouldn't."

Susan shut her eyes for a moment.

"It isn't bad news?"

Mrs. Green fanned herself with a clean pocket-handkerchief.

"Stands to reason it wouldn't be. You wouldn't think so little of me as that! If I run myself out of breath, which I have and no mistake, it's on account of what you said to me this morning. 'Let me know', you said, 'if so be you hear anything'. And first minute I got Lily off and had a word with William Cole that come in behaving himself as if he was Hitler—that directly minute I put on my hat and run over."

Susan opened the dining-room door.

"Better come in here."

For the moment her relief was beyond words—just that immediate relief which does not look ahead. Then it changed to suspense. But there was no way of hurrying Mrs. Green. She would take her time and tell her tale in her own way.

The dining-room table was strewn with large sheets of drawing-paper. Bill Carrick, with a pencil in his hand and a determined frown upon his brow, was concentrating upon the possible plumbing problems of Mr. Gilbert Garnish. When he lifted his head and beheld Mrs. Green the frown deepened involuntarily.

Susan put a hand on his shoulder.

"Bill, Mrs. Green has come to tell us something—good news—you did say good news, didn't you?" Her voice implored Mrs. Green—or fate—to let the news be good.

Mrs. Green regarded them with benevolence. She was not offended by the frown, because men were all alike the way they looked at you if you interrupted them when they were doing anything. You'd think they hated the very sight of you if you didn't know better. She took the chair which Susan had pulled out for her, loosened her coat at the neck, and told them what Lily had seen on Monday evening.

"Oh, Mrs. Green!" Susan took hold of one of her hands and squeezed it.

Bill Carrick had turned pale. Gilbert Garnish's drains dazzled before his eyes. He pushed the sheets away.

"Lily is sure she saw Miss de Lisle—she couldn't be making a mistake?"

Mrs. Green turned a glowing face upon him.

"Now would I be coming here to tell you if she wasn't sure?"

"I don't know," said Bill. "That's the point—is she sure?"

"Certain sure. Lily isn't one to say she seen anyone if she didn't. A truthfuller girl doesn't live though I say it. The best eyes in the village too—and I don't mean for looks only. No, Mr. Bill, if Lily said she seen her, then she seen her and there's no getting from it. William Cole, he tried hard enough to stop her letting on, but I had it out of her, and I had it out with him when he come round just now. He needn't think he can come it over me like he does over her. 'No,' I said, 'Lily's not here, William', I said, 'and if you want to know where she is, she's gone back up to King's Bourne to tell the police what she did ought to have told them Monday night, and what she would have told them if so be as you hadn't carried on like you hadn't got any right to. Look at the talk and trouble you've brought on Mr. Bill and Miss Susan making Lily hold her tongue like that. You did ought to be ashamed of yourself', I said. Well, he flared up properly, I can tell you. Jealous, that's what he is. Said all Lily wanted was to get her picture in the papers, and to put herself forward to be took notice of by the London police. And I said to him, 'William Cole, you're just plain jealous, and a jealous husband's like having a stone in your shoe, it don't get any better as you go along, and if I've any say, you won't never be any husband of Lily's,' I said. And with that he said something he shouldn't and banged the door and off down the street on his bicycle."

Bill pushed back his chair and got up. Mrs. Green would go on like this till all was blue, and he couldn't stand any more of it. Was this story of Lily's going to make any difference, or wasn't it? Was it dawn after nightmare, or was it only a spark of hope which might peter out and leave them in the dark again?

He stood by Susan for a moment and pulled her round to face him. He was frightfully pale.

"I'm going out—I've got to think. I'll try and give Lane the slip. Don't build *too* much, Susan."

For a moment Mrs. Green might not have been there. Susan looked at him and said with quivering lips,

"I must have *something*."

He put his cheek against hers. The grip of his hands hurt her. Then he straightened up, let go of her, and went out through the kitchen.

Mrs. Green dabbed her eyes.

"Don't you take on, my dear," she said. "A nice walk'll do him all the good in the world. I could see how he was when I come in. I've often thought it funny about men. When a woman's upset in her mind what she wants is a lay down on her bed or a nice cup of tea, but men's all the same, they want to get outside—can't stay in the house, and don't want to be fussed round. Walk miles they will, where a woman'll set down and cry. Of course if they're the drinking sort they'll be down to the Magpie. But that's not Mr. Bill's way. He isn't the drinking kind, and you've got to be thankful for that." She dabbed her eyes and said in a choked voice, "Lily's father was. And that's why I take on about Lily. If you've had a bad husband yourself you know what it means. And I don't say William drinks, for he don't, but an overmastering, dictating, domineering king of the castle he is, and there's no getting from it. And that don't make for a happy life whether you take it lying down same as Lily does, or standing up and giving him back as good as you get, which 'ud be my way."

Susan was to look back afterwards and think how strange it was that with Bill's life, and her life, and all their happiness in the balance, she and Mrs. Green should have sat there for the best part of an hour by the clock talking about William Cole, and Lily's chances of happiness as his wife.

Chapter Forty

UP AT KING'S BOURNE Inspector Lamb continued his interrogation of the household. Mrs. Raby, Esther the other housemaid, and Doris the between-maid, had each assured him that they had neither seen Robert go out nor heard his motor-bicycle—"but then of course we wouldn't—we had the wireless on."

Old Lamb lost his temper. His red face turned plum-coloured and he brought his fist down with a bang upon Lucas Dale's blotting-pad.

"Don't anyone in this house ever stop playing gramophone records, or having baths, or listening to the wireless?"

"Oh, yes, sir." That was Doris, with a sniff. But Esther Coleworthy, small, dark-eyed, and uppish, flickered her eyelashes and said with a toss of the head, "Oh, well—once in a while—when there's something better to do." Mrs. Raby, stout and shapeless, opined in a good-natured voice that a bit of music kept things going and didn't do no harm to nobody.

Lamb dismissed them curtly.

"Well, that brings us back to Raby, who told Robert he could go out about six o'clock."

Frank Abbott nodded.

"It was just on six when I came out of the study and Raby told me he'd let Robert go."

"And that's all we've got. Raby no more than anyone else heard the motor-bicycle. They were all listening to that infernal wireless, and when Robert came in about seven I suppose it was still going on, and the water-pipes drumming into the bargain. Seems to me they could have a machine-gun going in this house and nobody'd hear it. Not that I think it was Robert. It might have been, but I don't think it was. After all, you've got to have a motive, and where's anything that begins to look like a motive for Robert?"

"You never can tell."

"No, but you can make a pretty good guess and see what comes of it. Take Carrick—he's got an overwhelming motive. He's overheard threatening to do what I believe he did do, and by his own admission and that of Miss Lenox he was on the spot when the shot was fired, or as near as makes no difference. As to this second business, if he hasn't got a cast-iron alibi, I'll say what I said before, it's ten thousand pounds to a halfpenny he knew Robert had a motor-bicycle and where he kept it, and with all those women sitting with their heads in a loudspeaker there was nothing to stop him running the bike out, and running it over to Ledlington, and running it back again. So you'll just step down to the Little House and ask Lane what comings and goings there've been. And then you will tell Mr. Carrick I'd like a word with him, but you needn't tell him why."

Frank Abbott strolled down the garden. Just across the village street from the Little House he came upon Constable Lane in an apologetic frame of mind.

"Come down the hill not five minutes ago, Mr. Bill did, and clapped me on the shoulder. 'I'm one up on you, Lane,' he says. 'We've had some nice outings, but I've a fancy for my own company tonight', he says. Then he laughs and off into the house, and I give you my word I didn't know he was out."

"Mrs. Green been here?"

"An hour and a bit over—only just gone."

Frank Abbott gave his Inspector marks. If Mrs. Green had been here for an hour, then the Little House knew as much as Lily did. He went across the road and used the knocker.

The talk in the drawing-room broke suddenly at the sound. They were all there—Mrs. O'Hara on her sofa, Bill and Susan standing together in front of the fire. Cathy in a low chair, leaning forward with her chin in her hand, eyes wide and lips parted. Susan had just finished repeating Mrs. Green's account of what Lily had seen.

"But that means—oh, Susan, if Lily really saw Miss de Lisle there—" Cathy's voice shook and trailed away.

"It might mean she shot him, or—" Susan hesitated—"or it might mean that she saw who shot him. I should think they would arrest her. Anyhow they're bound to find her—to find out what she knows."

Cathy's eyelids fell. Her lips moved stiffly.

"Arrest her?" she said.

Mrs. O'Hara gave a little cough.

"The thought of an innocent person being arrested is naturally disturbing, but nothing of that sort will happen, my dear."

Cathy looked up with a startled expression, and it was at this moment that the knocking came upon the door. Before anyone else could move she ran out of the room. Through the half open door they heard Frank Abbott's voice. A cold breath from the outer air blew in. Mrs. O'Hara pulled her shawl about her, and Bill put his arm round Susan for a moment and held her close. Then he turned with a jerk and went out into the hall, and she after him. There was a low, brief interchange of words, and the sound of the front door falling to.

Mrs. O'Hara shivered slightly. She pushed the rug off her feet. As Cathy came back into the room, she was putting her knitting away.

"Mummy—oh, Mummy!"

"Darling, what is it? You look very much upset. Have they really arrested that Miss de Lisle?"

"I don't know—I don't think so. I think something dreadful has happened. He—he looked like that."

"Darling, who?"

"That Mr. Abbott. He wanted to know where Bill had been since six o'clock and—and—why should he want to know that?"

"I can't imagine," said Mrs. O'Hara.

Cathy came quite close and stared at her.

"I know it's something dreadful. He's taken Bill up to King's Bourne, and Susan's gone too. I think they're going to arrest Bill."

"Oh, no, my dear, they won't do that."

Cathy put out her hands, and drew them back again without touching her mother.

"They will unless you stop them. Perhaps they'll arrest Miss de Lisle. Oh, Mummy, you can't let them do that—you can't let them arrest anyone!"

Mrs. O'Hara sat up and put her feet down.

"Darling, why not?"

"I saw you," said Cathy in a breaking voice.

"Dear me!"

"You came along to my room and looked at me, but I didn't open my eyes—I didn't feel as if I could talk to anyone. And then you went into Susan's room, and you put on the light there. Both the doors were open, and I could see right through. I saw you take her shoes and put them on." She paused and said with a sob, "Susan thinks it was me—and I let her—I didn't tell. There was a footprint inside the study—you must have stepped in the clay—and I let Susan think it was me—she thinks I wore those shoes."

"They were most uncomfortable," said Mrs. O'Hara. "So much too large. But I thought I should feel the damp in my house shoes—all mine are so thin. Of course yours would be a much better fit, darling, but I didn't want to disturb you."

Cathy gave a dry sob.

"I saw you pick up Susan's handkerchief from the dressing-table and tuck it into your sleeve."

"I am always dropping handkerchiefs," said Mrs. O'Hara—"and the interview might have been a very emotional one."

"What interview?"

"Darling, I thought you would guess. I was going to tell Mr. Dale that I couldn't possibly dream of letting Susan marry him. She was obviously very unhappy about it, and I was going to tell him so."

Cathy stood still and trembled.

"And did you?"

"No, darling," said Mrs. O'Hara in a practical voice. "I didn't get the chance."

"Mummy!"

Mrs. O'Hara removed her shawl and patted her hair.

"I think, darling, if you will get me my fur coat and those shoes of Susan's, I had better just go up to King's Bourne and talk to the Inspector. I felt no ill effects at all the other night. And I don't think I need trouble about a hat—this light shawl will do very well to put over my head. But I should like my gloves—the loose washing ones I took the other night will do. They are in my left-hand drawer."

Chapter Forty-One

MRS. O'HARA seemed quite to enjoy the walk, up hill though it was.

"I used to be very fond of walking when I was a girl, but of course it is many years now since I have done anything in that way—just down to church and back in summer. James was always so particular about not taking the car out on Sundays. But I don't know when I was out walking after dark until the other night, and really, darling, I had forgotten it was so pleasant. Quite a mild air if a little damp, but I had on my fur coat, and it doesn't seem to have done me any harm—in fact I really feel all the better for it."

Cathy listened in a sort of horrified astonishment. She said, "Oh, Mummy!" in a choked, protesting voice.

"Well," said Mrs. O'Hara equably, "one just goes on doing the same things every day because there isn't anything else to do, and when anything really happens, even if it's something dreadful, one can't help feeling as if it made a break, if you know what I mean."

They came out of the little orchard, skirted the tennis court, and after crossing the lower terrace came up the left-hand steps.

"This is the way I came up on Monday," said Mrs. O'Hara. "But when I was coming away I went down by the farther steps, because I thought I heard someone coming up this way, and I think from what I have heard since that it must have been Susan. I didn't want to meet anyone just then of course, so I went the other way. I see there is a light in the study, darling, so we will just knock on the glass door and go in that way."

At the sound of that knocking Inspector Lamb stopped short in the middle of a sentence. It was the sentence with which a police officer is bound to caution the person whom he is arresting. The hand he had stretched out fell from Bill Carrick's shoulder. He said in a tone of sharp annoyance,

"What's that?"

It was as if the knocking had broken something. Not a silence, for there had been no silence to break—the Inspector had been speaking. But something did break—the tension which held Bill with his shoulders squared facing arrest, which fixed Susan where she stood, one hand at her throat, the other leaning upon the writing-table, her eyes on Bill as if she was looking her last at him and could not look away.

Frank Abbott could not look away either. But it was Susan Lenox at whom he was looking—Susan with all the colour and beauty drained from her face and nothing left but pain. For a moment the pain was his own. Then the knocking fell and the tension broke. The Inspector spoke his sharp "What's that?" Susan's breast lifted with a long breath, and as Abbott went to open the door he was aware that she and Bill were moving, drawing together, and turning to see who was coming in.

Mrs. O'Hara came in in her fur coat with a small fleecy shawl over her head and Cathy behind her, a little exhausted ghost, bare-headed, her fine colourless hair all blown about. In spite of Susan's shoes, which were a size too large for her, Milly O'Hara moved with grace. She brought a social manner with her. As she came up to the writing-table, it became impossible to forget that the house, this very room, had been the heritage of her family for many generations. By the far door hung the portrait, a doubtful Lely, of the Millicent Bourne who had been one of Catherine of Braganza's maids of honour. From over the mantelpiece she herself looked down from Lazlo's canvas, young and lovely, with Laura at her side. She looked up at the picture for a moment, because she could never come into this room without that silent greeting for Laura. Then, as her eyes dropped, she seemed to become aware of something strange. She had been speaking, but no one else had spoken, until now as she moved towards a chair the Inspector said in a harsher tone than was usual with him,

"Mrs. O'Hara, I must ask you to leave us." He turned to Cathy. "Please take your mother away."

A look of gentle surprise crossed Milly O'Hara's face. Having reached the chair, she seated herself, removed the shawl from her head, opened her fur coat, unwound a long grey chiffon scarf from about her neck, and said,

"But, Inspector, I have something to say. I have come here on purpose to say it."

"You had really better go, Aunt Milly," said Bill.

He and Susan were standing together now, and Susan's hands were locked about his arm. Really Susan looked very pale—very pale indeed. Mrs. O'Hara shook her head slightly at Bill and turned graciously to the Inspector.

"I must apologize for interrupting you, but I really have something to say. Perhaps before we go any further you will tell me whether it is true that you are thinking of arresting someone."

"Perfectly true," said Inspector Lamb rather grimly.

"Then if that is the case, I am afraid I have no choice, because of course I couldn't let you arrest an innocent person, whether it was Miss de Lisle or anyone else, much as I dislike the idea of the publicity involved—and really the press seem to me to go into the most unnecessary details nowadays, though of course it is all quite interesting if you can look at it from the standpoint of an outsider, which in this case I most unfortunately cannot do."

Cathy said "Mummy!" in an agonized voice. She went down on her knees by the chair.

Mrs. O'Hara put out a hand and patted her.

"Now, darling, you mustn't upset yourself. You wouldn't want any innocent person to get into trouble, would you? And I am sure the Inspector will do all he can to keep your name out of it." She smiled faintly at Lamb, who had turned a really alarming colour. He put a finger inside his collar as if to loosen it, replied to the smile with a portentous frown, and said with as much restraint as he could manage,

"What are you talking about, madam?"

Mrs. O'Hara's eyes opened widely. She said in a tone of surprise,

"But, Inspector—I was talking about Mr. Dale—I thought we all were."

He said firmly, "If you know anything about the murder of Mr. Dale, madam, I must ask you to say so plainly, and if you do not, I must ask you to leave us."

"But, Inspector—"

"Mrs. O'Hara, do you, or do you not know anything about this murder?"

This time he got his plain answer. With her hands lightly folded in her lap and in a gently practical tone she replied,

"Of course I do—I was there."

There was a moment of profound silence. Probably no one breathed. Looking round with a kind of pleased surprise, Mrs. O'Hara encountered the apoplectic stare of Inspector Lamb, Frank Abbott's fixed pale gaze, Bill's frozen incredulity, Susan's horror, and the clouded anguish in Cathy's eyes. Incredibly, she appeared gratified by the effect she had produced. She nodded slightly and said in a conversational tone,

"Perhaps I had better explain."

Frank Abbott alone found voice.

"It might be a good plan," he said, and heard his Inspector snort.

Mrs. O'Hara smiled upon him. He really had quite a look of the Francis Abbott with whom she had danced through that brief season before the war. She must remember to ask him if he was a relation. The smile was a gracious one. She said,

"The only reason I didn't speak of it before was because of Cathy. So disagreeable for a young girl to have her name in the papers—though I must say a good many of them don't seem to mind that nowadays."

The Inspector broke in rather loudly.

"You say you were present when Mr. Dale was shot?"

"Oh, yes."

"And you wish to make a statement?"

"I am quite willing to do so. You see, I couldn't let an innocent person—"

"Quite so. Abbott!"

Addressed in this peremptory voice, Frank Abbott produced notebook and fountain pen. Mrs. O'Hara watched him with interest.

"I suppose I had better begin from the beginning?"

"If you will."

She settled herself comfortably and smiled at Susan, then began.

"Of course, Inspector, you will understand that I don't want what I am saying to get into the papers. Family matters—well, perhaps you have a family yourself. But so much has been in the papers already that perhaps it doesn't matter, and I must just rely on you to do what you can. You see, when my niece told me that she had broken off her engagement to Mr. Carrick and was going to marry Mr. Dale, I saw at once that it wouldn't do at all. She didn't even pretend to be happy, and I could see that it would never do. I made up my mind that I must have a talk with Mr. Dale and tell him so, and as there is no time like the present, I thought I would just walk up through the garden. It was a very mild evening—"

"What evening are you referring to?"

"Oh, Monday—the day Mr. Dale was shot. That is what I am telling you about. I just went in to see if Cathy was asleep, and I thought she was. And then I went into Susan's room, which is just opposite, to get some shoes because all mine are so thin. And it seems Cathy wasn't asleep, because she saw me."

Susan leaned forward.

"*You* took the shoes, Aunt Milly—*you?*"

"Oh, yes, my dear."

Susan began to tremble.

"Did you take one of my handkerchiefs too?"

"I believe I did—Cathy says so. But I couldn't find it afterwards, so I am afraid I must have dropped it."

Susan leaned back hard against Bill's arm.

"Fibs picked it up. He's been trying to blackmail me. He picked it up by Mr. Dale's body."

"What's this?" said Lamb. "Who's Fibs?"

Susan said, "Mr. Phipson."

"A very rude nickname," said Mrs. O'Hara reprovingly. "But blackmail—oh, he really shouldn't have done that!"

In a firm official voice Inspector Lamb said,

"Will you kindly proceed with your statement, madam."

Mrs. O'Hara appeared to be slightly taken aback. She said,

"Yes, yes—oh, certainly. But I am afraid that just for the moment I am not quite sure.... Susan dear, where had I got to?"

Lamb answered before Susan could.

"You had taken a pair of shoes and a handkerchief belonging to Miss Lenox, and you were intending to walk up the garden and have a conversation with Mr. Dale upon the subject of his marriage to your niece. I shall be glad if you will proceed."

"Yes, yes—of course—how stupid of me!" said Mrs. O'Hara with her faint gracious smile. "Cathy darling, I think it would be much better if you would have a chair and lean back. You know kneeling is apt to make you faint. Oh, thank you so much, Mr. Abbott. And now—let me see.... Oh, yes, I put on Susan's shoes—terribly loose of course, but I managed quite well—I have them on now as you may have noticed. And then I put on my fur coat, and this cloud over my hair—my mother used to tell me they called them fascinators when she was a girl—and I came out through the French window in the drawing-room, because of course I didn't want Susan or Bill to hear me."

"Did you know where they were?"

"Well, I knew they would be in the dining-room or the kitchen, and of course I didn't want them to know that I was going to see Mr. Dale."

"Go on, madam."

"Well, I managed quite nicely. Really it felt quite like old times walking up through the garden, and when I came to the terrace and saw that there was a light in the study—"

"How did you see it?"

"Well, I came up the steps at this corner, and looking along the side of the house, I could see that one of the windows in the bay was open and the curtain drawn back, so I knew that Mr. Dale must be there. I thought, why go round to the front door when he can let me in quite nicely and privately and we can have our talk without anyone knowing. There is such a terrible amount of gossip in a village, and I thought how much better it would be if no one were to know that I had come to see Mr. Dale."

Frank Abbott's head was bent over his notes. The light struck down upon his pale, sleek hair. Every other pair of eyes in the room was bent on Mrs. O'Hara's face, which retained its habitual expression though warmed by an unusual flush. She continued without hurry or confusion.

"I intended to knock upon the glass door, but when I got there I found that it was ajar. As you can see, it opens outwards. I pulled it towards me, and was just going to draw the curtain back, when I heard voices and realized that Mr. Dale was not alone." Mrs. O'Hara paused and looked from one to another. "I stood just where I was for a moment. Of course I had no idea that I might be overhearing a private conversation. I just felt that it was a little awkward, and I wanted a moment to make up my mind what I had better do next. I do hope, Inspector, that you won't think that I had any idea of eavesdropping—such an unpleasant thing—"

"What did you hear?" said the Inspector.

Mrs. O'Hara's flush deepened. It was very becoming.

"This is what I should so much have preferred not to repeat," she said. "And I do hope, Inspector, that it will not be necessary for the press—"

"What did you *hear*, madam?"

Mrs. O'Hara resigned herself with a sigh.

"I heard my daughter's name. Nothing else would have made me go on listening, but when you hear something like that about your own daughter—"

The Inspector jerked a handkerchief from his sleeve and passed it over an empurpled brow.

"Will you kindly state what you heard!"

Mrs. O'Hara looked at him with a faint surprise.

"Oh, yes. But I want you to understand what a shock it was. I really could hardly believe my ears, but he spoke so very distinctly—"

"Who spoke?" said the Inspector.

There was a hush in the room. Frank Abbott raised his head.

"Mr. Phipson."

The name fell into the hush and broke it. The Inspector made a quick movement.

"What did he say?"

Mrs. O'Hara gave a little cough.

"I really *couldn't* believe my ears—"

"What did he *say*?"

"He said—and, as I was telling you, I found it difficult to believe my own ears, only he spoke so very distinctly, though not in a very loud voice—"

"Mrs. O'Hara—*what did he say?*"

"He said, 'I saw you put the pearls into Cathy's bag'."

Chapter Forty-Two

EVERYONE EXCEPT FRANK ABBOTT made some sound or movement. Lamb said, *"What!"* Cathy drew in her breath in a sob. Bill Carrick said something short and sharp. Susan made no audible sound. A shudder swept her from head to foot. Frank Abbott's eyes were upon her. He looked, and looked away. Then he wrote down what Mrs. O'Hara had said.

To everyone's surprise Cathy spoke. She turned her eyes upon Inspector Lamb and spoke to him with the simplicity and earnestness of a child.

"That was how he got Susan to say she would marry him. He had the pearls out to show to the Veres and the Micklehams, and I had to put them away in the safe. Afterwards he said that some of them were gone. He sent for Susan and made her look in my bag, and the pearls were there. He said if Susan would marry him, he wouldn't prosecute. But I wouldn't have let her do it—I really wouldn't. I was ill—but I wouldn't have let her marry him."

Old Lamb looked at her kindly. When he was not angry his voice could be soft. He said,

"That's all right, Miss O'Hara—I'm sure you wouldn't. And now I'd like your mother to go on."

Mrs. O'Hara murmured "Cathy darling!" and proceeded.

"You can imagine what I felt like. I really couldn't go away after that. But of course I didn't want to stand in a draught, so I stepped inside and pulled the door to behind me—there is just room behind the curtain. Do you want me to tell you just what they said?"

"Yes, please. Who else was there?"

"Oh, Mr. Dale. And he said, 'What are you talking about?' And Mr. Phipson said, 'You know very well what I am talking about. You put those pearls in Cathy's bag on Saturday morning. She left the bag on a chair, and you put them in while she was over there at her table with her back to you.' Mr. Dale said, 'And where were you?' Mr. Phipson said the far door was ajar. Mr. Dale said, 'Eavesdropping, Monty?' and Mr. Phipson said there wasn't anything to hear, but he'd seen what he had seen, and perhaps Miss Susan Lenox would be interested. That was when Mr. Dale really got angry. He used the most dreadful language, and I hope you won't expect me to repeat it, for I don't think I could—such very odd words—it really didn't sound at all nice."

"I'm sure it didn't," said the Inspector heartily. "Will you please go on?"

Mrs. O'Hara went on.

"I felt very awkward indeed. It was most unpleasant. Mr. Dale said, 'You little rat! Do you think you can blackmail me? I could have smashed you any time this year.' I looked between the curtains—there was just a little space, you know—and Mr. Dale was in his chair and Mr. Phipson standing at the end of the writing-table on Mr. Dale's right between him and the fire. Mr. Dale looked frightfully angry, and Mr. Phipson was shaking. Mr. Dale took some papers out of a drawer and banged them down in front of him and said, 'It's all here. Did you think you could steal from me without my finding you out? Robson's contract'—I think it was Robson he said—'you made two hundred out of that. And a hundred from Mather. And how much did you sell me for to Levinsky over the last consignment for Spain? If you've forgotten, you'll find it all here. You've been selling me and double-crossing me for years, and now I'm going to smash you!' He got up whilst he was speaking and went over to the fire. I thought he was going to ring the bell, and Mr. Phipson thought so too. He called out to Mr. Dale to wait, and he put his hand down and took something out of one of the drawers. It was that drawer on your right, Inspector—the second one from the top. I didn't see which one it was at the time, but I did afterwards, because the drawer was open. And I didn't see what he took out, but of course it was the pistol. And of course Mr. Dale didn't see anything, because he had his back to him."

"Go on, Mrs. O'Hara."

"Mr. Dale turned round and came back again. I don't think now that he really meant to ring the bell—I think he just meant to frighten Mr. Phipson. Well, he came back and sat down in his chair again, just where you are sitting, Inspector. Mr. Phipson had come round to this side of the table, because when Mr. Dale turned he had backed away from him as if he was afraid. Mr. Dale was sitting at the table with the papers in front of him, and Mr. Phipson was between him and me with his right hand in his pocket—and of course if I had known that he had a pistol—"

"You didn't see the pistol, Mrs. O'Hara?"

"Not then, Inspector, or of course I should have thought it my duty to warn Mr. Dale."

"Go on."

"Mr. Dale said, 'Well? Anything to say for yourself, rat?'—and of course that was a very offensive way of speaking. And Mr. Phipson said, 'It's all a dreadful mistake, and if you'll listen to me, I can explain.' Mr. Dale said, 'Explain nix!'—at least that's what I thought he said. And then he said, 'You can make your explanations to the police. I'm ringing them up here and now.' The telephone was on his right. He couldn't reach it because his chair was pushed back from the table. I don't know whether he really meant to telephone or not, but he turned that way and he began to get up, and Mr. Phipson shot him. He took his hand out of his pocket and ran in quite close and shot him."

"You'll swear to that?"

"Oh, yes, Inspector—I saw it. And of course it was a most terrible shock. Mr. Dale fell down out of his chair—he was just getting up, and he fell right down with a crash. I didn't seem to be able to do anything except stand quite still. It was really quite a horrible experience, and I must say that Mr. Phipson's behaviour shocked me very much. Such a quiet little man, and so obliging, but he really behaved in the most callous manner. He didn't even feel Mr. Dale's pulse. In fact he seemed to think only of himself. It shocked me dreadfully."

"What did he do?"

"He took out his pocket handkerchief, and wiped the pistol with it, and put it down on the table."

"Will you show me where?"

Mrs. O'Hara indicated a spot, and he nodded.

"Go on."

"Then he grabbed up the papers and ran out of the room by the farther door."

"And you, Mrs. O'Hara?"

She looked at him with some reproach.

"Well, naturally, I went to see if poor Mr. Dale was really dead, and of course I saw at once that he was—I was with a hospital, you know, in France during the war. So when I saw that there was nothing I could do I came away, because I naturally didn't wish to have Cathy and Susan mixed up in such an unpleasant affair."

Lamb looked at her sternly.

"You did very wrong, Mrs. O'Hara."

"Oh, no—I don't think so. It would have been most unpleasant for two young girls to be brought into a murder case. I thought it would be much better for everybody if it was suicide, and I think so still."

The Inspector's colour deepened alarmingly. Frank Abbott bent his head.

"*Suicide?* Madam, how could it be suicide—with the revolver on the table and completely out of his reach?"

An expression of surprise flitted across Mrs. O'Hara's face.

"Do you know, I never thought about that," she said. "What a pity! Because I could so easily have put it on the floor beside him, or even in his hand."

Lamb's very neck became suffused. He opened his mouth to speak and shut it again. The inadequacy of words held him dumb. He heard Mrs. O'Hara say with a sigh, "So I came away," and at this he roused himself.

"You went out through the glass door?"

"Oh, yes."

"Did you shut it behind you?"

"I don't think I did—oh, no, I left it open."

"And how did you return to the Little House?"

"I ran along the terrace and down the steps at the other end."

"Why did you do that?"

"I thought I heard someone coming."

Bill Carrick said in a puzzled voice, "Would that be me? I don't quite see—"

"Not *you*," said Frank Abbott, looking up. "You must have crossed the terrace while Mrs. O'Hara was behind the curtain or returning to the shelter of the curtain, because the glass door wasn't open then. By the time you got to the side window and looked in Mrs. O'Hara had opened the door and was out on the terrace. What she heard must have been Miss Lenox crossing the terrace below her. She went the other way and missed her, and you came along from the window and found the glass door open. It all fits in." He looked at his Inspector and got a frown, because, whether it fitted or not, it wasn't his place to say so.

Lamb rose to his feet clothed with authority.

"The question now is," he said—"where is Mr. Phipson?"

It was as he spoke that a most curious sound of bumping and scuffling made itself heard. The door was bounced open, banging back against the wall and thence rebounding, and Mr. Montague Phipson shot into the room propelled by the toe of Vincent Bell's right boot. The square American pattern lent itself admirably to this display of force. Mr. Phipson, clawing at the air, fetched up against the Inspector's massive form. He clawed and clutched at the Inspector. Vincent Bell's voice followed him.

"The little skunk's been trying to blackmail me, Captain. I'm giving him in charge."

Mr. Phipson straightened himself. He stood back a pace, recovered his dangling glasses, and opened his mouth to speak.

But the Inspector spoke first. His hand fell upon a shrinking shoulder. His voice came loud upon shrinking ears.

"Montague Phipson, I arrest you for the murder of Lucas Dale, and I warn you that anything you say may be taken down and used in evidence against you."

Chapter Forty-Three

TWO DAYS LATER, in the middle of the afternoon, Frank Abbott walked up to the front door of the Little House and knocked upon it. He looked like any young man who has come to pay a social call. There was nothing about the set of his coat to suggest that it harboured notebook and fountain pen. His well cut shoes shone with polish. His hair was a reminder of the fact that his nickname of Fug had been gained by what his schoolfellows considered an excessive devotion to hair oil.

Cathy opened to him and showed him a pale, scared face which brightened a little when he said, "Please don't look like that—I've really only come to say good-bye."

Reassuring, but really quite unnecessary. A funny little spark of pride flicked up in Cathy's mind. Policemen didn't come and say good-bye. The inquest on Lucas Dale had been yesterday. The inquest on Cora de Lisle was to have been at two o'clock this afternoon in Ledlington, which meant that the London police had no more to do with King's Bourne and its affairs, and that Mr. Abbott could very well have caught an afternoon train and gone back to town.

She took him into the drawing-room, where Mrs. O'Hara appeared delighted to see him. Instead of being on the sofa she was sitting up in an arm-chair with her knitting in a billow of pale pink wool upon her knees. Susan and Bill Carrick were not there. Frank Abbott's light eyes went round the room, found it empty of all he had hoped for, and came back to Mrs. O'Hara's welcoming smile.

"Mr. Abbott—how nice of you! Draw up that chair and sit down.... And now you can tell us what happened at the inquest. I can't help feeling interested, you know, though I would not have gone to it for the world, and nor would Susan or Cathy. I know people do all sorts of extraordinary things nowadays, but an inquest always seems to me to be most unsuitable for a woman. Of course we were obliged to go to the one on Mr. Dale because of having to give evidence—and I'm sure Dr. Matthews made it as easy for all of us as he possibly could—the Coroner, you know—such a very old friend, and his brother my own doctor, always so kind. He succeeded Dr. Carrick in the practice—Bill's father—but of course we knew him long before that, because their great-uncle, old Sir Henry Matthews at Bransley Park, used to have them to stay in the holidays, and very nice well-behaved boys they were. Only there was no money, and the Park had to be sold...." Mrs. O'Hara flowed on.

Frank Abbott said yes, he thought the Coroner had been very kind to her, and didn't say that she might thank her stars she wasn't in serious trouble for withholding important evidence.

Cathy, standing by the fire, wanting him to go, struck in.

"What happened in Ledlington? That's what you came to tell us, isn't it?"

Frank Abbott half turned, let his cool glance slide over her in the way she so much disliked, and said,

"It didn't take long. They brought in a verdict of wilful murder against Phipson."

Cathy shuddered.

"Did he—do it?"

"Oh, yes—there wasn't any doubt about that after Mrs. O'Hara had told her story. He must have come to the far door in the study whilst the Inspector was reading Lily Green's statement over to her before getting her to sign it. When he heard that she had actually seen Cora de Lisle by the open window just after the shot was fired he must have realized his danger. She might have seen him."

"Lily saw Miss de Lisle run past the window coming from the terrace after the shot," said Cathy. "Do you think she did see him?"

"I don't know. I think it happened this way. Dale had given her a fifty-pound note, but he had three others in his note-case, and she had probably seen them. Then she had a drink at the Magpie, and thought what a fool she'd been to let him down so light, and I think she went back to see what more she could get. We shall never know exactly what happened. She probably saw Phipson talking to Dale—she'd never have passed that open window without looking in. She may have seen the murder, rushed on towards the terrace, and then turned back in a panic because she heard Carrick coming up the garden. But I think it's much more likely that she heard the shot as she was coming round to the glass door, and that she then ran back along the way that she had come. She may have looked in at the window as she passed and seen what Carrick saw a moment later—

Dale's hand and arm stretched out along the floor from behind the writing-table. When I went to see her I was sure she knew that Dale was dead."

"How clever of you!" said Mrs. O'Hara. "You must really have a very interesting life. Please do go on. It is all most interesting, though of course very shocking too. I am really most disappointed in Mr. Phipson. Such a polite little man, though I must say he always did remind me of a ferret—and you can't trust them, can you? I was once quite badly bitten by a jill ferret belonging to William Cole's father. But pray do go on."

"Well, I can only tell you what I think. I think Phipson realized the danger he was in from Cora de Lisle and went off to silence her. Robert kept his motor-bicycle and a helmet and goggles in a shed in the yard. Phipson had only to slip on a Burberry and his best friend wouldn't know him. Now I can stop thinking and give you facts. He rode Robert's bicycle into Ledlington, hit Miss de Lisle over the head with the poker, and rode back. We've got an errand-boy who saw him turn out of Gladstone Villas. He noticed the number of the bike—boys do, you know. But what puts it fair and square on Phipson is just the lucky chance that Cora de Lisle had spilt the dregs of a bottle of brandy on the floor of her room. She was packing—running away, I expect—and the whole place was littered. Well, one of the things on the floor was a fag-end of lipstick, and the man who killed her had trodden it into the puddle of brandy. Most of it went into the carpet, but there was enough on his shoe to give us a cast-iron case."

Cathy said "Oh!" and shuddered again. Mrs. O'Hara sighed.

"It only shows how careful you have to be—I mean if you are committing a crime—and of course none of us would. It does show, doesn't it, that even with the greatest care it can never really be safe. I expect Mr. Phipson thought he had been much too clever to be found out, but being a criminal can never really be safe, and it must be a continual strain upon the nerves. And now perhaps we had better talk about something else. Cathy darling, you look very pale—she is sensitive, Mr. Abbott. And there was something I really did want to ask you. The moment I heard your name I wondered whether you could be related to an old friend of mine, Francis Abbott. We used to dance together in 1914, just before the war. He was reading law, but of course he joined up, and he was killed in 1915. Tall, fair, and very good-looking, but you remind me of him—"

Bill Carrick, opening the door in time to overhear this compliment, surprised an unmistakable gleam of humour in Frank Abbott's light blue eyes. He supplied a nod and a grin himself. Abbott said,

"I had an Uncle Francis who was killed in the war, but I'm afraid I don't remember him."

"So nice, and so very good-looking," murmured Mrs. O'Hara—"but there is quite a likeness." She turned to Bill. "Where is Susan, dear boy?"

Bill made a face.

"Entangled with Mrs. Mickleham. I fled."

After a little talk Frank Abbott made his farewells. Cathy's cold hand just touched him and withdrew, Mrs. O'Hara smiled graciously, and Bill shook him warmly by the hand. The door closed upon him.

He stood at the gate and looked up and down the village street. Away to the right Mr. Cox the butcher stood on his doorstep, a stout figure in a blue apron, conversing with Mrs. Green. Away to the left young Mrs. Gill was wheeling her twins down the hill in a double pram. If he had been a native of Netherbourne he would have known at a glance that she had been up at High Farm visiting her aunt Mrs. Paige, and that it was a hundred to nothing she had half a dozen new-laid eggs and a pot of honey tucked away under the pram cover. Over the way from behind a neat curtain of spotted muslin old Mrs. Bogg was watching him, as she watched everyone who came and went along the street. It was twelve years since she had set foot to the ground, and fifteen since she had been downstairs, but she knew everything that went on. She could have told Detective Sergeant Frank Abbott that Miss Susan and the Vicar's wife had turned in at that very gate a matter of seven minutes ago—and Mrs. Mickleham beginning to cry right out in front where everyone could see her, and wouldn't go into the house not for nothing Miss Susan could do, so they went round into the garden, and unless they'd gone up to King's Bourne they'd be there yet. But since Frank Abbott did not even know of Mrs. Bogg's existence he had to do without the information. She thought him a well-looking young man for a detective, and quite the gentleman. She went on watching him, and all at once she saw him turn about and go up round the house the way Miss Susan and Mrs. Mickleham had gone.

It was the sound of a rending sniff that made Frank Abbott turn his back on the street and go round into the garden. He met Mrs. Mickleham hurrying like a hen, with her nose very red and her long neck poking. She sniffed again as she passed him, and dabbed at her face with a wet crumpled ball of a handkerchief. Frank went on round the corner, and came upon Susan disappearing into the scullery. She came face to face with him as she turned to shut the door.

"Oh—Mr. Abbott—what is it?"

He said with a trace of bitterness in his voice, "I'm not always on duty, Miss Lenox," and saw her change colour.

"I'm so sorry—"

"You won't be when you hear that I came to say good-bye."

She seemed a little taken aback. He thought, "She didn't expect that. Why should she? None of them expected it. I don't really know them—I'm just pushing in."

She said gravely, "That was very nice of you. Won't you come in?"

But in the kitchen he stopped. It was, after all, the most suitable place for her to entertain a policeman. He said,

"I've been in already—I've said good-bye to the others. I just wanted to see you."

Susan looked at him. The strained patience had gone from her eyes. The deep blue was serene again, but he saw a faint distress just touch the surface. That was all he could ever hope for—just to touch the surface of her thought. The deeps were not for him.

, before she could say anything, he was talking as if they
.timates.

℘'s going to be all right now—for you and Carrick. You'll be
.ing married."

She said, "Yes."

"You'll be happy—"

"Yes." Just the one word, gravely and sweetly.

"King's Bourne will be yours now. Shall you live there?"

"Oh, no—I'm not taking it."

"But it's yours—Dale left you everything."

She shook her head.

"We couldn't take it. Bill would hate it, and so should I."

He looked at her with a curious feeling of pride. If you put
someone on a pedestal, you want to see her stay there. He said, out
of his thought of a moment ago,

"I'm pushing in—asking things I've no business to ask—"

"I didn't think of it that way."

"Because I'm a policeman and it's my job to push into people's
private affairs."

"Oh, no, Mr. Abbott." She paused and added gently, "You
have been kind. You didn't really think that Bill had shot Mr.
Dale, did you?"

"No—I didn't."

"I could feel you not thinking it—and it was such a help. I could
feel you being friendly. I've wanted to thank you."

He was silent.

She said, "We are going to have a little flat until we can build.
Not London—somewhere outside. It will be very small, but we want
to see our friends. Will you come?"

He said, "Yes."

Susan put out her hand. She smiled. The distress was gone.
Bill's job—the little flat—friends coming and going—blue skies and
happy times—

"I'll send you the address," she said.

Frank Abbott took the hand, held it for a moment, and the most astonishingly, bent his head and kissed it. He stood up, no flushed but pale, and went without a word.

Susan was still looking at her hand when Bill came in.

"I couldn't think where you'd got to."

"Nor could I," said Susan.

"That fellow Abbott was here—came to say good-bye. Nice chap. I've an idea he stood up for us to old Lamb. Pity you missed him."

"I didn't," said Susan. She could feel the kiss on her hand.

"Oh, then he told you all about the inquest."

"He never mentioned it, darling."

Bill stared.

"Then what did you talk about?"

There was the faintest spark in the dark blue eyes.

"He asked me a lot of questions."

"Oh, he did? What sort of questions?"

"About when we were going to be married, and whether I was happy now—he seemed to want me to be happy—and whether I was going to take King's Bourne and the money—"

"He had a nerve!"

She shook her head.

"It wasn't like that. He wanted us to be happy, and he'd have hated us to take the money. He's coming to see us when we get our flat."

"Oh, he is, is he?" Bill put his arms round her. "Woman—have you been flirting with this young man?"

The spark became slightly more pronounced.

"Darling, I don't!"

"You do something," said Bill gloomily. "Whatever it is, it does them in."

"I don't mean to. And, Bill, he's nice. He'll be friends—he really will."

"We've got to get married first. How soon will you marry me?"

"I don't know."

week—Wednesday or Thursday. It depends how long
t a licence. We'll go up to town first thing on Monday
d find out."

looked away.

, it's too soon—"

o you want to stay on here—to have everyone talking to you
about you, and wanting to know about King's Bourne and that
nned money of Dale's—and old Mother Mickleham going on like
sick hen every time she meets you, and saying the Vicar thought it
was her duty to try and get me hanged? I tell you I won't have it! The
sooner you're gone, the sooner they'll stop talking." He dropped his
head upon her shoulder. His voice came to her muffled and broken.
"Don't you want to marry me? *Susan!*"

All the pain came back like a sudden breaking wave. They
remembered how nearly, how very nearly, it had drowned them.
They held each other desperately and hard. Susan felt the tears run
hot and blinding. She said,

"Yes—yes—let's go away. Oh, Bill! Let's get married and go right
away and never come back!"

THE END